LAKE DESIRE

To Carol—
Enjoy!

2.18.05

LAKE DESIRE

by Dāv Kaufman

CROTALUS
MINNEAPOLIS

LAKE DESIRE

Published by:
CROTALUS PUBLISHING
3500 Vicksburg Lane North #302
Plymouth, Minnesota 55447-1333
www.crotaluspublishing.com

Cover design by Marti Naughton
Book design by Michelle L. N. Cook

ISBN 0-9741860-0-7

Crotalus and the Rattlesnake Colophon are trademarks of Crotalus Publishing.

First Printing, July 2003

Printed in the U.S.A.

All characters in this book have no existence outside the imagination of the author and have no relation whatsoever to anyone bearing the same name or names, living or deceased. They are not even distantly inspired by any individual known or unknown to the author, and all incidents are pure invention.

THIS NOVEL IS DEDICATED IN LOVING MEMORY
OF MY FATHER,
AL KAUFMAN,
WHO, WHEN I WAS EIGHT, SHIELDED ME
FROM THE FREEZING OCTOBER WIND
WHILE I STOOD ON THAT SHORE
OF LAKE MINNETONKA WITH THE FISHING ROD
HE HAD JUST BOUGHT ME. HE WASN'T EVEN
FISHING WITH ME THAT TIME.
HE EVEN KNEW
I WASN'T GOING TO CATCH ANYTHING,
BUT THAT DIDN'T MATTER.
HE STILL STOOD THERE AS MY WIND BREAKER,
PROTECTING ME FROM THE COLD SO THAT
I COULD FISH FOR A FEW MOMENTS MORE.
MY FATHER WAS LIKE THAT.
HE CELEBRATED MY LOVE OF FISHING
AND THE OUTDOORS, AND MADE SURE WE SPENT
AS MUCH TIME AS WE COULD
ON THAT LAKE, DESPITE HIM WORKING
TWO JOBS TO PUT FOOD IN OUR MOUTHS
(ONE OF THEM BEING A FULL-TIME HIGH
SCHOOL TEACHER). HE READ EVERYTHING
I WROTE WITH A PRIDE UNEQUALLED
BY ANYTHING I HAVE YET KNOWN,
AND HIS INFECTIOUS LAUGHTER CONTINUALLY
TAUGHT ME TO ENJOY LIFE—WHICHEVER LIFE
I WANTED.

༄༅

THANK YOU FOR THE PRIDE, DAD.

CHAPTER ONE

ELLE RAVENWOOD WAS A POET. SHE WAS A TRUE POET who wrote her poems because she, herself, loved them. That's a rare thing to find in any artist. She enjoyed only one thing more than writing her thoughts and inspirations, and that was nursing them to the town who had come to not only recognize her greatness, but rely upon it. She ended every conversation with "We are all capable of greatness." It was how she said "Amen."

There was no one who either lived in Desire, or just passed through on a fishing trip, who didn't gain something more than what they had before she began to immerse them in her healing words. Elle Ravenwood was an artist. At almost sixty, she still had a youthful beauty about her that could only be awarded with a life lacking in foolish worry. She often laughed and played with children. She took long naps in the afternoon. She saw beauty in everything, even the ordinary.

She lived as a poet.

She even died as a poet.

But that was never her intention, her fault, or even anything she could have avoided. Someone else, on the other hand, could have avoided it for her, but that's another heartbreak altogether.

On that bright April day, a few weeks after the ice melted back into the lake, when the northern Minnesota cold still clawed at your eyes, Elle rejoiced that she could once again take her boat to Arrowhead Island to do one of the things in life that filled her with the most fixational sense of beauty, and that was to write her poetry in solitude from the most beautiful place she had yet found.

Elle walked down the dock to her new boat that her husband, Arnold, had bought her just last fall. She loved that new boat because it was much nicer than the old wood-sided canoe with the outboard clamped to the stern that she had used for decades. Arnold was never one to play it cheap when it came to his wife's happiness. Therefore, he had the boat upgraded to the model that had the side console steering column complete with an electric starter and windshield. The console even had a cup holder that was a perfect fit for her ever present coffee cup with the cartoon of a dripping brown moose that read CHOCOLATE MOOSE just below it. Behind the console, the wooden seat that was cushioned by her life vest was raised another few inches so that Elle could see better over the bow. It also had a 100-horsepower outboard engine so that she could get out to the island faster than in that old canoe. Returning was never a race, however.

As Elle climbed aboard, she lamented that something was noticeably missing that morning: Bear wasn't sitting on the dock with his journal. Like her, every day since ice out, he'd been there. She had come to rely upon the fact that his was the last smile she saw on her way out to the island. Bear's absence gave her pause, but she figured it had to do with Cherie Tester, his girlfriend—or as Bear was fond of saying only to Elle, "his girlfriend until someone better came along." Elle had never understood why Bear put up with Cherie. She'd never judge him, however; she just missed her friend that morning.

She was right about Bear's absence being tied to Cherie. Late last night, she drove her truck off the road into a bog. Having managed to crawl out before the truck sank into the swampy water, she walked the five miles back to town and demanded that Bear take her to work on his Harley, because she was scheduled for the breakfast rush that morning. Bear, didn't even ask if she'd been drinking; he didn't need to.

On board her boat, Elle reached into the utility box that Arnold had drilled under the steering console. Her pens, journal, and an assorted disorder of junk were there, but no boat keys. Perplexed, she glanced at the ignition, and there dangled her keys with the yellow float key chain stenciled with a large muskie on its side that Arnold had given her with a toothy grin when he presented her new toy. He knew as he handed her the keys that at the very least, he'd get a dinner that night that would bring jealousy to royalty. He also knew that the most he'd get—well, with Arnold and Elle, that was never something he'd need to buy her a boat for.

Elle stared at the keys for longer than she realized. She could have sworn she hadn't left her keys in the ignition; she never did. But there was the proof. Without a second thought, she turned the key, and her new boat awoke to life.

Throwing off the bow line, Elle put the boat into gear, and made a beeline directly to a small island of protruding rocks about fifty yards from shore where she abruptly crashed with such force, that she was thrown over the bow—headfirst into a protruding rock face.

Elle floated face down in a mess of drifting debris—including her life vest—for fifteen minutes before a group of fisherman saw her and the half-sunk boat from their approaching truck. Two of them jumped into the water and swam out to her. The other called 911 on his cell phone. Strangely, no one responded to the dispatch. It didn't matter anyway; by the time the two men reached Elle, it was long past too late.

No one saw the accident to say for sure what happened. Bear should have been there that morning, or so he believed, and that further damaged how he felt about Cherie, even if the fact remained that there was nothing he could have done to prevent it.

Even so, he couldn't escape the self-inflicted contempt that he wasn't there to rescue his friend.

Deputy Bret Newstead hadn't been on the scene, either. Hours later, he'd been found passed out in his patrol car reeking of a fine Canadian whiskey with a 911 distress call paging him on the radio.

It seemed as if all that happened years ago, but it had only been three months, and the town of Desire would not suddenly heal from it.

CHAPTER TWO

L IFE LURCHED RELENTLESSLY FORWARD ON LAKE DESIRE, and the symphony of morning had always been that encouraging promise of new possibilities. Somewhere in the elusive distance, off into the forest, the call of a white-throated sparrow echoed serenity over the lake—a soul-feeding call to all who listened that hope was not an impossible desire. Like complimenting oboes, a pair of loons joined in, calling out over the hypnotizing purple silky water. The clarinets of the red-winged blackbirds were followed closely by the plucking of cello strings heard in the calls of the green frogs beckoning from reeds that danced in the nurturing wind. The cymbal crash of a largemouth bass returning to the water from its reward of a dragonfly gave climax to the percussion of the waves lapping against the rough, sandy-stone shores and the soothing thud of the fishing boat knocking against the dock. The strings were the breeze as it tore through the needles of the gigantic white pine and spruce ornamenting the shoreline. The symphony of morning heralded the new day, drawing night to a close as the sun languidly stretched its radiant bounty across the sky.

It was an arrogant sky. And the lake was its mirror, a reflective testimony to its majesty when it was at its crepuscular best.

That's the thing about lakes—they are forever clear and truthful in their reflections of what they witness—at least when it is enraptured by the tranquil mood of morning, before the wind irritates, and manipulates it, and the waves cause a distortion of that truth. Yet even then, the colors in the reflection remain true—particularly the colors of the sky.

It was a search for that uncompromising truth that had compelled Bear to return to that dock after avoiding it for too long since Elle's death. He felt as much at peace as he could again sitting there with his back resting against one of the dock poles—the last one on the right, so that he could look over that eutrophic lake that had been there, enjoying the sunrise since the glaciers created her almost ten millennia ago.

Over that time, the lake had witnessed everything that history could dish out. It smiled at the wooly mammoths and vast caribou herds that had come to drink from it before the pines and the spruce ever thought to set up camp. It witnessed thousands of years of Native American tribes—from the first Woodland tribes, to the Dakota, and then the advancing Ojibwa, who had a camp just south of its shores. They trapped beaver, muskrats, and otter from its bounty to trade for metal pots and hatchets with the French and British, and later, the Americans. It was home to huge fish, bigger than anything known today. There were still big fish in it, but not the huge fish that once were kings. The lake had witnessed volumes, and still retained that uncanny ability to always reflect the truth. As he sat on the dock, it seemed to appreciate Bear's company mainly because Bear appreciated it for nothing more than its beauty. He really was the first to sit on its shores in all that expanse of time, and not expect anything more out of it than what his eyes could feast upon.

His black Harley-Davidson (which, unknown to anyone, he'd named Emily after his most respected and adored poet, Emily Dickinson) rested on her stand on the shore just behind him, and to look at her was to think that even she loved it here. There was no other company he needed or wanted, except, of course, Elle.

During the countless hours he had spent on the dock, Bear had filled several journals with his thoughts and poetry, but the one he had on his lap now was different from the others. Not only was it nicer than the others with its brown leather jacket sleeve with a burned insignia of a plume on its cover and strip to tie it closed, nor was it even the fact that he had made that cover himself; the difference was that he'd had it for some time, but written nothing in it. It was as blank and as new as his life had become when he returned to Desire not too long before the accident.

Still, he saw this place as his temple, and it had become almost a religious ritual for him come to the dock each morning whether he would write anything or not. He began each vigil lost in the tranquility of the morning symphony, a tranquility that was sometimes broken by the memory of Elle's death seeping into his meditation.

Someone else shared the burden of that memory for a very different reason—someone who was as oblivious to Bear's presence as Bear was to theirs.

ON DOGTOOTH BAY, JUST AROUND THE POINT, OUT OF sight from Bear's dock, close to shore in only knee-high water, two barefoot legs with pants rolled up just above the knee languidly shifted through the water. A certain methodical quality marked their movement through the knee-high water close to shore— poignant, almost poetic. Quietly, the legs turned to face the lake and stopped while two hands gently set to sail a homemade birch bark boat, its hollow filled with flowers Elle knew and loved, among them Indian paintbrush, purple lupine, wood lilies, and violets. Tucked into the flowers was a torn, bleached white strip of paper on which was written two words: *I'm Sorry.*

AT THAT MOMENT, BEAR TOOK HIS PEN FROM HIS LEATHER vest, opened his blank journal and began to write. He didn't question why or what moved him to begin, he simply wrote, and the words appeared as though something elusive buried deep within him controlled his pen.

> It wasn't truth most of us were seeking because most of us had long ago invented our own truth. What it was now had manifested itself into a validation for our rights, and for our wrongs. It was a glorious abuse of the justification of our existence that turned into an on-going fight against the helplessness of being. And that compelled us to discover just what truth really was.

As the comfort of finding himself back in the cradle of creativity engulfed him, the unmistakable sound of hollow footsteps upon the dock broke his concentration. He turned to find Martin Ravenwood with fishing rod and tackle box ready for battle. His arrival was no surprise; he'd arrived on that dock ready to fish every morning for almost three years now.

Bear found a genuine smile for him, as he had every morning.

"G'morning, Bear," Martin said as he approached his boat.

"Martin. You're up early. What day does today make?"

Martin set his fishing rod and tackle box in his waiting boat and began to untie the bowline. "Nine hundred and sixty-eight days," he answered as he stepped into the boat that his grandfather had bought in '61 and grabbed the gas line from the ten-gallon gas tank he kept by the 5-horsepower outboard. He squeezed the center ball, filling the cylinders of the outboard.

"How many more days till the record?" Bear asked.

"'Bout another week-and-a-half yet."

"I take it your dad's not going with you today?"

"No. Shop's been pretty busy lately with the contest coming. I figure I'd let 'im sleep in."

Bear nodded while Martin untied the stern line from the dock, then cranked the pull cord of the old paint-chipped outboard. It began to cough. Another hard crank and the morning symphony was invaded by the two pistons knocking, then revving to life.

Since the accident, things were different between Bear and Martin; unlike before, their conversations consisted of nothing more than small talk. Bear was caught up in wanting the perfect words to say, but had no idea what to say at all. Maybe it was because Martin never talked about his mother's death, at least to Bear. Or maybe it was because he never showed any outward sorrow about it. But Martin was like that anyway; he was always very private, and spent most of his time alone. Maybe that love of solitude had something to do with him perfecting his craft to become the best taxidermist in northern Minnesota—quite possibly the whole state. Martin's love of solitude was the one thing over everything else that Bear did understand about Martin. Still, Bear, and possibly even Martin, was looking for something more from each other, but neither of them knew what it was. Maybe they just needed to talk to each other about something more than fishing.

Bear looked over the lake. The sun had completely risen over the horizon. "Looks like it's going to be a good day."

"Yeah," Martin yelled over the roaring engine, "maybe I'll even catch something today."

With that, he smiled, waved, and headed out across the water toward the promise of big fish. Bear watched until Martin's boat disappeared behind the point, then kept watching as the wake rolled over the protruding rocks that were still scarred from Elle's boat. He took another few solemn seconds to stare at those rocks and then continued to write.

The first time I was ever presented with the crippling loss of greatness was the day they pulled Elle Ravenwood from the water. But in her death, we all found a testament to her life that commanded the most pure and raw explanation of ourselves. It was the beginning that came from an end, and it offered us the power to live with our helplessness and rise from our self-orchestrated purgatories to finally explore the meaning of our own existence and the discovery of our own desires.

As he wrote, he thought about whom specifically he was writing about. It was really about everyone that he knew. His head filled with the images of the people of Desire—about those who loved it here, and those who couldn't find a way to leave. He thought about Main Street with its red and brown brick front buildings that hadn't changed much since they were erected just after World War I—the exception being the Lake Theater, which had opened with a huge gala event in the spring of 1960 with *Psycho* as its premier movie.

As Bear mused, a banner was being raised on Main Street that proclaimed, "25th Annual Lake Desire Fishing Contest—$25,000 in prizes—July 29th." Decorating the banner were the names and logos of the event sponsors—Gander Mountain, Minnesota Tourism, and the Minnesota State Lottery among others. Just out of town, the biker gang that frequently partied with Bear and his younger brother Earl, rode past another sign, one repeatedly scarred from shotgun blasts. Pine green letters wished visitors WELCOME TO DESIRE, MINNESOTA; however, the "c" and the "a" had been destroyed by a direct hit long ago.

Bear continued.

What is it about ourselves that keeps us buoyant despite our fears, and inspires us to carry on when hope runs out of ammunition? The answer is as simple as that which fuels our desires, for it is desire itself that is necessary to keep our lives in motion. It is the one thing we all share in common, and it is also the one thing that separates us all. And it is desire that encourages us all in its unique way, and inspires us to carry on.

He stopped and thought about his girlfriend, Cherie, as she tied her apron around her waist and prepared for the breakfast rush at the Sportsman's Café with a permanent cigarette wedged between her lips. There was something mysteriously symbolic about the way she dumped the old, black ooze down the drain that had been sitting in the coffee pot overnight, although the metaphor did escape her, probably on purpose. She looked old beyond her thirty-seven years, aggravated, fed-up. A "just deal with it" attitude was as foreign to her as the concept of a bigger picture. She hated this place, and everything around her seemed like one more visual reminder that her life did in fact turn out the opposite of what she dreamed it would become, but in the exact way she knew it would. Nevertheless, this place was the bull's eye of her comfort zone, and she knew it. Because of this, she struggled more and more in the glue trap into which her life had manifested itself.

Magic wands are only available to those who believe in them, but Cherie didn't believe in magic anyway, even though that's what she thought it would take to make her life what she once dreamed it would be. The only thing Cherie really believed was that everything was always someone else's fault. And sometimes, just sometimes, perhaps just often enough to keep her believing it, they were. But Cherie was never one to examine philosophical ideas too deeply. She preferred a bottle of rum to do that for her.

Even as Bear thought of her, Cherie was reaching to flip the CLOSED sign to OPEN, then gazed out the window at the gray world, trying to understand why it had given up on her. That morning, as with every morning, a smile was nowhere in her agenda.

As Cherie lit her fifth cigarette of the day, Bear continued.

For some it is the desire to rise from an incarceration of self-indulgent animosity, lifelong in the making, and finally achieve a point to where the renovation of vitality becomes palatable for the first time despite the lack of knowledge necessary to accomplish this form of enlightenment when the only knowledge that's possessed is that there is no pain as great as simply being alive.

He then thought about Stella Holmstead, although even within the confines of his own mind, he was surprised to once again find himself a bit timid in doing so. He did, however, smile at the irony that the thoughts of her would follow the thoughts of Cherie. He thought about the gravity of Stella's loneliness, and the liability of the perpetual malaise that accompanied it as she walked out the front door of her white, Victorian-style house to face yet another day.

Stella's house was a true friend to her, standing alone on an acre-and-a-half lot just north of Main Street where she owned the town's used bookstore Forgotten Memories. To Stella, her house was a friend on whom she lavished time and attention. Window boxes overflowed with flowers or greenery, depending on the season. The flower garden, a three-season haven of astounding color and peace, flowed toward pink and white roses that climbed up and over the front door. Sentry evergreens stood in welcome, decorated with tiny white lights that in fall and winter replaced the floral welcome of summer.

As abundant as the display in front was the bounty of the vegetable and fruit garden in the back. And each year, as the other vegetables and fruits gave way to fall, the bright orange of pumpkins emerged ever more prominently. She planted more pumpkins than anyone else in town, and it made sense. She loved Halloween. It was by far her favorite holiday because for one day out of the year, she had a constant flow of visitors.

The spotless house and lush garden stood out in Desire, and it would not be surprising if the entire property wound up on the cover of a magazine someday. Still, Stella knew mostly loneliness, but she learned to accept and tolerate it, convincing herself that doing so made her strong. But she was becoming sick and tired of being strong—and there was nothing Bear could do about that. He didn't know how, and even if he did, would he? He was expected to be so much more than that.

Even as Bear sat on the dock thinking of her, Stella stood on her front step, sighed, and prepared to face another day alone. It was best not to think too much on Stella, Bear decided, and went back to his journal.

> Perhaps it is the desire to simply give into desire itself and for one glimmering moment, harness the power to live with your helplessness, and cling to an irresistible hope that loneliness is only a temporary disability.

Next in his thoughts was Bret Newstead, who needless to say was no longer the deputy. In fact, he was lucky that firing him was all Sheriff Dwayne Walker did to him. Everyone knew that Elle's maiden name was Walker, and everyone expected the Sheriff to do something much worse to Bret than to simply dismiss him from duty for not being there to save his sister. Bear understood Bret's problems, or he thought he did, but just because we understand someone's plight, does that mean we can simply forgive them for their failures?

Bret was a war hero, but only because he survived his thirteen-month tour in Vietnam. Still, no one really knew why Bret came back from Vietnam a broken shell of his former self like so many others that made it out alive. There was a lot of speculation as these things always generate, but no one had it right.

For the first month of his tour, he sent many letters home to Elle who would read them aloud to everyone in the café. In them, he made it seem life on the front was at least manageable. Bret wrote to Elle as often as he could, but still as time went on, they became less frequent. Elle found it more and more difficult to cope with never knowing if her fiancé was dead or alive. As the time between letters grew longer, she lived between the hope of a reassuring letter from Bret and the dread of the catastrophic possibility of one from the State Department.

Over time, the letters that Bret would send were reduced to one or two lines that gave the same simple message: "I'm alive. But I don't know for how long." After three letters like that, spread out over a month and a half, she simply couldn't take it anymore, and found comfort in the only place she had since Bret had left—Arnold. Eventually, the letters stopped altogether, and as Elle and the town prepared themselves for the news that Bret might be KIA, in a small gathering on the lake shore, Arnold and Elle had exchanged their vows. It wasn't easy for either of them as Bret had a place in both of their hearts, but Elle's secret pregnancy with Martin made it easier to justify, and their marriage lasted happily until that day just a few months ago.

Bret's platoon was one of the last to leave Vietnam. In fact, the war was unofficially over before Bret got his walking papers. He didn't write home to let anyone know—not even Elle. Somewhere in his gut he knew that he had lost her, and he didn't even know if she'd be there when he returned. He didn't want a parade, or even a welcome home party (he was actually afraid to let anyone know because he heard people were spitting on GIs at the airports, calling them "baby killers" and those that believe they're guilty never liked having it rubbed in their faces). He just wanted to go home, stare out over that lake one more time, and figure out what he was going to do with the rest of his life—or more to the point, what the rest of his life was going to do with him.

When Bret did return, almost a year after he had been discharged, just in time for Christmas 1974, he walked into the café to the sight of necks wrenching as they whiplashed in his direction, and the sound of a plate crashing to the floor. Everyone welcomed the hero home, but with a pound of trepidation as they didn't know if Bret knew about Elle and Arnold, and nobody wanted to be the first to tell him about that.

It was soon apparent to everyone that this was not the Bret who had left them. This was someone who looked like the boy they sent to war, but came back a ghost. Everyone knew that war stripped a person down beyond his foundation, leaving him a mere fraction of his former self so that a bigger political objective that really had nothing to do with him would be achieved. That was the explanation everyone accepted. It was just that Bret had survived a terrible war. When they heard Bret had thanked Arnold for taking care of Elle and making her happier than he ever could, the town knew that they would have to get to know Bret all over again, because the Bret that was sent off more than two years before would never have been so accepting, even indifferent, to losing something he considered his.

Up until Elle's death, when the word of his incompetence spread like a fire in the Rockies, the townspeople had developed a growing respect for Bret, especially when the sheriff hired him as his deputy in the spring of 1975. The sheriff, as did everyone in town, respected Bret even more when he refused to carry a gun. All of this respect, however, was when he was off the bottle. Bret wasn't a drunk, but it was only at the bottom of a whiskey bottle that he found escape from what he dubbed "the cycle."

The only one who really knew what he was talking about was Barney Whitmore, the owner of the town's only bar—The Lunker Lodge—which Barney purchased upon his return from Korea. Bret knew that he personally would have done to himself what the war couldn't do if he didn't have Barney as a sounding board.

Barney genuinely cared about Bret, regardless of his mistakes, and therefore watched over him like a father. Vets have a bond like that. They understand each other more than anyone else can, and with that understanding comes an amnesty that can't be found anywhere else. Barney really cared about everyone in town, and although he didn't realize it when he opened his bar, he had stepped into the shoes of being the town's psychologist, and he was wise enough to wear those shoes well.

But even Barney didn't know exactly what had horrified, and more to the point, ruined Bret in Vietnam, and he never asked; he knew better than to do so. All he knew was that when something reminded Bret of what really happened all those years ago that caused a cancerous wound in him that sometimes even alcohol couldn't heal, Bret went on the cycle. And on the morning of Elle's death, Bret was yet again a prisoner of it. No, Bret wasn't a drunk, even though he had every reason to become one. He fought his demons as best he could, and most of the time, he won. But there are some things in our past for which there is no magic healing potion to make us feel better about ourselves. Most times, you just have to get sick of living with it.

Now, fueled by the blame of Elle's death, Bret's cycle had become a hurricane. As Bret stumbled from the wreck his shack had become (it was never that hard to turn that place into a wreck in the first place) with a black, folded flag loosely dangling from his barely clenched hand, that magic potion was as nonexistent as his own sense of self respect. But he was a soldier, and that was something he would never forget, even if he did some day beat the cycle, or end up succumbing to it. Tying the flag to the flagpole in his front yard and hoisting it with the cord, he watched as the black POW flag unraveled and began to proudly ride the waves of the wind. He stared up at it for a few minutes, which to him might have well been hours. Like a resilient soldier, he found the strength to salute it as it reminded him YOU ARE NOT FORGOTTEN.

Bear continued to write.

> For others, the disability lies within a past paved with the cement of regret that our only salvation lies within a tangle of synthetic devotion of who we believe ourselves to be. Unbalanced as it always is, it boils over to a point where the only desire becomes the pursuit to end the war within ourselves.

A smile crept over Bear's face as he thought about the old ice fishing house that sat at an angle behind the Lunker Lodge. He thought of the boy who each morning kicked the always-stuck door open, yawned, shook off his sleep, and then walked out to the huge burr oak and unzipped his fly to give the tree its morning drink. In summer, he always wore cut-off jeans, and one of three t-shirts—the only clothes he owned. His t-shirt selection of the day had a smiley face with a bleeding bullet hole through its forehead that he drew with a red marker that he stole from the café. Below the smiley face were the words HAVE A SUPER DAY.

Within seconds, the door was kicked open again and, like a living doubletake, his identical twin walked over to the oak to join his brother. The town didn't think of the two as permanent residents; they simply tolerated their presence. But because they were both dating Cherie's nineteen-year-old daughter, Annie, and because everyone in Bear's biker gang loved having them at parties, they were accepted as part of the community—not that they needed that acceptance to stay.

They followed Annie home from a club in Duluth about a year ago, and set up camp in Barney's icehouse after it was dragged off the lake at the end of February. Barney didn't care less if they stayed, just as long as they found a new place to live by the time the lake had frozen again. Even Annie wasn't sure why they didn't just get a regular place, nor did she really care, just as long as they stayed. They gave her something that no one in town had ever given her, even her mother—especially her mother—and that was a sense of importance, and in return, she followed them habitually.

The boys' parents never left the commune that they had established in the early seventies on a farm in southwestern Minnesota. As they had no reason to think their parents ever would move, the boys had a relentless confidence that they would always have that place to call home. Two years ago, on their eighteenth birthday, the twins' parents wished them well with what they called a "gift of the earth" and sent them on their way to explore it. So far, they had never left Minnesota, because to a Minnesotan, where else was there?

Never believing in the ideals of individual conformity, their parents named each twin Steven, and after the first few months of trying to work that out, Annie decided she was going to call one of them Stee, and the other Ven, and patted herself on the back for being so clever. Annie herself could have been a throw back to the free love movement, complete with a wardrobe of long dresses, fringed accessories, halter tops, and strings of beads she'd made herself. Her hair hung straight and long and she was almost always barefoot, sometimes even in the winter. Her mind was free but just enough to comprehend that which she could see in front of her. Things really didn't exist to her otherwise.

Stee and Ven never knew what being apart was like so they shared everything, from clothes to food to living quarters. Why would it be any different with women? Jealousy between them over sharing Annie was never admitted to their consciousness, and as time progressed, Annie, like everyone else, saw them as they saw themselves—the same person, just born in separate bodies.

The twins also saw themselves as constant students of astronomy. They knew everything about the stars and the constellations right down to their given trajectory on any given night. It was an interest their parents had given them, and something that Elle perpetuated in them. Because of who they were, they were particularly entranced by Gemini, and although Annie was just beginning to learn all this, the three of them became inseparable.

The thing about them that Bear liked so much was that they didn't think like anyone else he had ever met. They had ideas and dreams that were impossible to contain. As far as Cherie was concerned, she didn't really have an opinion about them other than she thought they were really weird. She just liked the fact that the twins kept Annie out of her hair until they were hungry or needed money.

Having completed their morning routine, the twins jumped aboard their snowmobile that they had attached ATV tires to the drive train for summer mobility. They could have stolen the whole ATV, but who would be able to identify just the tires? As far as they knew, no one was looking for this old snowmobile. But even if they thought someone would be, it would not have stopped them from taking it. And now that they had tied the skis up so they didn't drag and repainted the body, who was going to recognize it anyway?

They pulled to a halt outside an old red double-wide trailer and entered it without knocking. As they crawled into bed with a still sleeping Annie, Bear continued.

Or even more, it is the desire to explore the meaning of your own existence, and to impress your mark on the world as you demand it to acknowledge your own breed of reality, and to challenge every obstacle, and every fear as a personal anthem, and to leave a record of your legacy to let the future know that you did, in fact, exist.

Bear's thoughts drifted again, this time to Martin and Arnold who now only had each other. He thought about the worry in Arnold's voice when he talked to his son that the tragedy of Elle couldn't bring them closer to each other. Martin was like that, though. He hardly ever showed what he was really feeling. He took for granted that his father would always own the town's bait shop, and he would always have his taxidermy studio in the back room, even though he should have learned how impermanent life was by his mother's fate.

Arnold had the same undying love for his son that he had for Elle. In fact, now with Elle gone, it was only Martin's happiness that he considered in all he did. And Martin's seeming lack of emotion just made Arnold try harder. The shop had become a shrine to his and Martin's fishing and hunting accomplishments, with the trophies and ribbons Martin had won in fishing contests and taxidermy shows prominently displayed on a shelf just above the register counter so that they would be the first things a customer walking in the door would see. The other thing that immediately caught a customer's eyes was the huge dry-erase board on the wall behind the counter. On the top of the board, a homemade sign read NUMBER OF CONSECUTIVE FISHING DAYS BY MARTIN RAVENWOOD. The board was divided down the middle by a blue line creating two columns. The column on the left read NUMBER OF DAYS, and written below it was the number 967. The column on the right read MINNESOTA STATE RECORD, and written below that was the number 978.

Martin's deer heads and a huge bull moose head (that was actually taken by Arnold on a hunting trip near the Boundary Waters when Martin was too young to legally hunt) hung from place to place coupled with Martin's three walleyes more than thirty inches, a smallmouth bass that was twenty-five inches, a largemouth bass that came in at twenty-six inches, and two of his northern pikes that were more than twenty-five pounds—all caught on Lake Desire. The only thing missing, and one of the reasons Martin began to fish everyday, was a muskie. He secretly felt incomplete, and sometimes inferior as a fisherman, without one on the wall.

Photos of Arnold and Martin fishing together were placed everywhere around the shop. Looking at them as he prepared the shop for the day's business, Arnold was saddened by the realization that in those pictures were the last time he'd seen his son truly smile.

Right on schedule, ten minutes before the shop opened, Charlie Swanson, who in his sixty-seven years of life had never lived in a house that had plumbing or electricity, knocked on the door. He was a chainsaw artist who knew everything there was to know about fishing, but only in his own mind. He was the artist who carved the sign on the front of the store that read RAVEN-WOOD'S BAIT SHOP AND TAXIDERMY STUDIO with the 3D walleye carved from a piece of red pine jumping from the sign after a jig and leech that Arnold had later put up. As he always did, Charlie would spend the entire day in the shop "teaching" Arnold how to fish. Despite this, Arnold came to enjoy, and later rely on his company. While Charlie began his lesson of the day, Bear continued.

> But still, for others it is the desire to keep a firm grasp on contentment and stability while celebrating a capacity of intelligence that dictates that fear is something that logic can destroy, and often does. But that type of uncontrollable desire can breed a fear all its own that can threaten the very possession of happiness.

The word *happiness* carried Bear's thoughts to Ernie Brown. Ernie had always been one of Elle's favorite people, because, like her, Ernie didn't have the capacity to judge anyone, and that made them perfect friends. Ernie inherited the town's gas station from his father, despite the fact that he knew just about as much about cars as Charlie did about fishing. It was never really known if his father died, or just abandoned him and the station, and no one really cared. Ernie's father was, by almost everyone's standards, a first class asshole. Ernie, on the other hand, was adored by all. Even those who just stopped for gas grew to like him within the time it took to fill their tank. He was simple, but by no means the stupid kind of simple. He just didn't ask much from life, and therefore life took care of him.

One thing that could be said about him was that he was a creature of habit. His day consisted of three parts. Part One was preparing for the day by pushing his duct-taped recliner and old black and white television on its folding stand out onto the front step of the shop. Having done that, he made sure his Polaroid camera was full of film, with more in the magazine pocket on the arm of the chair.

Part Two was to spend his day pumping gas, checking tire pressure and, when asked, acting like he was checking the oil, although he had never yet actually seen a dipstick. Through it all, he had a beautiful talent for making everyone who came to his shop smile. When someone came by the station, Ernie would take their picture, and post it on the "Wall of Fame" that he had just inside the door in the entryway of the shop. There were hundreds of pictures there, and in them all, everyone was smiling. It was actually rather melancholy for him seeing families smile, something that in his youth he never was able to do. But true to his nature, he believed that if everyone else was happy, so would he be—as if some of it was sure to rub off on him. And from time to time, it did.

Part Three of Ernie's day consisted of closing the shop, microwaving himself a TV dinner, and watching as many of *The Twilight Zone* episodes as he could before he fell asleep. He loved *The Twilight Zone,* and had just about every episode on tape, even the new ones, and had seen them all dozens of times.

That was what he did everyday without variance. That was what made him simple.

As Ernie pushed his duct-taped recliner out to it's spot on the front step, Bear continued his writing.

> But happiness in itself is a relative term that can only be translated by individual experience—and that can be found in the simplest of places. However, simplicity has it's own desires, like the struggle to prove one's worth not only to themselves, but to have it recognized by the world.

That applied to Bear as well—but differently. Bear had already proven his worth to himself, and therefore, felt no need to prove it to anyone else, much less his brother, Earl Massey. Earl was constantly testing the boundaries of his brother's worth, but then Earl wasn't really happy unless he was picking a fight with someone. Earl's personal depth seemed to go only as far as the needle of his tattoo gun would pierce the skin of any one particular client. Bear never intended to go into business with his brother at the tattoo shop, but he was good at it, and at the time of his return, it made sense. It was a comfortable situation—at least it was then.

Earl, with his everlasting hangover, walked through the shop from his room in the back, his hand digging in his off-colored briefs scratching himself. He took a bottle of rum off the tattoo chair, probably one that Cherie had left lying around, and turned it upside-down to confirm that it was empty. Throwing it on the counter, he walked to the window, and gazed out into the world of Desire, and let the world of Desire gaze in on his near-naked splendor, stretching his arms above his head just in case anyone was, in fact, watching.

He hated that he had to wait for Bear to get back before they could go to the café for his usually balanced breakfast of beer. But he'd never walk into the café alone, at least not while Cherie was working. He never understood why Bear spent his mornings on that dock anyway. He found it completely antisocial and never missed an opportunity to let him know that. But he did take a certain comfort in the fact that he had found yet another thing to be annoyed at.

Bear did feel a sense of pride when he and his brother shook hands, and bear-hugged each other when they put up the sign outside the shop that read DESIRE TATTOOS BY BEAR AND EARL. Some of that pride lingered still. However, since Elle's death, Bear had been searching in his mind for an excuse to leave the shop without it crushing his brother. What he was really looking for was a way to leave what he had become, and what he was expected to be. It really wasn't who he was anymore, and maybe it never was. He really didn't know, and as he asked himself why he was writing all these things about all these people, it slowly dawned on him: What he was looking for within the pages and in the lives of those around him was himself. He wasn't writing the poetry he usually wrote as he sat on that dock, but then again, poetry was never all that he ever wrote. He was writing again, and that's what was really important. He had taken the first steps to finding something magical within himself, regardless if he didn't recognize it at first.

One thing that Bear knew for sure, was that there, on that dock, looking out over that truthful lake, was the place he loved like nowhere else on earth. He wanted to stay on that dock and keep investigating himself. He wanted to stay and write those thoughts and inspirations all day, but stopped in mid-thought, and put his journal away.

Earl was waiting.

CHAPTER THREE

THE SPORTSMAN'S CAFÉ WAS THE CENTRAL MEETING place of the town since it opened in 1955. Any story, usually stories—or more to the point, bragging—about fishing could be overheard, especially during the breakfast rush. Weather was always a hot topic as well. Especially in the dead of winter when temperatures might bottom out at seventy-below windchill. The biggest complaint overheard then was that the propane heaters in someone's ice fishing house wasn't working like it used to. Likewise, in the dog days of summer when it was not unheard of for the mercury to soar to more than one hundred degrees accompanied by miserable dew points and humidity levels really gave the people of Desire something to complain about, because, as it was well known, life in northern Minnesota didn't come standard with air conditioning.

Desire was like most small towns: everyone in town knew everyone else's kid's grades in school; who hadn't come home for dinner the previous night; who was pregnant, sick, in trouble, getting married or dying; who had money and who didn't; and the café was the verbal bulletin board by which most of this local knowledge was shared. But oddly, no one really ever talked about Elle's accident.

The original owner and founder of the café was Edwin Stockton, a man who had big dreams, but unfortunately didn't have the means or the discipline to make them bear fruit. Edwin had been a traveling salesman leading a lonely life of selling condiments to roadside cafés across the upper half of the state. His travels had made him a veritable travel guide of the North woods; he knew which no-tell motels had the cleanest bed sheets, the most stain-free towels, those free little bite-sized bars of soap, or free coffee in the morning. He could tell you, too, the best place in the whole of northern Minnesota to get a steak or a whitefish sandwich caught fresh from Lake Superior.

Edwin had never really had a permanent home, and it was the one thing he really wanted out of life—a permanent roof over his head, and God willing, a wife and family. When he arrived in Desire in 1954, he was surprised that a town that had already acquired a reputation for attracting the fishing tourist didn't have a café, or really anywhere that a fisherman could get a bite other than cold sandwiches and a beer at the newly opened Lunker Lodge, and although Barney was a client of his, he really didn't need a ton of condiments. The corner of Main Street and County Road 2, he recognized, was the busiest intersection in the town because it was the quickest way to get from the lake to the shops on Main Street. However, at the time, all that stood on that corner was a lone red pine in a vacant lot. He bought the lot for what was reported, although not confirmed, for only a hundred dollars. By the spring fishing opener of 1955, the Sportsman's Café was open for business to feed the hungry mouths of the touring fishermen. He showed a profit within the first year—probably because he didn't have much overhead in the condiment department.

Profit is the single biggest motivating factor for small men to become big dreamers, and in the spring of 1956, Edwin spread himself a little too thin as he set out to create a chain of Sportsman's Cafés across the upper Midwest. It backfired on him when he failed to recall why he'd built the first one in Desire in the first place—it was one of the only towns that hadn't already had an established eatery. As good as the Sportsman's Café might be, the concept couldn't compete with the established eateries in other communities, and one by one, his new cafés failed. Edwin was overheard late one night as he sat at the counter sipping his brandy-spiked coffee saying that he was better off as a condiment salesman. Shortly after that, in the winter of 1963, Edwin signed the café over to his nephew, Jack Hanson, as a gift for Jack's eighteenth birthday. Edwin came by frequently to show Jack the new line in condiments and to give his nephew some uninvited business pointers until cancer took him in 1976. Jack still owned the café, but only this one—the first and the last of his uncle's dream.

Edwin would be proud if he could see the café today. Even though it was smaller than when it opened, it hadn't changed much in general. About the time Bret returned home, business wasn't what it was even two years earlier, and Jack had to do something fast to save the café from going under. There's an old saying that things happen because they're supposed to happen, not because we want them to, and both Jack and Arnold became a guest to this philosophy one night as they sat over coffee. The building that originally housed Ravenwood's Bait Shop was one of the oldest and most dilapidated in town, and every morning that Arnold went in, there seemed to be new evidence of that fact.

They complained about their predicaments for a good hour before the answer to both their predicaments sprang into Jack's mind with a ding and lighted bulb. The last summer's flock of fishermen had barely left the town before construction began to section off a third of the café to create the new space for Ravenwood's Bait Shop. The agreement was that Arnold would pay a third of the property tax, and rented the space from Jack for a rent-controlled amount of four hundred dollars a month.

The arrangement, as both of them knew, saved both of their businesses. The only source of conflict between the two, if it could have even been labeled conflict, as Arnold put it (though he said it only on his side of the wall), was that Jack was sometimes a real ass. He considered the waitresses and cooks as beneath him, and made sure that they knew this. But this was none of Arnold's business, anyway. It just irritated him a bit.

In spite of its smaller size, the café looked pretty much the same as Edwin had left it. The neon sign on the flat roof with the neon fishing rod doubled over fighting the neon bass was the same sign that Edwin had always had there. The red awnings over the big picture widows were from his day as well. Inside, the V-shaped counter with the twelve stools around it remained. The biggest change was that the tables that occupied what is now the bait shop had been replaced with booths along the dividing wall. Still, Jack had only had to sacrifice three tables in the deal. That and four hundred a month was as win-win as anything Jack would likely ever have again.

The red and white striped vinyl booths bandaged with duct-tape that lined up against the picture windows still had the table-top jukeboxes attached just over the condiment caddies. Although none of them worked anymore, they still had the original menus in them from greats like The Rolling Stones, The Beatles, The Doors, and too many from Elvis. Jack always made a few bucks on the quarters of out-of-towners hoping the machines still worked, a ruse he justified by putting a small, inconspicuous piece of masking tape on the boxes that read NO REFUNDS. It was safe to say that Jack was pretty much an ass to just about everyone.

As he walked from his back office to discover that the tables were filling up faster than Cherie could get to them, and that on the cook's line plates of sunnyside up eggs, pancakes, and omelets were dying under the heat lamps, he proved once again, at least to Cherie, that he was king ass. "Cherie! You got food dying up here! You wanna quit moving like you're underwater?" he blasted, then just stood there, not touching a plate.

Cherie, the coffee pot now a seemingly permanent appendage grasped in her hand, balanced a couple of plates on her forearm, and walked out to the row of booths. "Thanks for the help, Jack.

You're a real fuckin' hero, you know that?" she said under her breath as she set a plate of pancakes and an omelet on the table and moved to the next booth before she could hear the couple at the table say, "Cherie, this isn't what we ordered."

As she flew back to the cook's window to pick up some more plates, Jack just stood there staring at her with his arms folded in front of him. She didn't see him shake his head at her, but she knew he was doing it. As she passed the table that she had delivered the wrong order to, she still didn't hear, "Hey Cherie! This isn't our order." She even ignored the booth two down from them say, "I think that's ours." She just kept going, delivering the plates on her arm to a couple of oversized fishermen at the counter, while behind her, the man got up from his booth to deliver the pancakes and omelet to the booth two down from them.

Jack did nothing.

Sitting alone in another booth was a woman in a powder blue dress. Cherie hadn't approached her, much less served her, even though she'd been sitting there for quite awhile. But she didn't complain or even try to stop Cherie as she passed by; she just sat, and stared at the chaos. Anyone watching might have noticed that she seemed overly observant of what was going on, almost as if she was investigating something—or perhaps was just finding it all entertaining.

As Cherie refilled the coffee cups at the booth closest to the door along the dividing wall, Bret cautiously walked in, and sat where he always did at the booth on the other side of the door— the first one in the row by the big picture window and the broken jukeboxes. Cherie spun around and flipped the coffee cup on Bret's table and poured him a cup. "How's life treatin' you today, Bret?" she said, her voice laced with flirtation. Cherie flirted with everyone innocently until Bear was around.

"I don't know," he mumbled, "why don't you ask someone who has one?"

Cherie soaked up what Bret was going through, and what the town now thought of him, as it seemed to take some of the scorn off her shoulders. She bathed in it, just skirting the edges of rubbing it in his face. Bret didn't really care. Even in his dumps, he still had the strength to dislike her.

"Good one. I'll have to remember that one," she said, and then half-heartedly hustled back to the cook's window.

For those who came into the café every morning, the sound of the door crashing open had long ago ceased to startle them. It simply meant that Bear and Earl had arrived. Cherie didn't show any special attention to them. That was her game. She wanted Bear to show special attention to her, and it continued to frustrate her that Bear wouldn't play that game. They sat at the counter, filling a lot of space. Nonchalantly, Cherie walked over to them.

"If you want coffee, you're gonna have to wait. I'm just making a fresh pot."

Earl stabbed a snide look at her. "Does it look like we want coffee?"

Cherie sighed with a bleak "shoulda known" and planted two bottles of Summit Great Northern Porter in front of them.

After his first swig, Earl slammed his already half-empty bottle on the counter with a belch. Bear just took a gulp, not as wolfish as his brother. Cherie looked directly at Bear for some kind of attention, anything. He looked up at her, but it was a short-lived acknowledgement as his attention was diverted to Stella who had just come in, her shyness instantly apparent as she took in how busy it was. Her eyes on the floor, she scurried to the front counter, and stood waiting for Cherie. Stella felt as if all eyes were on her, judging her, but the truth was that only three people even noticed she was there.

Bear looked at her with a touch of compassion, but not so much that people, especially his brother, noticed. Watching her in a similar way was the woman in the powder blue dress who was still waiting to be served. She noticed Bear looking at Stella, and Stella looking back at him, quickly turning away when their eyes met. It's amazing what can be learned by just sitting and watching, and as the woman watched the exchange between Bear and Stella, her face broadcasted a degree of sympathy. The third person who saw Stella standing there was Cherie as she callously greeted her at the counter with a twenty-ounce Styrofoam cup of coffee.

"Morning, Stella. Here's your coffee—buck sixty."

Plates were still dying in the cook's window. Jack still did nothing. This was the only place in town, and he had a café full of regulars. He really didn't have to do anything.

Stella reached into her oversized canvas shoulder bag, and dug around the bottom, pulling up dimes, nickels, and quarters as she found them.

Cherie rolled her eyes. She wasn't impatient, she just thought it pathetic. "You know a few words from you once in a while would be nice," she said snidely.

Stella tried not to look at her, but did for a brief second, and then resumed her coin collecting. Cherie rolled her eyes again, and landed them in Bear's direction. She instantly caught the way he was looking at her and tried her best to ignore it, but couldn't, and true to her form, she stabbed at Stella. "I mean, you do know how to talk, don't ya?"

Stella cautiously stole another glance at Bear, but hadn't expected to actually make eye contact. Almost paralyzed by shyness, she quickly looked away, grabbed her coffee and began to leave, almost smashing into Sheriff Dwayne Walker and his new deputy, Eddie Brewster, as they were walking in. Bear watched her leave, and then threw a cold stare at Cherie who didn't notice it. He tried to think of a reason he was still with her, and the only one he came up with was that he had become comfortable. He had to laugh to himself at that weak excuse. He could've been a professional wrestler with his size and strength, but to his discredit, he had no strength when it came to this.

The sheriff and Eddie walked to their places at the counter where Bear and Earl sat, but not before the sheriff sent a cold look in Bret's direction. Even though he was the law in town, he still couldn't stop people from going where they wanted to, and Bret's being there, as the sheriff saw it, was a challenge aimed directly at his lack of that ability. Bret returned the stare, without a flinch, directly into the sheriff's increasingly slanted eyes. Bret did have guts, he'd give him that.

The sheriff sported a big girth about him, which he used and admired as a trophy of his own strength. Eddie was small and scrawny. In the sheriff's mind, small scrawny types needed to constantly prove their strength, and fearing their own weakness, tried to force respect by throwing what little they had around until someone took them seriously. That was Eddie in a nutshell. How Eddie had made it through the police academy was a question in itself. Having done so, though, he was almost certainly better off in Desire where chances were slim that physical force would be needed. If Bret hadn't put the sheriff in an abruptly deputy-less position, he probably would have continued looking through the stack of resumes. But, as he was quickly learning, Eddie was a breeze with the paper work, and for the sheriff, that was worth more to him than his shitty pension. On Eddie's first day on the job, the sheriff gave him an option of wearing a gun, and he, unlike Bret, demanded it, and constantly wore it more conspicuously than his badge.

Eddie simply plopped himself on the stool, but Sheriff Walker wasn't nearly as unbound as that. Before he could sit comfortably, he had to complete the ritual of grabbing his belt with both hands and giving it a good, solid tug to hoist up his pants. He sat down as if he'd been on his feet for hours, then, finally comfortable, he looked to the biker boys. "Boys. What's new in the world?" he asked.

"Not a ton." Bear replied followed by a swig of his beer.

Before Bear could ask how Eddie liked his new job, Cherie approached them with her ever-present coffee pot, and poured the officers each a cup.

"Morning guys. Keeping the streets safe today, are we?"

"Well since you're in here, we figured we don't need to be out there." Eddie quipped.

"Ha ha. You want your coffee in a cup or on your head?"

"Haven't seen Annie around lately, where's she been?" the Sheriff inquired.

"Why are you always so concerned with where my daughter is?"

"It's my job to be concerned."

As hard as he tried, or more to the point as little as he tried, the sheriff couldn't let the fact that Bret's presence there was a damaging reflection of his own authority. If he had it his way, Bret would be sitting in his jail cell dining on cold coffee and a stale bologna sandwich, but there was really nothing that tied him to Elle's death, from a legal standpoint, anyway. It pureed his gut knowing that there was nothing that he could legally do to punish Bret for his mistakes, other than send him to the unemployment lines. It was something that he would *find* a way to remedy, and his angry eyes, as they once again met Bret's, communicated loud and clear. Bear noticed the silent exchange immediately; Earl just noticed that he was out of beer, and motioned to Cherie for another. Bear knew that the growing confrontation between the sheriff and Bret could get ugly real fast, and always the empathetic peacekeeper, he tried to calm the approaching storm.

"Bret. You comin' down to the shop later? I'll finish your ink."

Bret took his eyes out of the dead-lock of the Sheriff's and landed them in Eddie's supercilious gaze. Eddie relished in this, as he now had an opportunity to assess his authority over Bret. He was younger, quicker, and better educated as an officer of the law than Bret was, and he had been waiting for an opportunity to let Bret know that he was having no problems filling his shoes. Bret didn't intend to give Eddie that chance, however, and just rolled his eyes at him. Eddie took that as a sign of insulting disrespect. He felt spat upon—just what Bret wished to accomplish. But, still, if the sheriff wasn't sitting next to him, Eddie wouldn't have the balls to go one-on-one with Bret. In fact, just yesterday, Eddie saw Bret walking toward him down Main Street, and ducked into a store-front before Bret noticed he was there. To say he was afraid of Bret was like saying Cherie was competent at her job. But under the gut-shield of the sheriff, Eddie found the confidence to challenge him, and he looked deeper into Bret, menacing. "If you got something you want to say to me, why don't you just say it right now?"

Bret raised an eyebrow at him. Soon, the tension overtook everyone in the café, everyone, that is, except the woman in the powder blue dress who was still waiting to be served. Sheriff Walker felt the looming explosion as well, and decided that while he couldn't control Bret any longer, he could control Eddie, and this just wasn't the time or the place for this to happen.

"Eddie, it's not your fight," he said with a shake of his head, and a sloped brow. And in that one sentence, he defused the tension and headed off the confrontation. Despite his new-found hatred for Bret, he still was the peacekeeper in town, and he was, for the past thirty years, the best Sheriff that could be remembered, even by the old-timers.

For the people in the café, this was excitement at its finest, and would be grist for the gossip mill for weeks to come. But for Bret, it was just the beginning of having to endure, among everything else, a life in the shadows of a scrawny, cocky, undeserving replacement. Giving a dismissive snort to Eddie, Bret looked to Bear. "I'll be up there this afternoon," he said, making sure Bear understood his irritation wasn't directed at him.

Bear nodded, and looked at the Sheriff who looked back at him appreciatively. Bear slightly lifted his bottle in a gesture of "no prob," then drained the contents. Glancing at the door, his thoughts returned to the woman who had just left. He slammed his empty bottle on the counter with a dull, wet thud, and slapped his brother on the back. "Go open the shop without me. I gotta go check something out," he said as he rose from his stool to leave.

"What, we're going already? I ain't drunk enough to stick a needle in nobody yet."

Like so many times before, Bear looked down at him like a father looked at his whining child. "Earl?"

Like that whining child, Earl returned with a heavy sigh of forced compliance. "Fine."

Earl stalled by taking his time to finish his beer, then slammed his bottle on the counter top, gave a loud, audible suck of air, and offered the patrons an off-key and gratuitously long belch. Bear rolled his eyes, but couldn't help laughing a little. So did the sheriff, and to a greater degree, Eddie.

"See you boys later," Bear said as he led Earl toward the door. Cherie stared at the retreating pair, feeling like an abandoned bag of trash. She stopped them before they could get to the door, and moved in seriously close to Bear.

"Aren't you forgetting something. . . ?" she said as she leaned into him, not giving him a chance to refuse her.

She invaded him with a kiss.

It was one of those gratuitous, wet and sloppy kinds of kisses, given without an ounce of romanticism. It was intrusive, forced— the kind that spawned an uncomfortable disgust in anyone who was unfortunate enough to witness it. It was a kiss not to show each other that they meant something stronger than rock to each other. It was a kiss that had the flavor of shackles being locked tight. It was cheap and showy and far from appropriate in front of all the patrons; more than one of them pushed their half eaten plates forward at the sight of it.

And Jack did nothing.

His was the only game in town. Everyone there would be back tomorrow morning, just as they were every morning. Still, if nothing more than for his own amusement, Cherie would hear a mouthful about that crude display at the end of her shift. It was always at the end of the shifts that Jack let 'em have it. Why chance someone walking out in the middle of a shift?

When Cherie finally released him, she, as she had known for sometime now, again detected a certain distance in him. She kept telling herself it couldn't be her; it probably had to do with him working at the shop too much.

"What's wrong? Are you mad at me?" she asked with pouty lips.

He smiled sarcastically. "I'm always mad at you," he answered, giving her a good, hard slap on her ass before turning his attention back to Earl who, creating his own little scene, twisted to reach into a family of four's table, and snatched a piece of toast off the father's plate. Having shoved the whole thing in his mouth, he smiled a smile of wet bread squishing through his teeth, and asked, "Er ju golna eat dis?"

The father gazed at him with wide, almost fearful eyes, and the kids just snickered as Earl laughed, and walked out the door.

Bret, finding a last refuge of humor, couldn't help a little laughing smile himself.

CHAPTER FOUR

RNIE'S SERVICE STATION SAT IN THE OXBOW OF THE curve in the road that led north to Main Street. It was the first building that visitors saw as they drove into Desire, and the last they saw as they left, that is, if like most visitors they were either heading back down to the Twin Cities or taking that sharp left turn toward Duluth. Directly across the street from the station were the remnants of a long abandoned iron ore mine that closed just after LBJ was inaugurated. Now all that existed on that once productive site was a twenty-five-hundred-foot hole in the earth with miles of tunnels in all directions. An overgrowth of trees, shrubs, and climbing vines had grown up and around it, shielding it from view for those who stopped at Ernie's, and no one who didn't already know it was there probably never would.

Over the decades, the accumulation of rain and snow had filled it so that an entirely new lake was formed, but not any that the Department of Natural Resources had stocked with lake trout hybrids or "splakes" as they were known locally, as they had done with so many other abandoned flooded mine pits across the area. This one was home primarily to nothing more than floating islands of gooey green algae. It really wasn't a pretty sight, but that didn't matter, because to most of the tourists, anything that couldn't be seen from the road really didn't exist anyway.

Ernie knew that mine pit lake well. In his youth, the creature at the bottom of the pit threatened to swallow him whole by scattering the outer lip of the lake with loose rocks so that any kid walking too close might fall in and be devoured. His fears came from the stories his father told him about the buried treasure at the bottom of the pit that was left when the Vikings raided Canada. That's what the creature was protecting. Anyone who could get to it before the creature knew they were there would be rich beyond his dreams. He wasn't sure he should believe his father's stories, but did anyway. As often as he could after his father set him free from a day of home school, he would run to the pit and walk the edge, getting closer each time. A few times he got a little too close, but he didn't care; if he fell in he might get to the treasure before the creature found him. Ernie still thought often about those stories and how if he had fallen in, he might still be there to this day. Maybe that was what his father had in mind all the time.

As he sat in his duct-taped recliner, lulled by the television but not really paying attention to it, his thoughts came back from his youth and the pit lake. It was a slow morning; only a few cars had stopped, most to ask the way into town. Maybe if he went out to that pit one more time, he might see something shining on the bottom. But those were just stories. He had a shop to run, and TV to watch, and that, in and of itself, was his treasure. He smiled at the thought of that, and then, the alert hose dinged and broke his reverie.

An SUV, one of the big ones that seemed its only design was to guzzle more gas, rolled to a forced halt at the pumps. Towed behind it was an eighteen-foot fully-loaded bass boat equipped with a front-mounted trolling motor, the kind that had a foot pedal for hands-free steering. The outboard had 150-horsepower engine under its hood, with a side console steering wheel with all

the gauges, gadgets, bells and whistles available. Ernie was immediately taken with the boat. Its console was nicer than some dash-
boards he'd seen on a few cars. Hell, the whole boat was nicer than
some cars he'd seen. Usually, around here, people only towed
beaten up old tiller boats with small horsepower outboards, or
simply had canoes strapped to the roof of their cars. This was
truly a treat for his eyes, and he stood and dumbfoundedly stared
at it until the driver, short on patience, stepped from his gas guz-
zler, and reached for the pump.

Still mesmerized, Ernie walked to the pump. "That's okay.
This is full service here," he said as he grabbed the hose from it's
holster.

"Great. Fill 'er up," he said, in a demeaning tone. But the tone
missed its mark, getting tangled in Ernie's brilliant simplicity. The
man wouldn't let it go, though. He thought this slouching gas
jockey was beneath him, and couldn't resist the opportunity to let
him know it. "Also the tank in the boat. And we hit a lot of bugs on
the way up here, why don't you wash the windshield while you're
at it. When you're done with that, why don't you fill the washer
fluid and check the oil. Got that all?"

Ernie turned to face him, caught off guard by the request. Was
it possible to check the oil in a boat? He didn't know. "In the boat
or in the truck?" he asked cautiously.

The man looked directly at him, then he pointed to the hood
of the truck. "Um, in the truck," he said, his tone nicely matching
the perplexed look on his face.

"Okee," Ernie said as he plugged the nozzle into the truck's gas
tank. The pump began to sing that all too familiar *Ka-chunk, Ka-
chunk* sound that had become music to Ernie. To him, it sounded
like *Ka-ching! Ka-ching!* Like it did every time he heard that music,
the opening bass line from Pink Floyd's "Money" crept into his
head, and would stay there all day long.

Ernie took off his cap, and wiped the sweat from his brow with
the top of his forearm. He looked at the driver who looked back at
him, expecting him to pop the hood and continue, but Ernie just

stood there, wondering why the man was staring at him like that. Ernie then moved over to the boat. "Now this, Sir, is a boat," he said, leaning over it. "Look at this. You've got everything on this thing. Those fish don't stand a chance with you on the lake."

"Yes. Well, we like it," he remarked, then impatiently motioned to the truck. "Could you just . . ." He made a sweeping motion with his fingers in the direction of the hood.

"Oh, yeah. Check the oil, right?"

Ernie hadn't really forgotten, although he was known to have a little whoops-a-daisy of his thinker every now and again, especially when it came to having to act like he knew what he was doing. He reluctantly moved around to the front of the truck. He was smart, though. He knew the more he dilly-dallied around with this, the less chance there was that the man would stop the gas flow until his tank was ready to geyser.

"Yep. Don't see a lotta boats like that around here, I can tell you," he said as he lifted the hood, and looked around at the incomprehensible maze of tubes, and wires, and various metal things. "I've lived my whole life here, and I don't recall seeing one that nice," he continued as he fumbled around just enough to get his hands dirty.

"You've lived here all your life, on this lake, and never seen a boat like this before?" the man asked with a curl of his lip, trying to keep some distance from the open hood as if a blob of grease might jump out and affix itself to his L. L. Bean fishing vest.

Ernie slammed the hood shut and wiped his hands with an equally dirty towel that he yanked out of his back pocket. "Just makin' conversation," he said as he gave the nozzle another squeeze, topping off the tank.

"That's an odd way of making conversation."

Ernie had a lot of practice tuning out insults over the years, and although this guy wasn't directly insulting him, his tone was. He tried his best to ignore it, and just grabbed the hose, plugged it into the gas tank on the boat, and changed the subject. Still, he was a little nervous as to where this might go.

"I haven't seen you up here before, you from outta town?"

"Doesn't that answer your own question?"

"How do you figure?"

"If you live here, and if you haven't seen us up here before, doesn't that tell you that, yes, we are from out of town?" He laughed a little at how stupid he just made Ernie look, and Ernie knew it.

"Just making conversation," he replied softly.

"You're not the brightest bulb on the tree, are ya?" the man said, and then looked over his shoulder to see if his wife, sitting in the passenger seat reading a magazine was listening. She wasn't. From the look of how engrossed she was in her magazine, she may not have even realized the truck had stopped moving.

"I get by," Ernie said even softer, deflated.

The man rolled his eyes but this time not at Ernie. He did it at himself because he knew he had gone too far, and a rush of guilt swept over him.

"Look. I'm sorry. I didn't mean that."

"It's nothin' I haven't heard before. I get used to it, I guess," he said, purposely not making eye contact with him as he plugged the hose back into the pump.

"That'll be thirty-nine seventy-five."

The man dug into his pocket and produced a volume of bills bound by a gold plated money clip with a pewter dry fly emblem on it. He stripped off a fifty. "Here. Keep it."

Not knowing what else to say, the man gave a half smile, and turned to slip back into his truck. Ernie, never one to be comfortable letting someone go without a smile, no matter if they deserved it or not, stopped him.

"I don't suppose you'd like to join my Wall of Fame, would ya?"

"What's that?"

Ernie found his old capricious self again. "In the shop, I take a picture of everyone that stops by. I'd love to add you, your wife there, and that boat to my collection."

The man's hand was already on the door handle of the car, but Ernie achieved his goal. Instead of getting in, the man stuck his head in the car and said, "Honey, get out of the car for a second."

Ernie smiled and rose into action. He lined them up along side that beautiful boat, framed them perfectly in the viewfinder, and Flash! A perfect photo of a happy couple about to enjoy a day of fishing.

To Ernie, that's what it was all about. As he waved goodbye and pocketed the fifty, he smiled at himself for a job well done. Yes, he may not be the brightest bulb on the tree, but with two full tanks in one stop, a juicy tip, and making a real sourpuss leave with a smile, he felt as smart as he needed to be.

But most of that glory faded as he posted the photo on the Wall of Fame, and ran his finger along the smiling, happy couple standing in front of the greatest boat he'd ever seen. They seemed as if they never knew the meaning of the word *want* or *worry*. What they did seem to know was contentment, something Ernie knew only in fantasy. Maybe if he were smarter, he could have what that man took so much for granted. But people don't simply become smarter, do they?

He walked back over to his recliner, and plopped himself into it making a windy sound as the air rushed out of the cushions past the duct-tape. In time, the virtuous feelings of today would again lose the match to the next bout of painful ones, but as he always did, he'd stuff the pain into that lockbox deep within him where just the mere thought of exploring scared him from thinking about it any further. However, he had learned more than once that boxes stuffed full tend to leak.

He sat with his camera at the ready.

⊙⊙⊙

EVERYONE HAS A LOCKBOX, AND PEOPLE PUT ALL SORTS OF horrifying things inside of them. Everyone does it. As Stella sat behind her counter, sipping her still hot coffee and watching Bear rummage through the shelves of books, she tried unsuccessfully to stuff her anxiety in her own lockbox. Stella's lockbox was so stuffed already, though, that the anxiety didn't only leak out, it grew greater fed from having noticed that Bear was paying more attention to her than he was to the books. Every time their eyes met, she looked away, and landed them on the computer screen bordered by pastel Post-it Notes on which she'd hand-lettered personal affirmations.

Do something wonderful just for yourself.

Smile for no reason.

There is beauty around you and in you.

She'd written them to herself too long ago, but she still found them to be necessary. At that moment, they were necessary for her to find her nerve to go over to him. Calmed by the affirmations and a deep but quiet breath, Stella slowly rose off her chair and walked toward him, finding more confidence with every step.

This was, after all, her store. But still, there was something about him that was beginning to contradict her confidence. Maybe it was the way he was looking at her. Or maybe it was the fact that she really hardly knew him, other than he was Cherie's boyfriend. Maybe it was all the random gossip she had heard around town, but who on earth knew if all that was true?

No, this was her shop, and Bear was a customer no matter who he was, and it appeared as if he was searching for something.

"Bear?" she said, walking up behind him. "Can I find something for you?"

Bear turned, seeming a bit nervous himself. "Ah, no. Well, Maybe. I'm still looking for a book I haven't seen in a while."

"What's it called? I may know it."

Bear paused, not sure of what to say next. *Should I tell her the name of the book, or tell her the real reason I came in here?* "Listen, this is going to sound kinda strange, but would you want to—"

The door chime rang him out of his question.

Arnold stumbled in, managing a cumbersome box of books. "Morning Stella, Bear," he said as he hurried to the counter and dropped the books down with a hollow thud. He tried to catch his breath, but was impatient with it. "I was going through some of Elle's things," he took a deep breath and continued, "and I thought you might want these books."

Stella reluctantly walked up to the counter as she didn't want to leave Bear hanging, but at the same time she almost welcomed the diversion from the awkward affair of standing there alone with him. She dove into the box and began to take out a book at a time. She was familiar with every one of them, and neatly placed them on the counter before taking out the next. There were several books she wanted, and even some that she knew would sell, but these were Elle's books. Could she bring herself to do that?

Arnold reached in the box and pulled out a journal that was sitting on one of the stacks that Stella hadn't gotten to yet. It was an old, faded, battle-worn journal with time yellowed loose leaf pages tucked here and there between the pages. Two old rubber bands bound it closed that looked as if to touch them would cause them to disintegrate.

He looked at it for a reflecting moment, and handed it to Bear. "I'm glad you're up here, Bear. It saves me a trip down to your shop."

Bear took the journal, almost afraid to touch it. "I know that you and Elle loved each other's poetry. I think she would have liked you to have this."

Bear slowly took off the rubber bands that even when separated from it, retained the rectangular shape of the book. Gently, he filed through the pages, careful not to touch them for more than a second. Without giving it more than that simple once-over, he closed it, not wanting to make that moment any more melancholy for both himself or Arnold.

He had never in his life received a gift that meant this much to him. Not even when he was incarcerated and Cherie had bought him his leather biker jacket on which she had sewn his old denim vest, on the back of which she'd added embroidered red chevrons that read DESIRE on the top and MINNESOTA on the bottom. He thought about that jacket everyday as his salvation, and couldn't wait to slip into it upon his release, which he did on the very day he was set free. Now, only on the hottest days of the year was he seen without it. But this gift was something more special than he'd ever had in his possession. Moved beyond expression, the great connoisseur of poetic verse could only find the simplest of words. "Thank you, Arnold."

Knowing that he would cherish it as he did, Arnold said, "You're welcome" with a gratified smile.

"I didn't know Elle had this book," Stella said as she held up a book that Bear took great notice of, probably because of it's title.

The book had a sky blue cover with a single arrow with red fletching and a sandpaper sharp metal arrowhead running diagonally across its face. Embossed in black with yellow trim, the title read *Love, Elusive*. In the same embossed fashion, the author's name, Rob Harper, filled the bottom half.

"That was one of her favorites," Arnold said with a fond smile.

She opened it and let the pages ripple over her thumb. "She told me about this book before she . . ." She stopped, then dropped the book back in the box, and began putting the others back as well. "I can't take these. I don't feel right about selling her things."

"Then just keep them for yourself. You'd be doing me a favor by taking them."

She paused, and then understanding his need to give them to her, smiled and nodded her thanks. Then she looked at Bear.

A silence fell, that kind of silence that binds so closely as to be uncomfortable if allowed to linger too long. Bear broke it with a deep inhaling breath. "Well, I should really get to the shop before Earl burns it down or something," he said and began to walk out, then turned, and held up the journal to Arnold. "Thanks again for this, Arnold."

"Enjoy it."

Stella watched until Bear disappeared out the door into Desire, leaving Arnold in awkward silence. "All right then, I'll tell Martin you said hello."

She snapped out of it. "I'm sorry, please do," she said, visibly embarrassed.

Arnold noticed the exchange between her and Bear. How could he not? And although it was not his place to nudge it, he smiled his approval at her. Then turned and, with a continuous smile, walked out the door.

"Oh Stella, 'fool' doesn't even begin to describe you," she whispered to herself, then opened *Love, Elusive,* and lost herself in the first page. As she did, she didn't notice that the woman in the powder blue dress was standing outside seemingly window-shopping, but more so was looking in at her.

CHAPTER FIVE

THE TWINS AND ANNIE HAD STAYED IN BED, WITH their arms wrapped around each other like a pack of hibernating wolf cubs, until just after noon. Usually they were up and out and adventuring much earlier than that, but it was hot outside, and that always bred lethargy in those who had no specific place to go.

One of the twins' "thinking" places was underneath the wooden walking bridge that spanned the Birch River, which fed into the lake. It was always low this time of year, but still beautiful nonetheless. At any given time, schools of silver sucker fish, and even a brown trout or two could be seen darting in and out from the cover of the bridge.

As for the bridge, although it still held its structural integrity, people nevertheless threw salt over their shoulders before they crossed it. But, no one in town really ever used the bridge anymore, especially on a hot day like this, so it was a perfect place for the three of them to frequently abandon themselves in seclusion from the rest of the world.

The bridge's legs were constructed from the same kind of pine poles used to make telephone poles, with cross beams, some of them now missing, to support the plank surface of the bridge. As a preserving agent, the legs were coated with a sticky tar, but most of it had eroded away over the years. Still, for this reason, Annie never went near the legs. She couldn't stand that hot tar and rotting timber smell anyway. She just waded, barefoot as always, in the transparent waters of the river. Of course, every so often, she couldn't resist the urge to kick water up at her boyfriends who had wedged themselves in the crossbeams under the bridge.

"You know what the number-one problem with this country is?" Stee offered.

"I can think of about a million," Annie replied, prancing in the water.

"It's not the economy or our government or insurance companies. The problem is that there is not one unexplained mysterious thing about our civilization," Ven continued.

"There is nothing to demand a sense of wonder for future generations to awe at," Stee added.

"Except at how we managed to survive the twentieth century," Annie quipped.

"Exactly. There is no Stonehenge—"

"No pyramids, or any kind of effigies."

"What about the golden arches?" Annie laughed—a quip that garnered her a bout of happy laughter from the twins.

"The biggest house of mud in Nebraska," Stee laughed.

"The corn palace in South Dakota," Ven offered.

"Mount Rushmore," Annie added.

Stee and Ven became serious at that example. "You know what future generations are gonna say about that?"

"Here's the most sacred land to the Dakota people—"

"This is their Jerusalem."

"Then the American masses murdered their way across it and carved four white, dead aristocrats into a mountainside."

"That'll leave 'em with a sense of awe. That's not how I want our culture to be remembered," Stee asserted.

"We have envisioned something that is primitive, yet futuristic," Ven said.

"What, like the pyramids, or the Easter Island heads?" Annie asked.

"Exactly," offered Stee. "We still have no clue why they exist, but the one thing we do know is it proved that the people once existed."

"Future generations will react in awe of this, saying 'Here's a beacon of culture from the greatest culture-starved society in the history of humanity,'" Ven preached.

"Our instructions will be easily decoded, and societies will form, and pilgrimages will be made every February to celebrate our vision."

"But at the very least, it'll be something that proves we once existed."

"Because the very essence of our existence, through which we will all live forever, is that which we create."

Annie was confused, but excited. "What are you guys talking about?"

The twins smiled a big, toothy grin at her. They had accomplished what they set out to do, and that was to find out if their girlfriend was going to be receptive to their idea.

"C'mon. It's about time we show you."

Off into the forest, on that lonely stretch of dirt road that went past Bear's dock, the twins, with Annie sandwiched between them, kicked up clouds of dust as they drove their self-customized snowmobile to a spot in the woods that finally opened up to a huge clearing that was obviously clear-cut by the lumber companies. The evidence of an old, broken-down deer stand suggested that the clearing was used by hunters until being abandoned altogether, probably when the state purchased the one hundred acres north of the lake for the addition to the Bear Island State Forest. But the twins didn't know for sure, nor did they care. This was one of those spots that, because of the years of abuse to the forest was destined to be a permanent hole in the thick woods. It was perfect for what the twins had in mind.

Piled at the south end of the clearing was a large mound of what at first appeared to be abandoned junk. But as the snowmobile came closer, Annie made out three full-sized telephone poles, scattered lumber, a chainsaw, a spool of cable, and a variety of power tools. The snowmobile sputtered to a stop just before the clutter.

Stee and Ven stepped off the snowmobile, but Annie stayed for a minute, trying to figure out what the excitement was all about. She had thought that she and her boyfriends told each other everything. Why hadn't they told her about this? Her hesitancy perplexed them—they figured she'd be more excited than she apparently was.

"This is the place," Ven said with a look that asked for approval.

"What place?" she asked as she climbed off the vehicle.

"Where our history will meet our future," Stee announced with enormous savor.

Annie walked around, staring at the various pieces of clutter. "Guys, isn't this Mr. Swanson's missing chainsaw?"

The twins smiled a "yes" at her, as she continued to rummage. "Telephone poles. Cable. Nail guns. What are you guys up to?"

"We're going to build that beacon of culture."

"Right here."

"Why didn't you tell me about all this?" Annie said, obviously annoyed.

"Because if we got caught, you'd go down with us."

"We have nothing to live for but this. You do."

"Like what? Guys, now that Elle's gone, I have nothing to live for but you. If we go down, we all go down together."

The twins smiled because of the way Annie continually made them feel genuinely wanted, and that was more important to them than they would let on. They walked to her, stood on either side, and as they put their arms around her, she wrapped an arm around each of them. Together, they stood, staring silently at the pile of materials and at the infinite possibilities flooding their imaginations.

"Elle always told me I'd do something great with my life. This has gotta be what she meant," Annie said with a reminiscent smile.

"Then let's consider this a monument to her," Ven said.

"The problem is that we can't steal everything we need," Stee hinted.

"We're going to need capital."

The answer dawned in an instant on Annie: all she had to do was find out when Cherie was next in charge of closing up the café. She smiled at her devious idea.

"Leave that to me," she said, giving them a final squeeze before she let go of them, and headed back to the snowmobile. One thing that could be said about her among everything else was that when she got something in her head, nothing could stop her. You had to give her stars for that. "Take me home. I have to check something out," she said as she leaped on the snowmobile.

The twins looked at each other, shrugged and smiled, and did as she asked.

As they sputtered around the corner, passing the bait shop and café, Annie looked in through the big picture windows and saw Cherie sitting at the counter, probably waiting for Bear to come and get her, but as he had told her several times, she could either wait or walk when he had a client. Annie took comfort that her mother was trapped in the café, because now she could find out what she needed without interference.

ᘒᘓ

NEXT DOOR, CHARLIE DUG THROUGH THE BAIT REFRIGERATOR looking for a snack among the stacked containers of night-crawlers, angleworms, waxworms, and leeches each on its own marked shelf. The other half of the refrigerator held the same types of things most do—a container of half eaten lasagna, a head of lettuce, half a loaf of bread, a few apples, an open package of salami, jars of strawberry jelly, peanut butter, and in the back, a jar of opened mayonnaise with a knife sticking out of it. Charlie's attention was diverted to the containers of worms. He grabbed a Styrofoam container of nightcrawlers, and a plastic one of angleworms, and brought them over to the counter where Arnold was working diligently on something with a lot of colorful feathers, wire, and hooks. Charlie never once inquired what he was doing, and Arnold never volunteered it.

"Arnold, Arnold, Arnold. How many times do I have to go over this with you?"

"What's that, Charlie?"

"I'm tellin' you, fish're smarter these days then they usta be. These worms gotta be fresh, or the fish'll smell it."

"You think so?" Arnold replied, not bothering to look up from what he was doing.

"I know it. I've seen it. They know if the worms are in Styrofoam or in plastic. They can smell the Styrofoam, but the problem is, they stay fresher in Styrofoam than they do in plastic. So they gotta be real fresh if you put 'em in plastic."

"How 'bout I put 'em in a paper bag for you, Charlie?"

"Naw. Fish'll smell that, too. I tell ya, they's smarter now. They've seen just about everything we've come up with to throw at them."

"Is that right?" he said, twisting a hoop in the wire with a pair of needlenose pliers.

"That's right. I should charge you a consulting fee for everything I do around here."

"And I should charge you rent for all the space you take up around here," Arnold said with a smirk as he looked up at him.

Charlie didn't have a quick rebuttal to this, and that caused a pause that with every passing second, the smirk grew bigger on Arnold's face.

"I've got money, you know," was all he could come up with.

"You've got money? You take a bath in a bucket in your living room!"

"Not anymore. Not since the ice melted on the lake," Charlie countered.

Arnold burst into laughter. He really did like having that old codger around.

The door chime rang followed by Martin walking in with a stringer of largemouth bass, three small walleye, and a small northern pike in hand. The color had faded out of them which meant that they had been long on the stringer. His morning was packed with action, but as the day progressed, the fish just seemed to turn off. He'd seen that happen many times before when a pressure front moved in and the fish just hugged the bottom, unwilling to chase anything down no matter how hungry they were. But with a lake in his backyard that he knew he'd be on every day until his record was broken, it was best to call it a day instead of sitting out there getting eaten alive by bugs.

"Hey, Dad. Morning, Mr. Swanson," he announced as he walked over to the aerated minnow tanks, and hooked the stringer to the edge of the sucker minnow tanks, dropping the fish in the water.

"Martin! Looks you like you hit the jackpot!" Charlie said, actually impressed.

"Yeah. No records broken, but at least it's dinner."

Charlie looked directly at Arnold. "Did you catch those with worms that were in Styrofoam or plastic?" he asked with high eyebrows.

Arnold just shook his head and went back to forming the wire.

"None of the above. Spinning jig tipped with a power leech," Martin said as he walked behind the counter to the dry-erase board.

"Spinning jig? That's plastic. Fish can smell that."

"Those didn't."

Charlie's logic had been unintentionally challenged, and he scrambled in his mind for something to say to save face or Arnold would never let him live it down.

"Well, that's 'cause those are probably dumb fish."

Both Martin and Arnold laughed just a touch at his logic. Martin grabbed the blue and red-stained cloth hanging from the edge of the board and erased the 967 in the NUMBER OF DAYS column.

"Yeah, well, dumb or not, it wasn't a bad morning for day nine hundred and sixty-eight." He said as he wrote 968.

"You're in the home stretch. I'm so proud of you son," Arnold said, giving his son a hug and mussing his hair. "This is my boy!"

Martin smiled, then playfully pushed him away. "I gotta get to work. John called twice this week asking about his head."

Arnold watched him proudly as he disappeared through the door into his studio. After the door closed behind him, there was a silence that Arnold never minded. He just went back to work on whatever it was he was making. Charlie, on the other hand, couldn't stand silence. When he wasn't in the bait shop, that's all he had.

"Yup. These worms already got the Styrofoam smell on 'em. They're no good anymore."

"You know Charlie, in all the years I've known you I've never once seen you out on that lake."

Charlie thought about that fact for a moment. The truth might as well come out, and he delivered it with impassive grace. "Yeah, well, I don't like to fish much."

Arnold raised yet another eyebrow at him as the door chime rang with the considerable entrance of Sheriff Walker. A sudden seriousness filled the room.

Playtime was over.

"Dwayne," Arnold said, giving him his full attention.

"Arnold, Charlie," Dwayne nodded.

"What's the news?" Arnold inquired.

The sheriff took off his hat, set it on the counter, and then leaned his weight on his elbow. He was never a man who beat around the bush or sugar-coated what he had to say. That's why everything he said demanded belief. "The news is it looks like it may not have just been a simple boating accident."

The color drained from Arnold's face.

"What do you mean?" Arnold asked seriously, softly.

"I just found something. Elle's boat hit those rocks head on. The bow was ripped apart."

"That's right . . ." Arnold said with a tone that expressed he was a little afraid of what might come next.

"But the outboard was damaged."

"What!?" Arnold said a little louder than he expected.

"Yeah. There was damage to the prop, the cavitation plate right above the prop was broken almost in half, and the trim tab was also ripped completely off."

Arnold took a step back. He stared in silence unable to swallow the weight of that news.

"What's a trim tab?" Charlie cautiously asked.

"It helps control the steering. I think she did see those rocks, and couldn't do anything about it. From the scars on those rocks, it looks like she just made a bee-line from the dock to those rocks, and by the time she figured there was something wrong with the steering, she couldn't do anything about it."

"What does that mean?" Charlie asked.

"I don't know yet, Charlie. Right now, it appears as if someone took that boat out the night before Elle did."

"Wait a minute. Are you saying someone sabotaged her boat?" Arnold insisted.

"No. Not necessarily."

Although he hated doing it, Arnold couldn't help but begin to compile a list of suspects in his head. The sheriff had already completed that exercise—and for him, only one name had surfaced.

"Well couldn't that damage be caused by her hitting the rocks?" Arnold asked, searching for another explanation.

"No. There was no scarring on the stern or on the outboard from those rocks. Do you know who else could've used that boat the night before she did?"

"Me, Martin. Just about anyone. Everyone in town knew she went out to Arrowhead Island every morning to write her poetry. The boat was always tied to the dock, and people who knew Elle knew she kept the keys in it. It could've been anybody."

"Well, right now it looks as if whoever used that boat the

night before Elle did may have done something to it that caused the accident."

Arnold just stared at him. This was Elle they were talking about. Everyone loved her. Desire became a ghost town on the day of her funeral. Why would someone want to hurt her? It was all simply just too much for Arnold to comprehend.

"Who would have the motivation to do something like that to her?" Charlie asked. Arnold had no more words at all.

The sheriff paused for a second. One name kept repeating itself in his head. He looked at Arnold who had turned clammy white, then back at Charlie. "I can only think of one person. I'm going to dig some more—I'll let you know what I find. In the meantime, keep quiet about this. The last thing we need is a witch hunt on our hands."

CHAPTER SIX

BEAR AND EARL'S TATTOO SHOP TOOK OVER THE restored building that had always been alleged to be a house of ill repute from the turn of the century all the way through the end of prohibition. It was said that the loggers and railroad workers used to line up at the brothel's door every payday, and that it was a second home to the gangsters and liquor runners between Chicago and Canada. Situated in the middle of nowhere, the location was perfect for such goings on: The law either couldn't find it or more likely knew exactly where it was, but chose to partake of its pleasures as opposed to raiding it or closing it down.

Bear and Earl's cousin, Ted Molly, bought and renovated the abandoned building, dividing it into the tattoo shop in the front, and a three-bedroom apartment in the back. He did the work himself, and was rightfully proud of the result. In spite of conducting his own "archeological" research during the remodeling process, Ted never found any real evidence of the former brothel, just rusty nails and door hinges. Truth was, he wasn't much of a digger, and Earl really couldn't care less what was there before, so he never gave looking into it a second thought. Bear, on the other hand, would have simply found it interesting. So the story went unproven, but people still believed it, which wasn't bad for business at all.

When Ted opened his doors for business in late '79, he had quickly earned himself a reputation as one of the best ink pokers in the upper Midwest, even though when he started the fad was still a decade away, and he would be a few years retired by then. Even so, business was good enough from the beginning that there was always bread on the table and beer in the fridge. At first, his clients were mostly bikers and military personnel who drove up from Fort Ripley, which was about an hour drive south of Desire. As time went on and his reputation spread, his client base expanded, and soon he had people coming over from Wisconsin, the Dakotas, and even Chicago who made the ten-hour trek just to get their ink done by Ted.

Bret was at the tattoo shop regularly; he'd begun collecting body art in his teens. Only two of Bret's tattoos were Ted's work, though. Bret hung out more for the ambience than to get himself inked.

When Ted retired to Miami in '87, the shop went to Earl. Ted couldn't think of any other way Earl would be able to earn a living, and he believed Earl would keep the business true to what Ted had begun. And for the most part, he had. Ted offered half the business to Bear as well, recognizing that he had the greater artistic talent. But at the time, Bear had other plans.

Bear really never had a permanent home since he was old enough to fly from his parent's nest, and quickly found that the Kerouacian lifestyle fit him well. He knew that with Earl taking over Ted's place, he'd always have a place to lay his head and settle for awhile if he wanted it. And so, with that security in his back pocket, Bear hit the open road. Until it was stolen, he lived in his tent, or if he'd gotten hold of some cash, the occasional cheap motel. Often, he'd crash with people he met at bars or at parties— sometimes for days if the girl was worth hanging around for.

Whenever night fell, he'd have a place to lay his head even if it was just in a sleeping bag on the side of the road. He ate when he was hungry, slept when he was tired, and never once did he have anywhere in particular that he needed to be. But over the years, that in and of itself had become tiresome.

Eventually, the open road became its own prison. Bear was the type of person who sized up situations almost instantly. If things weren't good, he found a way out, usually by just getting up and leaving without ever looking back. He never once tried to stay with a bad situation and try to make it right; life was just too short. So, as the town-to-town, flophouse-to-flophouse lifestyle started to feel more and more like a bad situation, Bear knew it was time to look into something that he was missing in his life, and that was permanence.

There had been everything out there to challenge his brawn, but very little to challenge his intellect. Bear had always intended to get a college degree in something or another someday, and that challenge turned out to be the next logical step in his life's journey. He realized two things pretty quickly: One, he wanted to major in literature; two, there was no way he could afford it. That was, until he started shacking up with Melissa.

Melissa managed a flower shop. She decided that she could use some good karma and that she'd help Bear earn his degree any way she could. They lived together for four years—right up until he graduated as magna cum laude of his class with a degree in literature. But because of the way in which Melissa acquired the money for his tuition, its glory was short lived, and true to his truthful nature, he took the fall, and spent the next few years behind bars.

When he was released from prison six months ago, he moved in with Earl, taking one of the rooms in the back of the shop, but after about a week, Earl asked him to either sleep in the shop, or out in the yard. He'd even spring for the tent. The problem was that Earl was not a heavy enough sleeper to deal with Bear.

Bear got his name in prison, and thought he could confide in his brother that the name "Bear" was not given to him by the other inmates because of his huge muscle-laden physique, but because he snored like a hibernating bear. Needless-to-say, he didn't make a lot of friends among the other inmates after lights out.

When Bear told him about the nickname, he also told Earl to keep it to himself. When he returned home, though, Bear was the name everyone called him. To his credit, Earl did do Bear right by telling the town that the other inmates called him that out of respect for his strength. Earl might have been an asshole, but at least he used a sliver of good judgment every once in a while.

At first, Bear hated the name. But as more and more people called him that, and knowing they considered it a respect to his size and strength, he began to like it. After a while, most people seemed to have forgotten he even had another name. He was Bear, and that was that. The only downside was having to live up to the name, and that was never how Bear saw himself. Furthermore, it wasn't how he wanted everyone else to see him either.

After a few sleepless nights, Earl, in his own abrasive form of diplomacy, suggested that because Cherie usually passed out every night, Bear should stay at her place more often. Now he stayed there or on the dock almost every night, and Earl was all the happier for it.

Earl had done some redecorating since taking over his cousin's place. He put in new reclining chairs that looked a lot like those in a dentist's office, figuring comfortable clients were happy clients. Besides, he got sick of people falling out of the folding chairs and knocking their heads on the floor when they'd pass out at first prick—a situation so common that he kept a container of aromatic ammonia on hand for just such occasions.

The shop's walls were papered with various tattoo design sheets, among them were topless mermaids and mystical designs of wizards, skulls and angels, colorful butterflies and animals. The majority of them were biker and tribal designs that rang of true American patriotism just to look at them. Only a few of them were from a supply company, but because those were usually cheesy and generic, Bear and Earl created originals.

Pictures of their work, not unlike Ernie's Wall of Fame filled two huge cork memo boards just behind the counter. Nailed to the wood frame of one of the boards was a biker calendar opened to March 1996, because the picture was of two naked women straddling the Harley Bear had before he got Emily. Earl was actually the one who insisted the calendar be kept up, saying that every time he looked at it, he wished he was that bike.

Just below that, next to Bear's computer, was a glass front wood cage that housed Earl's pet corn snake, Nicasa. Earl had always liked snakes, and in their youth, he and Bear knew the best places to find hoards of garter snakes as they came out of their hibernating dens in the spring. Although it had been a while since they'd been to the dens, they were probably still there, and going back again was one of those things they always said they were going to do someday, but probably never would. They used to catch one or two garters to keep over the summer that they'd release back at the den in the fall. Earl used to paint a few of the scales with red nail polish to see if they would catch the same ones again in the spring, and a few times, they did. Since then, Earl has never been without at least one snake as a pet.

The work counter, like the chairs, looked as if it belonged in a dentist's office with needles soaking in stainless steel pans of sterilizing solution, and a stainless steel autoclave sitting behind them. Behind that, lined against the back wall were bottles of germicidal Benz All for cold sterilization, disposable razors, alcohol swabs, non stick pads, rolls of tape, boxes of latex gloves, foil pack dispensers of Bacitricin packets, Vitamin A & D ointment, and Vaseline.

Bear and Earl still used sticks of unscented deodorant for applying the ditto paper design to the client which were lined up with everything else on the bleached Formica counter top. In a locked drawer under the work counter were bottles of ready mixed colored pigments with colors like Dragon Green, Aztec Brown, and Roman Red with bottles of Earl's own concoctions.

Earl spent months experimenting with mixing colors until he had thirteen original colors that only he had in his shop arsenal.

Those colors were what made him famous in the tattoo community, and he'd been offered several thousand dollars for the formulas, but Earl found more value in that he had something unique that brought more clients only to him. He had the formulas memorized so that no one, not even Bear, would find the recipes for them. He was proud of saying that they would die with him.

The equipment was also all updated since Ted retired. When their cousin first began, he had homemade guns made from the body of a ball point pen, duct taped to a dual coil motor that he took from the body of electric race car sets, with a sharpened E-string from an electric guitar running through the body of the pen. It was slower and duller than the guns they now used, but no one really complained about the added pain. No one knew any better. Now both of them used J-Frame tattoo guns not only because they could be taken apart and sterilized, but also because the fine detail of their work would be next to impossible without them.

Earl took another swig of his beer, looked around the shop, which was slowly becoming harder to keep in focus, and eased himself back in the reclining seat as he watched Bear pierce the skin on Bret's arm. Earl didn't have any clients scheduled today and Bret was the only one of Bear's. Therefore, Earl decided that the best way to spend his day off was to sit at the shop and get drunk. Bear didn't appreciate that, because he knew what a mean drunk his brother was, and this wasn't just another client, this was Bret, and the two of them had always been like a spark and gasoline. But it was Earl's shop too, and Bear really couldn't say anything about it.

Bear meticulously tattooed the outline of the twelve-point buck that Bret had harvested in last year's hunt on Bret's upper arm. He used a basic black for the outline, then would move on to draw every individual hair. It would take a while, but Bret took a sort of morbid comfort in the fact that the physical pain would be a welcome relief from the mental pain that still tormented him during the last few months.

He reclined in the seat, shirtless, with a pair of his trade-marked lichen pine colored camouflage pants. A cigarette that dangled from his lips jumped every time Bear dug a little too deep. All up and down his arms were tattoos of mostly game heads that he had harvested over the years. He found it to be more of a tribute to the animal by having them permanently preserved on his body instead of giving Martin his business with the real thing. A tom turkey in full display sat on his right pec, and on his left a big bruin black bear that he took in '88. War tattoos were mixed in with them, including one of a skull with a bowie knife in its mouth with the words DEATH BEFORE DISHONOR below it that he got on a whim in Bangkok. It was the least of his favorites, and every once in a while, he entertained the thought of having Bear cover it up. The only war tattoo he got after the war was the one that Bear did on his upper arm of the waving POW flag.

Bret leaned over and mashed out his cigarette in the ashtray that was balancing on the arm rest. Bear, once again annoyed that Bret kept moving, pulled the gun away from him.

"Sit still or I'm gonna screw this up," he demanded.

Bret ignored him as he took the pack of cigarettes sitting next to the ashtray, and shook another one loose, letting it dangle from his lips without yet lighting it. "How come we never go out fishing anymore, Bear?"

Bear paused trying to find a way to sugar coat the reason. It wasn't that he blamed Bret for Elle, but since that day, he hadn't stepped foot in a boat, and probably wouldn't again. But he couldn't let Bret know that; he would take it the wrong way. He knew that Bret was eating himself alive for what happened, and therefore he felt like he had to watch his words.

"I don't like boats anymore," Bear said without looking at him.

Bret did take it the exact opposite way Bear intended it. "Bear, don't you turn on me. You're the only one in this town that hasn't blamed me for what happened to Elle."

Before Bear could say anything more, Earl's half drunk wisdom reared its obnoxious head. "That's 'cause my brother's a retard," he slurred.

"Was anybody talkin' to your drunk ass?" Bret immediately stabbed back.

"Least my drunk ass didn't kill anyone," Earl responded, under his breath but loud enough for them to hear as was his intention.

Bret's eyes slanted thin. He looked directly at Earl, challenging him. "Wha'd you just say?"

The fuse was lit, and there was little that anyone could do to stop the approaching detonation, especially because Bear was the only one who wanted it stopped.

He looked sharply at his brother. "Earl, don't."

As he expected, Earl ignored that he was even there. He sat up in his chair, ready for anything. They looked at each other like two rival wolves, circling each other, sizing each other up, just waiting for the first sign of weakness.

Earl couldn't wait for that sign. He had to provoke it. "You heard me. Is it any wonder why you're no longer called deputy? I'm surprised the sheriff didn't just shoot you. Hell, if it was my sister you killed, I wouldn't even ask any questions. Just—bang! No more loser."

Bear was wise to take the gun off Bret. He knew all too well what was about to happen, and was helpless to stop it.

"Earl, listen close. You say one more thing about that and we will no longer be having words."

"What? Whassa matter, huh? Am I lying? Or is it that I'm just the only one with any balls to say it?"

"You're drunk Earl, and you don't know what the hell you're talkin' about," Bret said, giving him a chance to back down although he knew he wouldn't take it.

Earl swung his legs over to sit on the edge of his seat, hunched his back, and drooped his head looking at Bret from the tops of his menacing eyes. "You wanna take me out in the street and prove me wrong?"

Bret would have liked nothing better than to do that, but after all that had happened to him in the past few months, all he needed was to have people talk about how he put poor ol' Earl in the hospital, or worse. He chose to throw an empty threat to not only see if that would make Earl back down, but to make sure he understood that he wasn't about to either.

"I'd break you in half," Bret said through his teeth.

"Let's go soldier boy," Earl slurred.

"Knock it off, both of you!" Bear fiercely charged but was ignored.

"We had a guy just like you in my platoon in 'Nam. Never knew when to shut-up. You wanna start this? I will finish it."

Earl laughed. "Let me tell you something about Vietnam. That was the best war in history, you know why? Because it gave the government a chance to flush you fucks outta society."

Bret gave his last warning to Bear in a wide-eyed look that read "shut your brother up now." It came through loud and clear.

"Earl, shut up!" Bear tried.

"You know what POW stands for?" Earl continued without acknowledging Bear's demand. "Pee-Ons at War. That's right. By snapping your ugly neck, they'd give me the metal that your baby-killin' ass could never earn!"

Earl wanted the fight. It wasn't because he really disliked Bret, and it wasn't even to defend or gain some retribution for Elle. He just wanted to fight. He was drunk and full of piss and vinegar as they say, and Bret just happened to be the perfect candidate, but more so, it was just because he was there. And with that remark, a fight was what Earl got.

As fast as a rattlesnake strike, Bret grabbed the tattoo gun out of Bear's hand and lunged at Earl like a predator attacking its prey. However, before Bret had a chance to stab Earl with the gun, he felt the brick wall restraint of Bear grabbing both his arms, pulling him back. But he wasn't about to put his sword back in his sheath clean. He was fighting to see blood, and nothing was going to stop that as he kicked his leg up, and met Earl's nose three times with the bottom of his heel within the span of a second and a half. It was a precise assault, and although his brother was on the receiving end of it, Bear was actually a little impressed.

Earl was lifted off his feet. He didn't even have time to grab his erupting nose before he was flipped backwards over the chair. Bear held Bret who tried his best to get another shot at Earl and, in the process, knocked the side table over spilling supplies and ink everywhere with a metal-thundering crash.

After it was apparent that he was going nowhere under Bear's restraint, he calmed as much as he could, and put his hands up in submission. Bear slowly released him, and both of them pierced Earl with a dead stare. The fight was over as soon as it had begun, and although there would never be a day that Earl would admit it, Bear had just saved his life.

Earl lifted himself off the floor using the chair as a crutch. His nose wasn't broken, but it was gushing blood and swollen as if it was—but it was not as swollen as his ego was anymore. Bret just stood there as the rage dripped slowly out of him.

"You're damn lucky your brother's here," he said almost regretfully as Earl spit a thick wad of blood on the floor.

Bret looked at Bear as if to tell him there were no hard feelings, and then quietly walked out of the shop.

Earl clumsily pushed himself to his feet, and looked at himself in the mirror, horrified at the cantaloupe his nose had become.

"Agh. I think he broke my fuckin' nose!" he cried as he spit another thick clot of blood.

Bear just looked at him in unsympathetic disgust, then quietly began to clean up the mess. Earl had not only done that to a friend of his, but to a client as well, and Bear, being who he was, would have to either give Bret half off his price, or even finish it for free. Earl tried to regain what dignity he had as he went to his beer bottle only to discover it empty. He was more upset with that disappointment than he was with his nose.

"Good job," Bear said over his shoulder at him, shaking his head.

He threw what was in his hands on the counter causing a bigger mess than was there before.

"You can clean this shit up," Bear said as he marched out the door.

Earl threw his hands up in confusion. "Hey! I'm the one with the busted nose! I'm the one that's wounded here!" he screamed after his brother as the door closed. Bear heard it, but had no trouble ignoring it, and kept walking down the street, leaving Emily on her kickstand in front of the shop. He just needed to think, and walking was better than riding for that.

As he walked, he thought about heading over to Bret's to apologize for his brother's conduct, but it was still too soon for that, and he didn't even know if home was where Bret had gone. Besides, Bret's house was a good three miles, and Bear didn't want to walk all that way just to find an empty house. He knew the one place Bret hadn't gone was to the Lunker Lodge. He been avoiding it for a long while because the tendency to stay there all day and drink himself stupid was just too tempting. Besides, Barney probably wouldn't allow him to do that if even he wanted to.

Bear didn't feel like going anywhere right then other than the fated destination that one foot in front of the other would take him. At that moment, as it was long ago, he didn't have anywhere specific he needed to be, and he took a great amount of comfort knowing that.

Meanwhile, Cherie, giving up on the hopes that Bear was coming to pick her up, attempted to leave the café for the long walk home before Jack asked her to work the night shift. She did hesitate, but also knew that saying no to Jack was as good as saying no to her further gainful employment. Besides, the asshole never came to get her, and she would rather make some *kaching* than walk all the way home. But Bear wouldn't know this until later, so his semi-guilty feelings about not picking her up were unfoundedly taking up space in his thoughts when he would rather have spent them pondering more intoxicating concepts.

With Cherie troubling his mind, Bear wondered what was wrong with him that he couldn't find a woman that was more independent, and philosophically intelligent. He knew they existed, but most of them that he'd come across grouped all men into one stereotype and hated them for it. That wasn't the intelligence he was looking for. He wanted to find that elusive other that he could have an electric conversation with just for the sake of conversing and not because they simply wanted something from each other. He wanted someone who would share his company without making demands as though he inherently owed them something.

More often than not, he felt like property to Cherie, or more to the point like a servant. But he did realize something about himself just then that he hadn't considered before. There wasn't a time that he was on the road, in college, or anywhere else in his adult life that he wasn't with someone, and what's more is that he was never in love with any of them. Truth was, he'd never been in love. He had no knowledge of what real love was like outside of his imagination.

So what was it then? Was he afraid of being alone? No, he was too tough for that. But maybe it was the truth. Maybe that was why he put up with Cherie for so long. Or on the other hand, maybe he was the one she put up with. Perhaps he should really try to be nicer to her. Being with her was, at least, somewhat comfortable. It wasn't all as bad as he made it out to be, and God knows he's had worse. They did laugh together every once in a great while, and they did talk about things other than her loathing for her job, and how the rest of her life had never been a real lottery winner. But if he got even somewhat philosophical, he lost her. But was that her fault?

No, it wasn't all bad. Sex with her was as fun as a tilt-a-whirl, and that had to go for something, didn't it? What really got him was the fact that he knew he didn't love her, but was that so important? Millions of people were with each other without that part of the equation, so why should he and Cherie get to be any different? He didn't know. All he knew was that Cherie needed him now, and he couldn't do anything about that. He just had to try and be happy with it.

He had always appreciated the fact that he was truthful to himself, and wasn't afraid to go to those thorny places within himself that other people had boarded up after their first visit within themselves. He'd begun to tell himself that he was one of those people who just didn't get to have happiness, much less the money, security, his own house, and all those other things that happy people seemed to have.

He didn't even get to fall in love.

"You'd better teach misery to play cribbage, Bear," he thought to himself, "because it's going to be around for a long, long time. Perhaps forever." But that wasn't being truthful to himself either, and he knew it. Things were awful in that thorny place. Lies were there. Hopelessness was there. Insecurity was there. Misery with a deck of cards (rigged so it would always be dealt tens and fives) was there. Self-defeating things that had leaked out of his own lockbox would play with him among those thorns. He found it a sign of personal strength to frolic in there and survive unscathed, and because of this, he was a constant visitor.

Going there told him everything he needed to know about himself simply by the way he responded to it all. He knew none of those wicked things were true that he was telling himself. He just constantly felt the need to test himself, and really wanted to see if he would be so weak as to believe any of it. He would get to fall in love, and he knew it would happen when he wasn't even looking, although he did have someone in mind. But still playing in that thorny place, he told himself that that would never happen.

As he came around the bend in the road, Ernie's gas station materialized out of the woods. That was just the simple diversion to his workout in the thorny place that he needed. Besides, he hadn't talked to Ernie in a while, and talking to him always reminded him how trivial negative thoughts really were. He picked up the pace in his gait, but Ernie had a customer, so he just walked across to the pop machine, and got himself a Coke.

Ernie was just finishing up with the convertible parked at the pumps in which three girls sat giggling at their quiet jabs at him. Ernie was instantly smitten by their attractiveness, and was oblivious to being the subject of their chuckling sarcasm. But Bear noticed it from across the parking lot, and wondered if he should say something. He stopped himself, thinking it would be more insulting to Ernie if he interfered, so he stood, and watched with a condemnatory glare.

The two girls in the front seat were wearing bikini tops with cut-off jeans, and the one in the back was wearing cut-off gray sweatpants with a half shirt that read PORN STAR in glittery girly-girl script. Her hair was in pigtails, the passenger's in a ponytail, and the driver's was long and unbound. They were all wearing cheap, gaudy sunglasses, and too much make-up for a day on the beach. Which beach Ernie didn't know. Lake Desire didn't really have a public beach other than the shoreline at the park, and therefore, he didn't have an ounce of experience with customers like this.

The girls shushed each other as he walked up to the driver. "Okee, that's nineteen dollars," he said, perhaps too politely.

The driver handed him a twenty which he simply slipped in his pocket. Not everyone tipped him, but most people knew it was expected. These girls, however, knew nothing of it.

"Um, the math on that would be that you owe me a dollar," the driver said deliberately trying to be snobby.

It rolled right off Ernie as he slipped a dollar bill out of his pocket, and handed it to her. He was more hurt by the lack of a tip than by the insult. In fact, he wasn't even sure that he was being insulted. He had no experience with girls like these.

The girl in the passenger seat tipped her glasses and looked at his ever-present camera dangling from around his neck. She curled her lip. "What's the camera for? You a big photographer, or something?"

Ernie smiled, his comfort restored. "I was jus' gonna ask you ladies if you'd like to join my Wall of Fame, seein' as how I 'aven't seen you guys up here before?"

The girls looked at each other for a dumbfounded moment, then broke out in laughter. Ernie laughed a little as well, mistaking their laughter for excitement. That was until the driver kicked the gas, and the car squealed away, but not fast enough for the girl in the back seat to shout, "Bye-bye, pervert!"

Ernie stood looking at the empty space before him. He didn't understand what he had said to make them do that, but didn't spend too much time on it as Bear's sudden presence interrupted his thoughts. "'Ah, women are a decorative sex. They never have anything to say, but they say it charmingly,'" Bear quoted, adding, "Oscar Wilde said that, but I doubt he ever met women like that."

"'Morning, Bear," Ernie grinned, heading over to his recliner.

"It's well past morning my friend."

"I know," he said as he plopped himself in his chair. "Just making conversation."

Bear sat on the steps before him, and took a healthy swig of his Coke. "Don't feel bad about those girls. There's no shortage of mean people in the world, I guess."

"I don't feel bad for them, I just feel sorry for them. It looked like they were going swimming, but I don't know where. Last time I checked we didn't have a beach. But I haven't gone down to the lake since . . ." Ernie didn't even want to finish that thought.

Bear paused for a moment of reflection. "I know. Arnold just gave me a book of her poetry. I haven't done more than just flip through it."

"A book, huh?" Ernie said as if a book wasn't much of a gift. Thinking of Elle and gifts, though, he smiled, remembering the things she used to surprise him with. "She would always bring me these homemade pies she'd bake. Blueberry in the summer, pumpkin and apple in the fall. When I saw her comin' with those pies, I'd do just about anything for her. I don't think I ever once charged her for gas." He paused, suddenly solemn. "She was the kindest person I ever knew."

"Yes she was," Bear concurred.

"One time, she came without a pie. But you know what she brought?"

Bear shook his head as Ernie held up his Polaroid camera with a smile. "She said since everyone that came to town came here, I should start taking their pictures. She said one day she might write a book with them. It was my idea to put 'em on the wall until she was ready for them. That's how the wall of fame got started."

Bear smiled. "Perhaps some day you'll write that book."

There was something about that thought that Ernie preferred to avoid. Bear picked up on this, concerned that he had hit a still-raw nerve within him about Elle.

"Well, I'm gonna leave 'em up there anyway," Ernie said determinedly.

The two sat in silence for a moment. It wasn't really uncomfortable, they just both knew that they should abandon the topic of Elle, and neither of them knew where to take it from there. Ernie didn't mind. He just stared at the television.

"You ever watch television?"

"I have, but I don't own a TV now."

"I watch a lot of television. Sometimes all night long before I open up the station. I got one of those video units, so I watch a lot of movies, too. My favorite's *The Twilight Zone*. Ya know, both the television shows, and the movie."

"You know, Ernie, there's a whole wide world out there that's full of all that stuff you see in the movies. You should take some time off and go see it."

"I've lived here all my life. I've never even been down to Minneapolis before. Besides, I don't need to leave here to see the world." He motioned to the Wall of Fame. "You see all those pictures in there? The world comes to me."

Bear smiled at his perfect simplicity. He would give up everything he had to just possess that quality for a day.

"When I was a boy, though, I remember my daddy took us to Duluth once," Ernie said, suddenly disturbed. "He usta call me the biggest failure of his life. He was real mean to us. Me an' my ma."

"Well, some say that failure is more interesting than success. Don't you think?"

"I'm not much for thinking, I guess. My ma used to tell me that a lot. That's all she ever really said to me—'cept when she was calling me a fool."

Bear lifted his eyebrows. He had never heard of this before. "Your mother used to call you a fool?"

"I don't even remember her callin' me by my real name much."

Bear looked at him, trying to find the right words. He read the Bible several times long ago trying to find meaning in it but never could. He was by far not a religious man mainly because he found religion to be more imprisoning than liberating to the human and spiritual mind. But still, like so many other works of literature, there was wisdom in it. One of his favorite passages came to mind.

"Well, 'even a fool, when he holdeth his peace, is counted wise.' Proverbs seventeen twenty-eight."

Ernie thought about that for a moment. Not of its meaning, but that Bear had inadvertently challenged him with a quote, and he could only think of one to reciprocate. Besides, this conversation was getting just too serious for him.

"'Who's the bigger fool? The fool or the fool who follows him?' Obi-wan Kenobi, Episode 4," he offered with a genuine smile.

Bear was challenged in return. Not his words or his wisdom, but his own propensity to overcomplicate things. His rebuttal to that, and to Ernie's reply was something that he hadn't done in a long while, and that was to surrender all control to a burst of unadulterated laughter. It was the most soul-cleansing thing that he had done for himself in weeks. And as he hunched over holding his gut, Ernie couldn't help but join him.

Together, for the first time, their intellects were harmonized in a perfect libretto of laughter.

It was exactly what each of them had needed.

CHAPTER SEVEN

ARTIN'S SHOP WAS NOTHING FANCY—IT WAS simple and practical and had everything he needed. The walls were pegboard on which hung freeze-dried grouse, ducks, geese, and fish of all sizes and species. From the ceiling hung homemade racks in which foam deer head manikins in all different styles dangled from easy to reach hooks. The floor was cement that had been randomly camouflaged with sprays and spills of globs of paint and putty. Stacked in the corner were slabs of oak panels and tangles of driftwood that he had personally collected from the shores of Lake Superior. Next to those tangles was his freeze-dry chamber that Arnold bought him as a good luck gift on the day he opened for business.

On simple board shelves over his workbench, jars with the covers drilled into the bottom of the shelf contained, among other things, sculpting putty, glass eyes of every color and species, glycerin, razor blades for his exacto-knife, and various components for his airbrush system. Under that shelf, up against the length of wall, was his homemade workbench. It had taken him about an hour to make and had already lasted six years, ever since he began to do taxidermy professionally. On the bench sat his Dremel tool kit and his airbrush system with the small air compressor bolted directly onto the table. The place might be considered macabre to those who didn't embrace the outdoors, or those who just didn't understand. Martin knew of people like that, and he just felt sorry for them.

Martin showed promise in this profession from his first little yellow perch he did when he was eleven. He had always wanted to be a professional fisherman with his own show, but that dream took a back seat when people saw the work he was doing as a taxidermist. Soon, all summer long, people would bring him walleyes and crappies that they had caught in the lake, and because Martin always spent his summers helping out in his dad's bait shop anyway, he accepted every order, and Arnold helped to clear out half of the storage area for Martin's shop. After high school, he moved on to doing more complicated game heads and birds. When the bait shop moved to its present location, Martin announced that he had decided to turn his hobby into his profession, and Arnold, always supportive of anything his son did, had a room built in the back of his new shop for Martin's studio. The room quickly became Martin's retreat from the world. He spent more time in there than just about anywhere else except for the lake.

Martin looked around the room with that thought, then sank into his chair, and went to work on the foam deer head manikin that sat on the work pedestal before him. He took a gob of sculpting putty, and applied it to the cheek structure of the head, then took a carving tool and began to sculpt the muscle structure. He had already applied the fine detail around the eye sockets and nostrils. It was this extra detail before he even began to plaster the antlers that made him a sought after commodity and kept him busy throughout the year. Still, he could charge a lot more for his work than he did, but being fair in his prices was also one of the reasons he was considered the best.

Arnold walked in, and leaned in the open doorway. He had

nothing less than absolute pride for his son. "How's it coming?" he asked.

Martin looked up at him. "As soon as this dries, I'll be about ready to plaster the antlers."

"Good," Arnold said as he grabbed his chair, and dragged it next to his son. "I ran into John this morning. He was asking about it."

"For as lazy as he is, he sure is impatient."

Arnold smiled in recollection. "Your mother was kind of like that, too."

Martin gave his father a half-smile, but didn't look at him.

"She sure brought out the best in people, though." Arnold said as his smile got a little bigger.

But Martin's smile faded. He didn't want to talk about it, though he often felt he really needed to. Arnold knew this, and continued, hoping to help his son move past his sorrow. "You know, Martin, it's okay to talk about her. You never do."

Martin looked at him. If he couldn't talk about it to his father, whom else could he talk to? "Do you remember that bedtime story she would always read to me? 'Lights in the Forest'?"

"Yeah, I think so."

"She would read me that story all the time. It's one of my fondest memories of her."

"What was it about?"

"It was about this girl who lived with her grandfather who was a lumberjack. And just before he died, he told his grand-daughter that he would always be with her, he told her to look out into the forest, and she would see a big glowing light. That was him." Martin smiled, and then shrugged his shoulders. "I don't know, I was just a kid, and it was kind of a stupid story anyhow, but ever since the accident, I catch myself looking out into the forest. Maybe I might see that glowing light. Kind of silly, isn't it?"

"Not at all," he said empathetically.

Martin returned to carving the putty. "It was just a story. But I'm still looking."

Arnold could do nothing but smile. However, he hadn't come in just to reflect about Elle. He had something to tell Martin, and he knew his son was not going to like it.

"Listen, your uncle came in today. He, ah, said that the boat was damaged before she went out that morning."

"Really?" Martin said quietly.

"Yeah. I'm afraid so."

"What does that mean?"

"I don't know. I'm afraid he thinks Bret did something to it. But I don't. Bret and I have gone through a lot together," he paused in recollection of that fact, and then he sourly continued, "and a lot apart. He's got a lot of problems, but I just think that even drunk, he doesn't have it in him to do something to that boat. Personally, if I had my guess, I'd guess it was crazy Cherie. She hated your mother for all the time she spent with Bear, and for being more of a mother to Annie than she ever has. But, still, I just can't bring myself to believe that someone would deliberately do something to hurt your mother." He paused with a sigh. "I don't know, your uncle's a smart man. He'll figure it out. He didn't want anyone to know about this yet, so keep it under your hat."

Martin slowly nodded. That information brought him almost more distress than the trauma of her death in the first place. He hid it by returning to his sculpting in cold silence.

Arnold, never one for being the bearer of bad news without something sweet to balance it out, readjusted himself in his chair, and reached into his shirt pocket, pulling out two tickets. "Well, on a lighter note, I have something here that I think may be of some interest to you," he said as he handed them to his son.

Martin stopped what he was doing and took them. He knew right away what they were. At the top of the ticket was a stenciled drawing of a walleye, under which read 25TH ANNUAL LAKE DESIRE FISHING CONTEST. JULY 29TH, and then the long list of prizes.

"The fishing contest? Dad you're a judge. You've always been a judge. How can we enter this?"

"I stepped down this year so we could enter it together," he said with a proud, toothy grin, happy that he got the reaction he did.

"I've wanted to enter this since I was a kid!"

"I know. This year I'm making it up to you. Besides, I figure with a father-son team like us, there would be no contest getting another trophy for the wall."

Martin jumped out of his chair knocking it backwards. He bear-hugged his father. "This is great! Thanks, Dad."

Arnold laughed robustly and wrapped his arms around his son. For the moment, they were as happy as they'd been before the accident. They were father and son again, not entirely healed from the tragedy, but definitely on their way.

∾≬∾

BUT DEEP IN THE FOREST, SOMEONE ELSE WAS STILL TRYING to come to grips with that tragedy. Someone that wouldn't yet allow himself to heal from it. He couldn't; the cycle was in full hurricane force. However, after the confrontation with Earl at the tattoo shop, Bret had felt a little better for having released some steam by putting that little prick in his place.

Bret had gone home following the fight, but only long enough to grab his .22-caliber rifle and escape into the forest. For years, he had always hunted or fished for the bulk of his diet, and squirrels were always a bountiful dish. Over the years he'd collected volumes of recipes for squirrel, and as a bonus, he sold the tails to a lure manufacturer over by Leech Lake for ten dollars a dozen.

The forest was the only place Bret felt like he was in charge, where no one was pointing fingers at him or whispering too loud on purpose. He could escape and just be—and for the moment, that freedom was the very elixir he required to ease the crazies in his head.

It also gave him time to think. When the cycle came on in full force, he would pack a bag and disappear into the woods, sometimes for days, not knowing if he'd ever come back alive. That was just one of those things he couldn't guarantee to himself or, more to the point, care about.

For whatever reason, Bret hadn't seen any squirrels. Sometimes there were too many, other times not a one. He took the east fork in the path that led him down through a low land bog that invited him with the stink of animal and plant decay. On the other side of the bog, there was a red pine grove where squirrels were always plentiful. That grove was one of the only places he ever found contentment. There was something cathedral-like about the place with its huge stands of pines and the buttery sun-beams radiating through the needled canopy. Birds sang their hymns on a backdrop of serene silence, adding to the holy effect. Little other than the pines grew in the grove. There was no under-brush to impede his pace, and the dead pine needles made the ground as soft as carpet. It was the only peaceful place he knew, the one place that he truly felt pious, because how could God turn his back on him in a place like this?

Bret avoided the spot when he was caught in the cycle, because he didn't want to taint it with the association of the cycle's crippling paralysis. But the need for healing was greater, and so he came, carrying his burden into that sacred space. Soon, the for-gotten feelings of bliss seeped back into his being.

That was until he stepped on something.

Something that squeaked a synthetic whine. Cautiously, Bret looked down, and as he lifted his foot, any bliss he'd found was flushed with the fury of an erupting thunderhead. Panic, hand in hand with anxiety, rushed through him like a dust storm kicked up in the desert. There it was. A dirty, abandoned doll half buried in the dead pine needles. It was missing an arm, and one of its eyes hung from a thin piece of string. Dropping to his knees, Bret picked it up, gently brushed it off, and then cradled it in his arms as if it were real.

He stared at the doll in his arms, then at the gun in his hand, then back to the doll. He caught the panicked cry rising in his throat and tried in vain to swallow it back. "God! Haven't you made me suffer enough?"

He began to weep and nervously shake as he rocked the doll back and forth, cradled in his arms. In no time, his weeping turned to hyperventilating, and at once, an eruption of bile geysered up from his gut, but nothing more than would fill the crop of his throat and produce anything more than a distasteful swallow.

Then, as if the doll burst into flames, he threw it and his gun on the soft needle-carpeted ground, and terrified, pushed himself away from it, scooting along the ground, until the trunk of one of the pines stopped him dead.

He looked at the doll lying facedown over the barrel of his rifle, and the horror that had burned itself into his memory three decades ago returned. In one motion, he rose and began to run.

He ran as if the doll itself was chasing him. He ran through the pines, which took their turn slapping his face with their needles, cutting his skin. He ran through the bog, which grabbed at his boots, but never managed to actually steal them. He ran through the underbrush that tore at his camouflage pants and scratched his legs.

And he would keep running for what, to him, would seem like forever.

CHAPTER EIGHT

THE NEON SIGN ON THE FLAT ROOF WITH THE NEON fishing rod doubled over the neon bass suddenly crackled to light. The neon strip that made up the rod was flickering so it automatically caught the eyes of any passerby. The sign was a glowing beacon in contrast to the bruise-colored sunset with it's wispy strips of oranges, browns and thin ribbons of salmon pink. It was at this time of the evening, against that sky, that the sign was at its most beautiful.

The last of the fishermen were pulling their boats off the lake, but only a few of them stopped for an after dinner cup of coffee and a slice of pie, even though out on the lake, a fisherman's dinner was generally a bleak offering served up from the cooler (which also served as a live-well for some). PB&J or bologna sandwiches wrapped in tin foil, handfuls of Fritos, and a can of something to drink—usually cheap beer—coupled with the smell of fish on their hands made it a delicacy to any fisherman.

Cherie never understood why so many people who ate so little all day would still only come in for a slice of pie and not a whole meal. She saw it as money being taken directly out of her pocket for every table that filled a booth with a bill that was less that five bucks. Knowing that it meant that her tip wouldn't be more than seventy-five cents, she simply ignored them.

Because of the lack of the "fisherman's rush hour"—as it had been called in the inner circles of the café—Jack had informed Cherie that they were closing an hour early, something that she further translated as more money out of her pocket. Still, she was happy about it, because that just meant she could dive into a bottle an hour earlier than she had expected.

Bear and Earl sat at the counter, nursing their beers. Bear hadn't said more than two words to Earl; just mechanically nodded or shook his head at the one-sided conversation Earl was trying to have with him. Earl sounded funny talking through his bandaged nose, and Bear was internally amused by it, or he'd have told him to shut up long ago.

Although everyone had already heard what happened (by Earl bragging, and Bear countering with the truth), Cherie couldn't resist the urge to stab laughter at Earl every time she passed by, and it pissed Earl off something good.

That was at least one reason Bear was with her. She had a sharp sarcastic wit and the guts to take Earl on, and it made Bear laugh that Earl was absolutely defenseless against it.

Cherie walked back behind the counter and set the coffee pot on the burner, then turned to the boys. "Baby, wanna 'nother one?"

Bear finished off his beer in a gulp, and wiped his mouth with his forearm.

"Yup," he said, pushing his empty bottle toward her.

She looked at Earl. "And how 'bout you, Everlast?"

Earl really didn't know what Everlast was other than it probably had something to do with punching bags. Bear laughed loud and directly at him.

"I'll take another," Earl said, deflated that he couldn't think of an immediate rebuttal. He would think of one that would be more than likely be followed with "Bitch," but only after it was much too late.

Bear had to give Cherie credit. She had just put in an almost twelve-hour shift, her feet were swollen above her shoes, she looked like she had aged ten years since that morning, and still she didn't miss a beat when it came to tossing clever insults at Earl. Bear respected that. Not only that, but exhausted as she had to be, she'd still want to go and party until she collapsed. That was a stamina Bear only wished he had.

An impatient voice called at her as she set the reinforcements in front of the boys. "Could we finally get that refill, Cherie?"

That phrase, to her, was translated in her mind as *"Hey, you that hasn't done anything worthwhile with your life—be my slave!"* It burned into her ears and, rolling her eyes, she walked to the coffee pot.

"Yeah, that's exactly why the good lord put me on this earth— to get you another fuckin' cup o' coffee," she mumbled, yanking the pot off the burner and almost spilling it.

As she passed Bear on her way to the table, she looked directly and leaned deeply into him. "You better have plans to take me out and get me stinkin' drunk and laid tonight," she said with a seductive smile, then took her time getting to her complaining customer.

Earl looked at Bear, almost in awe. "Where do I find a woman like that?"

"Like what?" They were the first words other than a few obligatory "yeses" and "nos" Bear had said to him all night.

"She has a bad day, and you get your turtle waxed. She's the perfect woman."

Bear didn't acknowledge that— not with words, body language, or even a look out of the corner of his eye, even though there was a little place inside him, perhaps a place divided by a thin membrane from the thorns that agreed with Earl. But it wasn't something he'd ever admit—to his brother or anyone else.

The unmistakable crackling rumble of the twins' snowmobile stopped with a wheezing cough just outside the picture windows. Annie looked in the windows, pleased with how vacant it was. She got there just in time for a quick bite to eat—she nor the twins had eaten more than wild blueberries and raspberries all day—and to do what she came there to do.

She wasn't nervous about it, in fact, she wished she were. She, like the twins, always got off a little on that holy surge of adrenaline. Perhaps it would come just before she executed the deed.

They walked in just as the table that had insulted Cherie by asking for a refill were leaving.

Bear turned. He'd always liked Annie and the twins and tried to watch out for them when he could. In fact, that pseudo-father image he'd taken on made it a bit easier to justify his relationship with Cherie.

Annie never knew who her father was, so she took a bit of cautious comfort in thinking of Bear in that capacity. So did Cherie. She had always told Annie that her father was killed in a motorcycle accident before she was born. Truth was, Cherie couldn't honestly remember who Annie's father was. She had an idea, but thank the lucky stars he was gone forever. At least with Bear, both of their bodies remained bruiseless.

As a child, Annie thought of herself as having two mothers as a way of making up for the lack of a father. One, Cherie, she could rely upon for a roof over her head, and the other for solid advice, and a sense of significance only a mother could give her daughter, and Elle fit that glove as perfectly as Annie needed her to. Annie was the closest Elle would ever get to having a daughter of her own, and Elle was the closest that Annie would ever get to having what most would call a motherly influence in her life. Cherie hated that about herself, and therefore hated Elle for it as well. But she did have to admit that she took a certain amount of relief knowing that Elle was there for Annie when she never was.

"Hey Annie. Boys," Bear said, a genuine smile crossing his face.

"Hey Bear," Annie said with a slightly detectable trace of unease.

"What's up, Ursa?" Stee said as they slipped into a booth behind Bear and Earl.

Ursa. The twins always called him that. They felt smarter calling him by the Latin name of Bear, throwing their knowledge of Latin around like a Hollywood namedropper. Sometimes they'd go all out, and call him *Ursa americanus,* the Latin name for the black bear. Bear only found it mildly amusing. The twins adored him, and in some ways aspired to be him. He was one person they respected in Desire.

"Ain't nobody gonna say hi to me?" Earl said, acting just as upset as he was.

"Only if I hafta," Annie snapped back as quick-witted as her mother.

"What's with the bandage?" Ven asked.

"Keeping your dinner warm?" Stee added with a laugh, then looked directly at Annie with big, goofy eyes. "Thank you very much."

Bear broke into laughter, joining the twins and Annie. Earl slid off his stool, yanked up his drooping pants, and walked up to the edge of their table. He was oblivious to how intrusive he was being. "Very funny. You boys still livin' in Barney's old fish house?"

"Yup," they both said in unison, unenthusiastically.

Earl bobbed his head. Annie and the twins stared up at him, inviting him to leave with their eyes. But why would he go back to sitting over there when Bear wasn't paying any attention to him?

"So which one of you is the evil twin?" he said with a slight (and more to the point, poor) Vincent Price impression.

Again, the twins just stared at him.

Earl grabbed the steak knife on the table in front of Annie, and pointed it directly at Stee's chest. "So if I, like, stab you . . ." A quick flick of his wrist, and the knife was pointed at Ven. "Are *you* gonna feel the pain?"

Without a second of hesitation, Ven picked up the knife in front of him, and thrust it at Earl's mouth, holding it close enough for him to smell the dishwashing detergent residue on it.

"If I, like, take this knife and cut your tongue out . . ."

"Are you gonna stop talking?" Stee added.

Earl took a step back. He had just gotten his ass handed to him by a hardened war hero. That could be accepted. But what if it happened again by a weird set of twenty-something twins? That thought kept Earl from following his initial instincts to attack. Besides, he liked their spirit.

"I like you guys. You got nards," he said, patting Ven's back. Ven recoiled from the touch as though the cooties would take advantage of the opportunity to jump onto him.

At that moment, Cherie walked over and wedged herself between the table and Earl.

"Hi guys."

"Hey, Cherie," Annie said. It seemed like she had always called her mother by her name. Long ago, Annie decided that Cherie would have to actually be a mother in order to be awarded that title.

Earl was just standing a little too close for Cherie, and she stuck out her elbows in an attempt to detail the outlines of her personal bubble for him. He was oblivious to it, and therefore the hint flew right past him. "Is Earl bothering you?" she said more to Earl than to them.

"Not really, he's kind of entertaining," Stee said.

"In a Neanderthal sort of way," Ven added, and then looked up to see what Earl would do with that.

Earl had no idea what Ven had just said, so he had no clue he was being insulted. He turned to Bear with a slight half-drunk laugh. "Hey Bear! J'ou hear that? I'm entertaining!"

Cherie had already given Earl one warning of his invasive presence, and that, to her, was one too many. She jabbed her elbow into his ribs. "Earl, go si'down! You're being a fuckin' pest."

He ignored her and, to make it worse, took a step closer, pushing Cherie against the table. "Hey you guys should come down to the shop and all get matching tattoos."

"Don't even think about it, Annie. You're not getting a tattoo until you're eighteen," Cherie said directly to Annie, pointing a finger at her just to put an exclamation point on it.

"I'll be twenty next month," Annie said with raised eyebrows that called her mother pathetic.

"Don't get smart with me," Cherie snapped back.

Earl had now entirely invaded Cherie's space. Her lips tightened and her brow dropped. She clenched her fist and jabbed him in the ribs again, this time hard enough to sting. "Earl, damnit! Go sit down!"

Earl finally got it. "Yes Ma'am! Geez, they said I was entertaining," he said as he walked back to his stool. Bear shook his head at him with a smirk that called him worthless.

Cherie's eyes followed Earl to his chair before turning back to Annie and twins. "You guys hungry? You want some cheeseburgers before the kitchen closes?"

"Yeah," Stee said.

"I could eat," Ven added.

Annie looked at her mother suspiciously. Why was she being nice to them? Annie knew that either a favor was forthcoming, or Cherie was doing this to add to her arsenal of emotional weapons to be used later when she would launch one of her own perfected guilt trips.

"We don't have any money," Annie cautiously stated, expecting to go hungry.

"So, what else is new? You can owe me," Cherie said with a half smile and walked away.

Annie hated not knowing what her mother was up to, though you'd think she'd be used to it by now. But actually, Cherie wasn't up to anything other than trying on the mother clothes to see how they would fit. They fit a little baggy with room to grow into them, but on the whole, it wasn't a bad fit.

〇〇

WITHIN THE TIME THAT IT TOOK ANNIE AND THE TWINS to polish off their cheeseburgers and greasy fries, all the late night coffee hounds had called it a night, leaving only Bear and Earl. Bear had promised Cherie a night on the town, which meant closing the Lunker Lodge with the rest of the biker gang, and Cherie was scrambling to get her clean-up done so she could start the liver abuse party. Bear and Earl had started that party hours ago. In fact, more than once, Bear had to grab Earl by his shirt to keep him from slumping off his stool.

Jack walked out from his back office to collect the daily receipts that were impaled on a metal spike next to the register. He didn't acknowledge Bear and Earl, and simply passed by Cherie as she wiped down the cook's window. He did look up, however, to see Annie, and cast a perverted smile at the subject of his fantasies. "Annie. I didn't see you sitting there. How's it going?"

"Fine. Mr. Hanson. How you doin'?" She really thought he was creepy.

"Please, how many times do I have to tell you? Call me Jack, and I'm fine, thank you for asking," he said, then began tallying the receipts.

The twins looked at Annie with inane faces, motioning to Jack. They knew all too well what Mr. Creepy thought of her, and they couldn't resist the opportunity to give her shit about it.

"Stop it," she said with only her lips.

"I'm actually busy, real busy," Jack added extraneously long after Annie had considered the conversation over.

Annie just stared at her boyfriends and sucked her lips in, trying not to laugh. Jack suspected that he just made himself look like a first-rate idiot, and as he turned toward his office, caught sight of Cherie and took out his embarrassment on her. "After this place is shining, run a credit report for me, and bring it back to my office," he demanded.

"No problem," Cherie said. She was in too good of a mood to let his tone get to her.

He looked back at Annie one last time. "Good to see you, Annie. And your friends there, too."

"You too, Mr. Hans—Jack." Annie and the twins smiled at him until it seemed he disappeared back in his office. Then, at once, they burst into laughter.

"What the hell was that all about?" Ven laughed.

Cherie and Bear laughed a little as well.

"He creeps me out!" Annie squealed shaking her twisted fingers with a grimace.

"Hey, ze man's a gwashrack," Earl said in an incomprehensible drunken slur which, after a silent second of trying to figure out what the hell he just said, caused everyone to laugh a little more.

"Oh, call me Jack, cause that's what I'm gonna go back and do right now. Wanna watch?" Stee laughed.

Jack, however, did not go back into his office. He leaned against the wall just around the corner, and out of sight from everyone. He had heard every word, and every jab of laughter. The utter humiliation that seized his being percolated to the surface as anger, and as he peeked around the corner with teeth clenched tight at the sight of Cherie laughing at him, he vowed to himself to make her pay for that someday. And Jack always kept his promises, especially the ones he made to himself.

As the laughter dissipated, Cherie walked to the credit card machine, and as Jack had asked, pressed in the code that ran the credit report. Annie and the twins perked up as the long list of credit card numbers began to print. The *Mission Impossible* theme began to play in her head as Annie cleared the empty plates from the table. She walked the long way around to the dish room so she would pass the credit card machine just as it stopped printing.

Her timing was perfect.

Cherie walked up behind her and ripped the list from the printer. She looked at Annie with her armful of dirty plates. "Oh, thanks for doing that. Just set them in the dish room. I'll clean 'em off in the morning," Cherie said as she walked back to Jack's office with the printout.

But as she walked past Bear and Earl, Bear jumped from his stool, and grabbed her. She laughed with amusement as he began to maul her neck with nibbles and kisses.

The twins nodded at Annie, who nodded back, then looked at Earl.

His head was flat against the counter in a puddle of his own drool. He didn't even know he was still there. Bear was still carrying on with Cherie. Jack was nowhere.

It was now or never.

Everything that they wanted to do was dependent upon that one moment.

Balancing the dishes on her forearm, she reached down and pressed her index finger on the red DUPLICATE button. The same list of credit card numbers began to print. She looked back at her boyfriends with a super smile. Now, it seemed, the future would finally know that they existed.

CHAPTER NINE

THE WAXING MOON FADED AS THE RISING SUN STOLE its grandeur, and the lake again revealed its truthful impression of the sky. Loons, gliding on the purple silky water, joined the salutations of the green and mink frogs, and the red-wing blackbirds as the symphony of morning harmonized across the lake. Only one thing marred this opulence: Bear's dock was vacant.

Bear hadn't missed a morning since he returned after the accident. When he awoke from the sleep that he had passed out into, he would feel not only guilty for not being there, but worse, be overcome by that crippling feeling of loss that only came from failing to take part in an opportunity that would never again be regained.

It wasn't like he missed anything incredible, other than the sights and the sounds, and the tranquility itself. There wasn't a bald eagle that swooped down and caught a fish in its talons right in front of the dock, or a rare visit from the otters that sometimes played along the shore. Even so, he saw his absence as nothing more than a betrayal of Elle, and that would be a bitter pill for Bear to swallow.

But like Cherie, who was laying naked next to him in their bed, he would descend to the point where he would dissolve those thoughts into a bottle of something stronger than beer, and furthermore, until the guilt of dealing with that problem by hiding in a bottle would fade as well. They had, as Cherie had wanted, closed the Lunker Lodge, then headed out to party with the gang at the pit, an all-too-familiar spot just down the road from Cherie's trailer where the woods opened up just before the lake, and partied there with the gang and too many kegs until the eastern sky began to turn pink.

This particular party spot had always been called "the pit." Every small town in the country had one, and they all seemed to be known as "the pit." It must be something cosmic or maybe something simply mystical that all the party dwellers across the land came to dub their out-of-the-way party places that distinctively unoriginal name. It was the place where the young were never accepted, but those who at least looked old enough were never shunned away. It was the place where the sometimes sour stories were told with a brief lament for the lack of romance of how inebriated virgins lost their virtues in the woods to some guy they had just met, and would never meet again. It was a place that the law knew existed, but never paid a visit. It was neutral land in the battle against authority and freedom.

A party could be found there almost every night. Some were huge gatherings of fifty or more people with huge, raging bonfires, drunken laughter, skinny-dipping bikers, and that distinctive rumble of motorcycle engines echoing across the lake. At other times, just a few people sat around, knocking back a few brews in front of a small fire. And while bikers usually made up most of the people at any one party, especially the large ones, the pit was open to everyone. Even the woman in the powder blue dress sometimes made an appearance, but mostly only when Bear was there.

Annie and the twins often joined the parties. But last night found them waiting in their clearing to carry out the next step in their plan. And at exactly 2:22 A.M., the twins were laying on their backs positioning themselves perfectly by framing the hallowed spot in the sky with their thumbs and forefingers. Gemini, of course, wasn't visible yet, and wouldn't be until at least late November. But they didn't need to see it to know where it would be. While the twins laid on the grass, Annie did her part, outlining their bodies on the grass and weeds with white paint like the chalked outlines at a crime scene. Their trajectory was set. Now the real work could begin.

Bret sometimes heard the partying, but never joined in anymore. He'd thought about it once or twice, but after what had happened, he figured he wouldn't be welcome. And last night, he wasn't prepared to go anywhere other than to buy himself a coach fare to the hereafter. He'd spent his night in the middle of the chaos of war memorabilia he'd pulled from the storage area, creating a small mountain in his living room of clothes, magazines, books, and random military items. As he sorted through it piece by grueling piece, he discovered no sense of worth or pride. What had once made him feel strong now made him weak, and he was finding he couldn't deal with it anymore, not even with the aid of a fine Canadian whiskey.

At one point, Bret pulled from a box the helmet that had saved him from more than one piece of flying shrapnel and ran his fingers across the single word he'd written on it upon his arrival at that beach in South Vietnam. He had written it in thick, black magic marker as he sat on his duffle, dining on a steak and a beer with the other guys from his platoon, wondering if he'd ever make it out of that country.

Other guys wrote things like KILLER and DEATH FROM BELOW. One guy wrote CYCLOPS, which no one knew why, but it instantly became his new nickname. Other guys simply just wrote their names, or sometimes their girlfriend's names. But Bret simply wrote one word: DESIRE. That word meant something to him back then. It meant that he was going to survive that war. It meant that he was going to get to come home one day. Hell, it meant *home*. It also meant Elle. But now, it meant very little.

Without warning, the doll in the woods infested his thoughts, and that instantly fractured his ability to control his rage. He threw the helmet to the floor and furiously kicked it across the room, shattering a lamp. He turned next to the pile of clothes, and began to frantically kick and tear at them. Then, veins bulging from his forehead, he began to violently shred the piles of magazines. The bits and pieces snowed down around him like fallout.

With his heart physically aching from pumping too hard, he ran down the hall, into his room, and yanked his permanently loaded 30.06 Springfield from the closet. Returning to the living room, he shot at the piles of magazines and memorabilia, then emptied a shot into the pile of clothes, then the stack of pictures. He turned, and suddenly froze as he looked at the photo on the wall of him as a young, eager, shining-faced new GI. So full of pride. So full of hope. So respected. Now, by himself, so hated. Slowly, as if about to commit the real act, he lined up himself in the photo in the rifle's sight and fired. Shattered glass flew in all directions around him. His teeth clenched, and his veins pumping acid, he threw himself into the wall. His head hit a stud with the sound of a bowling ball thrown against a tree. He lined his back against the wall, and his body slid to the floor.

The pain had to go away.

The cycle had to be stopped.

He slapped the barrel against his forehead until it went numb, and then slowly, methodically put the barrel in his mouth.

He exhaled and pulled the trigger.

If he hadn't shot himself in that photo, he would have had a round left to do it for real. His hand released the rifle, letting it drop as he collapsed, tears flooding his face and sobs heaving through his chest. He had no idea how long he cried before falling exhausted into a state similar to sleep. But even in that exhaustion, he never actually did sleep. He was much too afraid to dream.

From where she lived, the only thing Stella ever heard on summer nights were the usual frogs and chirping insects, her only company at night. Normally, their music and the sweetly scented evening air wafting through the windows were all she needed to be lulled to sleep. But last night, sleep was not high on her list of priorities. She had a new book.

Cuddled under the white eyelet down comforter, she opened the book, and the soft light from the cinnamon-and-orange-scented oil lamp on her nightstand cast across the pages. Soon, she was entranced in the pages as if every word was written just for her, as though that author had tapped into her very being, knowing everything that she wanted and everything that was missing in her hollow life. She read late into the night, almost finishing the book, and before she finally gave in to sleep, she found herself falling in love with the author with every passing word.

Just around the point from the pit, on Dogtooth Bay, someone had heard the party breaking up in the early hours of the morning. Someone who stood in the knee-high water, pants rolled up just above the knees, just as it had been every morning since Elle's funeral. And like all those other mornings, two hands gently set on the water a small, flower-laden birchbark boat that floated away carrying the same message it always did, two words written on a small slip of yellowed paper tucked into the flowers: *I'm sorry.*

☙❦❧

THE BAIT SHOP HAD BEEN BUSY ALL MORNING AS MORE and more local fishermen came to liquidate Arnold's supply of nightcrawlers and fathead minnows. It seemed anyone who could be fishing that day was, getting in practice and planning strategies for the contest that was still more than two weeks off. Lots of those who came in were out-of-towners, or as the locals called them, *612ers,* a reference to the area code that for decades had been the only one attached to the Minneapolis/St. Paul area.

Business was always like that. It would get really busy in the morning, and then die down to a trickle of one or two customers who came in for extra fishing line once theirs had tangled into an unfixable bird's nest, or for a new rod after they slammed the trunk on theirs, or simply for a snack of chips and soda. In fact, it was so predictable, that often, Arnold put up his GONE FISHIN' sign in the window to go run his mid-day errands and return for the evening rush without ever missing a customer in between.

Martin figured he had it made. On any given day, he never had to wait to buy bait before heading out on the water, therefore he got to enjoy the tranquility of those early morning hours on the lake in solitude, before the lake was invaded by other fishermen. He also got first choice of spots, and Martin knew of several that nobody else had discovered. He knew every reef and mud flat, and the best spots to find each species of fish in the lake, information he kept very much to himself. Because of this, ever since it had become common knowledge that Arnold and Martin would be competing in the contest, there had been a rising uneasiness among both the fishing contest planners and the other would-be contestants. If the lower number of entries was any measure, there appeared to be real concern that no one other than Arnold and Martin thought they had a chance of winning the grand prize. The planners had hoped the contest's award scheme would overcome such skepticism: With the exception of the grand prize, the other prizes were staggered so that the most valuable prizes weren't awarded to only the top competitors.

Martin knew that there was a lot of concern with the other participants, but it didn't bother him a bit. It actually made him and Arnold laugh. But Martin felt as if he was somehow entitled to that grand prize trophy, as if it was restitution for having been denied it all those years, and the less competition from scared participants, the better.

As the encroaching sun began to bleach the morning colors, and all the other fishermen began to make their way onto the lake, Martin was just heading in. Having tied his boat to the dock, he turned and took one final gaze over the lake. With a peaceful sigh, he took a deep breath of the serenity, that was, until his gaze caught site of that particular island of rocks.

In the meantime, Arnold was listening to Charlie who, with a clear plastic container of fat black leeches in hand, was back on his soapbox. Arnold continued working with those colorful feathers, wires, and hooks. He was getting frustrated because although he had a design of what he was creating in his head, he still couldn't get it right. As a result, most of Charlie's one-sided conversation eluded rather than bothered him. Still, he liked having the company.

"I'm tellin' you, nothing beats leeches this time of year for walleyes. You can throw nightcrawlers, fatheads, rainbows—hell, you can even throw a fat crankbait at 'em, and nothing'll fill yer limit like leeches. But the secret is they gotta be tipped on a forest green colored jig head," he said, grabbing one from the display on the counter and holding it up to illustrate his point.

"Of course," Arnold replied blankly.

"'Cuz fish'er smarter these days than they usta be."

"You think so?"

"I know it. I've seen it. They know if these big, fat leeches is following somethin' that looks real or fake so its gotta be green because where in nature do you ever see purple, or chartreuse, or even white?" He looked to Arnold for a response that just wasn't there. "Green. That's what's natural, and that's what fills your limit," he continued, even though he knew he was pretty much talking to himself.

Arnold looked up at him with the smirk he reserved just for Charlie. "Green huh? I don't sell a lot of those."

Charlie paused, trying to decide if everyone else was just brain-dead or if it was just him. Certainly it wasn't him. "Good. More fish for me." he said with a sneer.

Arnold's grin got a little larger at that, then grew into a huge smile hearing the door chime ring and seeing Martin walking toward him holding a stringer of four fat walleyes. Their color wasn't faded, and those weren't the only fish he'd caught that morning. The action was rolling from first light until just about an hour before he called it a day. He'd wanted to stay out all day, but the unfinished deer head in his studio prompted him to call it a day.

"Hey, Dad. Morning, Mr. Swanson," he said, walking over to the minnow tanks and depositing the fish.

"Martin. Looks like you hit the jackpot!" Charlie said, genuinely impressed.

"Yeah. Lake's getting crowded lately, so I went over to that cove on the east side and fished all morning on that reef I found last year."

"Did those fish hit on leeches with a green jig head?" Charlie asked, looking right at Arnold with a smirk and raised eyebrows that warned him to prepare to eat humble pie.

"No. They all hit on deep-diving crankbaits."

Arnold threw the smirk back at him with a look that asked if he wanted whipped cream with his pie. But Charlie wasn't about to open wide yet.

"Where they *green* crankbaits?" he asked, casting another challenging look at Arnold.

"No," Martin laughed, wiping the 968 off the dry erase board and replacing it with 969.

Charlie knew that Arnold had won this round, but gave one last attempt.

"Well, this time of year you should be using leeches tipped with a green jig head, if you want my opinion."

Nobody could say anyone was wrong in an argument if they strategically slipped it in that their claim was *their opinion*. People could call them stupid, but they couldn't call them wrong, and Charlie was a four-star general when it came to knowing just where to slip it in.

"I'll keep that in mind. I gotta get to work," Martin said, then turned and walked into the studio before Charlie could see the laughing grin spreading across his face.

Charlie felt instantly slighted. He wasn't finished with this topic, and wanted to continue his argument.

Arnold inadvertently picked it up for his son. "You know, Charlie, for a guy who doesn't like to fish much, you sure are opinionated,"

"What are you talking about?" Charlie said with slanted eyebrows. "I love to fish."

Probably to Charlie's advantage, Sheriff Walker came in before Arnold could reply to that.

"Gentlemen," Dwayne said in a tone that immediately said this was business, not a social call.

"Dwayne. What's the news?"

Dwayne walked up to the refrigerator and grabbed himself a bottle of Coke. He figured that if people have to wait to hear what you have to say, it added a dramatic touch and authority that guaranteed your audience's full attention. Most found it annoying, and Arnold and Charlie felt no different. He twisted open his bottle and took a healthy swig before walking over to Arnold. "I just got the report this morning from county on the outboard," he began. "There were wood fibers found in the prop meaning Bret hit a log, or something."

"So you do think it was Bret?" Arnold asked.

Dwayne nodded confidently, which really concerned Arnold. Dwayne was too smart to be that sure of something so fast. There had to be something more to this, and Arnold suspected he knew exactly what it was: Dwayne was finding any way he could to punish Bret.

"But it was an accident?" Charlie asked.

"I don't call that an accident," Dwayne retorted.

Charlie and Arnold looked at each other. Both too afraid to ask *What do you call an accident, then?*

Arnold shook his head. "Dwayne, are you sure that Bret is to blame?"

Dwayne took another gulp. "That's my hunch," he exhaled with a little belch, "Bret's a talker. He'll tell someone what he did. Now it's just a waiting game."

Arnold had to say something. But what? This wasn't right.

Arnold knew it, Charlie knew it, and from a place deep within him, Dwayne knew it, too.

"Dwayne, I don't agree with you on this one. I don't think Bret did anything to that boat," Arnold countered.

"What makes you so sure?" Dwayne snapped, irritated by the confrontation.

"Well, for one, he was passed out that night."

"He was passed out that morning. Not the night before," Dwayne asserted.

"Still, I'm afraid that you're letting your feelings interfere with the truth," Arnold said, trying not to raise his voice.

"Why are you taking his side, Arnold? This is your wife we're talking about here," Dwayne said with a measure of anger.

"I am quite aware of who we're talking about, but I am not going to lynch someone just so that I can feel better about what happened," Arnold snapped back.

"I have been the sheriff in this town for thirty years. I've never let my personal feelings interfere in a case, and I have never doubted my hunches," Dwayne said as he stood straight up like a bear defending its fresh kill.

"Did you ask Cherie about it?" Arnold asked, unintentionally creating another layer of antagonism.

For the first time ever, Charlie felt like he should leave. He never did well in the face of confrontation, but he didn't believe Bret was guilty either. "What about Earl? He seems like the type," he said without any strength of conviction, as if he expected the next thing to come out of the Sheriff's mouth to be "Shut-up, Charlie."

Instead, the sheriff just looked at both of them, frustrated at what he took as a lack of respect for his profession. Not only that, but to him, his logic as a sheriff should never be challenged. It was inherent only to him, and it pissed him off when others outside law enforcement considered themselves a better sleuth.

"Like I said. I've never doubted my hunches," Dwayne repeated quietly, confidently.

Arnold knew that there was nowhere that that argument could go but bad. He had only hoped that he was right about Bret, even though he wasn't altogether sure he was. And even though there was something not right when it came to Bret, his gut told him that putting the blame on Bret was wrong. But unless other evidence came to light, that gut feeling was all he had. There was something else gnawing at him, too. Bret and Dwayne's relationship had been pretty much destroyed since that day, and he knew that Elle never would have wanted that.

Arnold shook his head at Dwayne, solemnly. "And to think you guys were as close as brothers once."

"Yeah, well. Brothers don't do what he did," Dwayne immediately responded with an unattractive snort.

From Bret's perspective, however, he and Dwayne never really had a brotherly relationship at all. He always felt like he had to be stronger than he really was around Dwayne. He hadn't even been comfortable asking for advice, much less confiding in him about what happened in those last days of the war and what it had done to his life. The only person Bret felt he could look to was himself, and fat chance he was ever going to find it there.

In Bret's front yard, next to the flagpole that stood empty this morning, a small bonfire raged. In it, burning in multicolored flames that produced plumes of sick, black smoke, was the memorabilia he'd partially destroyed the night before, including his uniform and piles of photos, books, and old magazines—all of it burning out of his life.

Carrying more books and magazines out of the house, he tossed them onto the fire, sending up sparks that flew like insects all around him. As he watched it all burn, without care for any sentimental or monetary value, he focused on the scrap of the photo of himself as a young soldier, the edges curling under the heat of the flames. He thought of the irony of shooting himself in a photo, which in turn, saved his own life. But he didn't take it as any sort of miracle; he simply considered it a mistake.

But still, Bret was a survivor, there was simply no denying that. He had survived that war. He had survived his years as deputy, and so far, he had survived the biggest enemy he had faced: himself. However, being a survivor comes with its own misery, and that misery was eating him alive now. He hated that word anyway—*survivor*, because survivors were people who went through horrific ordeals, and came out strong and proud. That wasn't him. He wasn't strong or proud anymore. All he'd done was manage to get out of that war alive, and nothing more.

He stood watching the fire consuming his past. He'd expected it would feel more liberating than it actually did; maybe that would come only with the last dying flame. His gaze fell on a pile of half-charred magazines and books that had spilled from one of the boxes. It had fallen on its side, creating a slide of glossy-covered magazines that extended past the reach of the fire. He slowly walked to pick them up and toss them back, but as he reached for them his eyes locked on one cover. *Time.* June 1972.

On the cover was one of the most horrifying pictures of the war. He'd seen that photo possibly hundreds of times before, but it had never sent the stony cold chill that streaked through him at that moment. It was the photo of a nine-year-old girl, Phan Thi Kim Phuc, running naked from a napalm blast by the South Vietnamese Air Force. It had been a terrible accident, and it was one of the photos that prompted him to join the army in the first place. He felt he had to do something, anything. He had to go and fight. Children were dying. He wasn't about to sit in his northern Minnesota living room and helplessly watch it happen.

Automatically, he flipped through the magazine. Other photos sparked memories of that brave, fearless kid he once had been, so full of life with endless possibilities stretching out ahead of him. He'd felt indestructible back then. But at that moment, he didn't stop his fingers from opening, letting the magazine fall into the fire, and incinerate. There was no emotion in the action; it was simply mechanical.

The fire still ablaze, he grabbed the knapsack that he had packed before he began to incinerate his past. Tied to the bottom was a bedroll; inside was all he'd need for several days. He tossed it over his shoulder, then picked up his .22-caliber rifle, and disappeared into the woods.

CHAPTER TEN

EVENING WAS CLOSING IN BY THE TIME BEAR FINALLY crawled out of bed. Cherie had tried to wake him several times, but Bear wasn't having any of that. He had slept more soundly than he had in months. Even a tornado would have had trouble bringing him out of it. His rare slumber had honored him with dreams, and as he stood in front of the bathroom mirror, trying to bring his image into focus, one of the dreams crept back into his memory.

In the dream, he was in the Arctic, sitting in Ernie's old duct-taped recliner on top of a flat glacier and surrounded by the Arctic Ocean seascape. The seascape, though, had a fake, almost computer-generated look. Sitting under the blue sky and wispy white clouds, he looked out over a black sea and endless sheets of ice. But it wasn't cold. It really wasn't any specific temperature. What it was, was deathly quiet. Quiet, not serene. Leaning forward in his chair, he caught site of Cherie's naked outline against a distant sheet of ice. She just stood there, emotionless, then lifted her arms over her head and took an Olympic-worthy dive into the black water. Her outline was visible beneath the water's surface as she approached him, moving through the water without swimming. Then, her outline became distorted by the waves, changing into a huge, menacing white shape that came right up to the sheet of ice Bear was floating upon and seemed to disappear under it.

Bear leaned forward again just in time to see the white paw of a polar bear with obnoxiously long and sharp claws grab onto the ice sheet creating a sound not unlike metal against metal. Slowly, it was followed by its twin paw. Bear jumped up on the chair, ready to pounce as the polar bear lifted its head out of the water. Its eyes slanted down at him as it rolled its lips back to reveal teeth the size of railroad spikes and intertwined with a grisly crocodile smile. Bear, neither feeling nor showing any fear, leaned forward as the bear began to pull itself up on the ice. Then without warning or hesitation, Bear closed his fist, clenched his muscles, and punched the bear directly in his nose. His fist was buried up to his forearm in the soft, almost foam-like nose. The bear growled. Bear pulled his arm back, and punched him again, just as hard and equally precisely. As the bear retreated and slid back into the icy water, he jumped off the chair.

"I'm the ape! You got it? I'm the fucking ape here!" He screamed and stood over the bear with a still clenched fist.

As he splashed his face with water from the filthy bathroom sink, he began to emerge out of the dream and back to reality. He never understood his dreams, nor did he try. He didn't buy into the bullshit that your dreams were trying to communicate something to you, and that there was a deep meaning in every one of them. Dreams were dreams, and that was that. But still, he couldn't deny the amazing symbolism in last night's slumber theater, and as he dried his dripping face with a towel as dirty as the sink, he stared at himself in the mirror.

"I'm the ape. What does that mean?"

There was no answer. Dreams were dreams.

He walked into the kitchen, and opened the fridge, hoping to find something palatable for breakfast, but didn't. It was then that he realized he was alone. Cherie obviously had to walk to work, and he couldn't figure out why she hadn't woken him up for a ride.

But all Cherie's attempts to wake him had failed. Even the cold water she dumped on his head didn't do it, but probably only made his dream all the more vivid. After an hour and half of trying, she could have either stayed and tried to get him up and been late again, or she could walk to work. Deciding her chances of being on time were better, she walked, but it was all for naught, since she was still twenty minutes late. To Jack, that was twenty reasons to let her go, but he didn't. He just told her to look in the mirror, as that was the only person who cared about her excuse for being late. Truth was, he didn't have a replacement for her, and he certainly wasn't going to do her job himself.

After looking at the clock and seeing it was almost five, Bear walked out to Emily, and kicked her to life. He tried not to let the gravity of missing a morning on the dock effect him. He was still in a party mood, and wanted nothing of reality to bring him down even though he was headed toward the shop were there was always plenty to cure him of his happiness. But he was only going there for a minute, then to go pick up Cherie, and then head out for another romp at the pit.

There was talk that everyone was going to be there, and when there was a huge crowd out there with bikers from all around, he could round up more clients for the shop. He and Earl always brought a few kegs of the good stuff in Earl's truck, a generosity that had never failed to reward them with a few new customers. That was the great thing about being in the tattoo industry; beer was a write-off.

Earl's third and last client of the day was a harebrained biker named Lorin. He was too skinny, with long stringy hair that only got the benefit of a washing when he would accidentally fall in the lake—which he did often. He was one of Earl's best clients, and a good friend—as good a friend as Earl could get, anyhow. Earl enjoyed hanging with him because neither of them had to be adults; they could be just as juvenile and reckless as Lorin always was. In fact, he was so reckless sometimes that people speculated that Lorin was only alive out of chance, as his stupidity simply hadn't caught up with him yet.

A few weeks earlier, Lorin was complaining to Earl that he was getting pissed that everyone was calling him "weasel," "skunk," or sometimes "the ferret." He wanted a name of his own choosing. Something a little more to how he saw himself, and what better way than to have your biggest tattoo call out your name loud and clear? So Earl went to work about a week ago on the huge coiled rattlesnake across his back. Earl knew nobody was going to call him that, but he never interfered with a client's wishes, or their wallets.

Bear rolled Emily to a halt right in front of the doors, then waltzed into the shop, and walked behind the counter. Earl looked up at him. "It's about time you woke up, you lazy bastard," he said sarcastically.

Bear just growled a little.

Lorin, lying on his stomach, looked up at him. "Hey, Bear. Rough night?"

Bear ignored them as he tapped at Nicasa's glass. She lifted her head up from her coils and looked at him. "How you doin' little girl?" he said, then flipped on his computer.

"Bruce waited over an hour for you to finish his wizard. He's really pissed," Earl said, almost more cautiously than the statement warranted.

Bear had never missed a client's appointment before, but didn't seem concerned, and merely shrugged his shoulders.

"That shithead's always pissed about somethin'. And who the hell gets a wizard tattooed on his inner thigh?" Lorin said, as if letting Bear off the hook.

Earl, paying more attention to whoever it was behind the counter that looked like his brother, but was obviously an imposter, ground the needle a little too deep into Lorin's back.

"Owww! You tattooin' my skin or my spine!" Lorin screamed, trying to turn his head toward Earl.

Earl just looked down at him as if he was a child bent over his knee. "Be a man," he scolded.

The computer beeped, alerting Bear that he had e-mail. He clicked to open it, and began reading.

Lorin looked confused. "What the hell was that?"

"E-mail. I keep in touch with my old buddies from the joint," Bear said without taking his eyes off the monitor.

"You got your own e-mail? How damn cosmopolitan," Lorin said with a ratty snort.

"He also gets free porn," Earl added cynically.

"I knew the Internet was good for something," Lorin said, and settled back down to let Earl continue the tattoo. But Earl had only just begun to shade in the rattle when the door flew open with the fury of a tornado, causing his hand to slip a little.

Cherie burst in, angrier than anyone there had ever seen her. Earl rolled his eyes, and quietly looked down at Lorin. "Speaking of free porn," he said, and shared a giggle with him.

Cherie ignored them. She had her cannons fixed directly on Bear.

"Bear, you are such an asshole! You know that? I was almost fired today because you couldn't get your lazy ass out of bed to take me to work like you're supposed to," she screamed so fiercely that her eyes began to water.

She didn't get the reaction she expected. Bear just turned and stared at her in disgust. He had never been in the habit of letting *anyone* talk like that to him, and Cherie knew it. But she was furious, and intended to get her point across any way she could. Even if it meant that Earl and Lorin sat there snickering like a couple of kids who just found daddy's stash of girly magazines.

"You do this to me all the time," Cherie yelled. "You tell me you're gonna do something, and then you do somethin' else. Why? Why do you have to be such an asshole? You know I don't have a ride other than you, and you told me not to worry about it, you'd give me a lift anytime I needed it. But no, 'I'm Bear. I'm the world's biggest fucking asshole,'" she said, caricaturing him.

Bear interrupted her, calm as a kitten's purr. "Cherie. I'm gonna let you walk outside, and come back in, and I'll act like you didn't just do that. Sound good?"

"Oh, fuck you! This is so totally not my fault! Don't try to turn this around on me like you always do! I have a right to be pissed off!"

Bear stood up from his stool. "Okay. That's all," he said as he marched towards her, which made her take a step back. Lorin and Earl watched with baited anticipation. They wanted to see a fight, but they were to be disappointed as Bear just picked her up, and effortlessly threw her over his shoulder. "I gave you a chance, and you didn't take it. You're going to have to learn one way or another," he said as he began to carry her to the door.

She kicked, and screamed, and pounded her fists into his back. "Put me down, you fucking asshole!" she screamed. It was like a mouse trying to fight a gorilla.

Earl and Lorin were loving this, especially Lorin. He thought he was just going to get a sore back out of his visit, he hadn't expected entertainment. Earl, even though he still found it amusing, was somewhat used to it by now. Still, he never missed an opportunity to mingle in it. "Hey Bear! You need some help takin' out the trash?" he yelled, and then erupted in laughter with Lorin.

Bear turned to them with a piercing, menacing look. "Shutup, or you guys're next," he warned.

In unison, they both waved their fingers at him. "Ooooooooo," they said with more laughter.

Bear shook his head, and continued out the door with Cherie still pounding and screaming.

He flipped her over his shoulder and deposited her none-too-gently on the tarmac of the parking lot.

"There. You're not allowed back in there until you can learn how to talk nice," he said, sounding like a father chiding his adolescent daughter.

She didn't even try to climb to her feet yet. "Quit treating me like I'm a baby!" she screamed, looking up at him towering over her.

"Then quit actin' like one!" he yelled back.

Her tactics hadn't worked at all. Bear had more willpower, and control than she did, and it continued to drive her nuts. If she was to win this, she would have to change gears, and try something else. She calmed down, but didn't yet get up. "I'm sorry. You're right. I shouldn'adone that," she said, looking up at him with puppy dog eyes and pouty lips.

Bear simply looked down at his pathetic girlfriend. He thought of apologizing, but what did he do wrong?

"I'm sorry, baby," she continued as she rose to her feet, stroking his chest as she rose. "Do you still love me?"

He stood there blankly. All he wanted to do was just walk away and get back to the e-mail about how the warden had just appointed four new trustees to oversee that there would be no gambling in the new game room.

Cherie leaned into him, and pressed her lips against his. Softly at first, then layering it on more feverishly. A good seductive kiss was the only weapon she ever knew to bring a man to his knees, and she thought it was working. But not this time. Bear was quickly getting sick of it all, and as Cherie looked up at him and smiled, thinking that she won, he just stared somberly down at her with the knowledge that there was little left for her to win.

◌◐

THE PARTY AT THE PIT THAT NIGHT WAS MORE FEROCIOUS than anyone could recall. At least seventy bikers had showed up as the Harleys rumbled in by the tens and twenties. Even the woman in the powder blue dress showed up.

Bear tapped another keg, and began to fill the empty glasses stretched out before him before filling his own. As he lifted it up to take his first sip, Cherie, already drunk, tripped into him, spilling his beer all over him. He looked at her with instant contempt. Hurt by both her deed, and his reaction to it, she bowed her head, and moped away as Bear refilled his cup and poured it down his throat before anyone else could spill it.

Metallica's "Blitzkrieg" was blasting from a boombox that was bungee corded to the back of someone's bike. The gathering was as wild as an Amazon feeding frenzy, and Annie and the twins hadn't even shown up yet. It was well known that with the twins, as well as Annie, came nothing but mayhem, and more than one person was keeping an anticipating eye open for them.

But Annie and the twins were hard at work unloading the trailer that they had attached to the back of the snowmobile. Their day had been spent going back and forth from lumber and hardware supply stores in surrounding towns.

They'd made their bigger purchases by phone, selecting a credit card number from the list to pay for the purchase ahead of time. If they were asked any questions when they showed up to collect the order, they explained they were picking it up for their father. It was the same story they used when they went into a store for the smaller items they needed, like nails, screws, shovels, hammers, gallons of waterproof sealant, and so forth. They'd just hand the clerk the sheet of paper on which they'd written one of the credit card numbers; once the number cleared the system, there was no longer any suspicion from the shop owner, therefore, no more questions were asked.

At their last stop, a cardboard box filled with random bullets sat on the counter next to the display rack of assorted candy bars. Written on the side of the box in faded blue marker, it read: RELOADS .75EA. Stee filed through the mismatched shells, and pocketed a 7mm bullet while the clerk was busy ringing up their order. He had plans for that little bad boy.

When the clerk handed Ven the credit slip, he signed it *Kurt Cobain*. No way the clerk knew who that really was. But the twins already knew that before they came. They had scoped this and the other places out ahead of time. They knew exactly what they could get away with, and what would cause suspicion. They were very smart about the logistics of pulling off their plan. They only used each credit card number once, then crossed it off the list and burned the receipt. They knew that paper trails were made by multiple purchases, and that could be traced directly to their clearing. But they had enough card numbers to purchase everything they would need anyway, in fact, they had also scoped out a lumberyard that sold telephone poles—they would need plenty of those, as the ones they already had would not nearly be enough. But that would be tomorrow's big purchase.

When they got back to their clearing, the party was going strong and loud. Even though the twins wanted to get right to work, the sound of the partying bikers were like the ringing bells of an ice cream truck to a salivating kid. They decided to call it a night and go join the fun, and a big cheer surfed over the pit as their snowmobile sputtered through the scene of partying bikers.

Bear walked around, looking for Cherie, expecting his mood to be taken down a notch by finding her crying in the woods. He did feel a little guilty for making her feel bad for spilling his beer, and for carrying her out of the shop like a bag of garbage, even though she deserved it. But still, this was his girl, and he was going to try to make something of it even though he knew in his heart it would never last.

He walked up to one of the regulars and shouted over the music and crowd noise, "Have you seen Cherie around?"

The biker shook his head. "Not in a while. I thought I saw her walking over there a while ago," he shouted, pointing into the woods.

Bear nodded his head in thanks. He walked through the crowd stopping at the fire pit where Stee and Ven, Earl, Lorin, and other bikers were huddled close. Annie and a group of other biker women were standing just behind them, anticipating a good show of nothing more than an act of sheer stupidity.

Stee and Ven loved to test people, and had an uncanny knack for separating the weak from the strong. In this audience, as they knew, no one wanted to be seen as weak. "Fear is an added disability to the weak minded," Ven said with a sadistic smile identical to his brother's.

Everyone, including Bear, knew a test was forthcoming, and a few people were entertaining the thought of walking away before they were trapped in the twin's challenge. But curiosity made every one of them stay, and listen.

Stee pulled the 7mm bullet from his pocket and held it up like an idol for all to revere. "This is a test of fear," he said sizing up those who would turn away, and those who would rise to their challenge. "The first man to break the chain will forever be dubbed a coward."

Earl was the first to rise. "We'll I ain't afraid of nothin'. I'm in," he said as he stood in front of the fire.

"I'm in," Lorin said with less confidence than Earl, but he wasn't about to be the first to be called a coward.

Two more bikers stood to the challenge. "I'm in," one of them thundered.

"Me, too," said the other, and took his place in the circle.

Stee looked at Bear. Surely he wasn't going to stand down. "Bear, how 'bout you?"

Bear didn't need to prove his bravery or his stupidity to anyone but himself. He had never lived a day in his life by what other people thought of him, and it was one of the things that everyone respected about him. Truth was, everyone actually would be more surprised if he took a place in the circle than if he walked away.

"You guys are fuckin' crazy," Bear said, shaking his head. No one even considered any disrespect toward him as he simply walked away, continuing his search for Cherie.

While his response hadn't surprised anyone, this hadn't been a typical night for Bear. Normally, he was a social butterfly, moving from group to group, talking about tattoos, bikes, or whatever, and drumming up business. But he'd been out of sorts all night, and now his only focus was to find Cherie, though he knew it was going to be a big hassle when he did. On the other hand, it would be an even bigger hassle if he didn't find her. For weeks he would have to listen to her bitch about how he never showed her any attention, never told her he loved her, never took her out anymore unless it was somewhere he wanted to go—and maybe she was right. Even though he knew there would eventually be an ending to their relationship, he had to try. He couldn't just go on being a zombie of routine with her. He had to know there was something more than that. He had to find her, and tell her that right at that moment. And as he walked into the forest, just far enough inside where the firelight didn't invade the darkness, he found her. But she was not alone.

Bear stood there, staring at her on her knees before another biker, with her head methodically bobbing back and forth. The immediate shock and infuriation exploded into a white blinding boil of rage that dissolved his control when Cherie turned to look at him, a glimmer in her eye and a Cheshire smile across her face. He charged at them like a lunatic, and grabbed her hard, giving her a nasty bruise in the process.

The biker grabbed his pants and lifted them to his waist. "What the hell are you doin', asshole?" he screamed at Bear, zipping up his pants, preparing himself for battle. His instinct to fight disappeared with his first good look at his opponent. Not only did Bear tower over him, he was a giant that looked like he wanted nothing more than to end someone's life. That, and it being his first time to the pit, it also dawned on him that his little rendezvous was with someone else's girl, and she had just been busted.

But Cherie didn't see it that way. She'd wanted Bear to catch them because, by her logic, it was the only way that Bear would show her any attention. And attention is what she got.

Bear could hardly see through his rage-soaked eyes. For the first time in his life, he cocked his hand back with the intent to hit a woman, and she angled her face, welcoming the consequence. But it wasn't who Bear was, not even in rage. Going down that road was more frightening to him than playing in the thorny place because unlike the thorny place, there might be no coming back once that first step was taken.

He stared at her with contempt as she braced herself for some attention. But Bear slowly lowered his hand, and without saying a word, simply walked away.

The smile on her face dissolved like honey in turpentine. Even now, after having to go down on a dirtball, he still didn't give her what she had wanted. She'd planned on getting hit and felt an odd hurt that she hadn't been. It would have at least been some kind of real contact, a sign she meant something to him, and now she was completely out of ideas on how to make that connection. Simply sitting down and talking to him about it never even entered her mind.

Bear's walk turned into a storm as he got closer to the fire pit. He passed the woman in the powder blue dress laughing with a group of bikers. Her face drooped as he marched by her, and she watched him with a sadness clouding her heart. In a circle around the bonfire, Stee, Ven, Earl, Lorin, and the other two bikers were preparing themselves for the test with their arms interlocked. "Let's begin," Ven said, but was interrupted as Bear tore into the circle between Earl and Lorin.

Everyone stopped and stared at him, wondering why he had changed his mind. They all knew it had to have something to do with Cherie.

"Do it!" Bear seethed.

The twins smiled at him, welcoming him to the game, and with that, Stee threw the bullet into the flashpoint of the fire. At once, arms interlocked with the dude next to them, the group began to circle the fire in a clockwise direction, each one more worried about breaking the chain than they were about getting hit by the bullet. The crowd around them kept its distance, but cheered them on with the fervor of riotous fans.

The bullet began to smolder in the fire. Its tip, pointed outward, began to glow red. It could explode at anytime, in any direction, and within seconds from now, one of these players of this reverse Russian roulette could be dead.

This intense fear was what Stee and Ven were feeding on. They were loving this. The fear was their medication. Their heads became light, and that cherished feeling of euphoria engulfed them as the adrenaline took over to the point that their legs felt limp, and they were almost being carried by the others. This wasn't their first time doing this sort of thing, but it was their first time with a bullet.

Bear was trying to will the bullet to hit him and put him out of his immediate misery. What better way to end his stalemate with Cherie than to have him lying dead in her arms? What a warrior's way out. What a poet's way out. Anger does disturbing things to your intellect, and at that moment, it was controlling his every move.

Lorin was but a second away from breaking the chain, which meant that everyone would win but him. But he'd rather die right here and now than forever be called a coward. The growing fear caused his breathing to become shallow and erratic, and that might just kill him if the bullet didn't first.

Earl felt the same way as Lorin, but masked it in a barrage of whoops and hollers, and an occasional *Yee-haw!* No way he was going to be called a coward either.

The two bikers, like the twins, were in their element. They had each been involved in more street fights than they could count, which made this seem like an innocuous merry-go-round to them. Their faces contorted in their growls of elation. They almost sang their shouts, seemingly certain they would survive the game without a scratch.

The longer it took for the bullet to explode, and the more revolutions the group made, the more the spectators cheered, waiting for a death, and caught up in a crowd mentality that wished for one. Standing apart from the others was the woman in the powder blue dress who just stood and watched with confidence, as though she had an ace up her sleeve.

Annie, on the other hand, had never felt this feeling of fear before. It fed on the growing terror that one of her boys was about to die. It was a terror she couldn't let anyone see, especially Stee and Ven, so she supported them by cheering on with everyone else.

Cherie, too, wanted to see a death—but only one. She didn't cheer for it, but in her mind she tried to will it to happen. She stood with her arms folded in front of her, glaring at Bear every-time he passed. He never saw her.

And then, without warning, a near-deafening explosion thundered from the fire as the bullet exploded in a mushroom cloud of sparks and cinders. The circle came to an immediate dead stop. Suddenly, it was graveyard quiet as a surreal sense of time in suspension took over the gathering. Even the frogs and insects stopped calling.

The only sounds were the crackling of the fire, and the fear-injected panting of the circlers who all cautiously looked at each other to see who had taken the bullet, but they were all too afraid to look down at themselves. Bear moved first, patting himself down. He was sure he hadn't been hit, but the shock of it caused him to check anyway. Cherie looked at Bear, and to her surprise, a rush of relief passed through her when it was apparent he was okay. Earl looked at Lorin who looked back at him; they weren't hit either. Their eyes went next to the bikers, who were as calm as if they were simply standing in line for another beer. They hadn't been hit either. Had the bullet missed *everyone?*

Annie's eyes had never left the twins. At first, nothing seemed to be wrong. But then Stee lifted the front tail of his jacket, and discovered a smoking bullet hole simmered through it.

Annie began to weep, and hid her face in her hands. Ven looked in horror at his brother. It wasn't supposed to be either one of them.

All the bikers in the circle stared with wide, helpless eyes, as silent as the speechless spectators. Ven was paralyzed as his brother twisted around, and grabbed the back tail of his jacket. An exit hole was burned through it. He laughed nervously, then slapped the side of his torso. There was no pain nor was there any sign of blood. The bullet just missed him by less than a rat's hair.

Stee threw an elated toothy grin to his brother, who slowly smiled back, and together, they threw their arms up and cheered louder than sonic.

Earl almost dropped to his knees in relief, and Lorin did collapse. The two bikers joined in the cheer, followed by everyone there who would never forget this night as long as they lived.

Annie ran up to her twins and held them in her arms while she repeatedly drenched them with kisses. Cherie looked at Bear, hoping he would come over to her and do the same, but he didn't. He just stood there, relieved to still be standing. He stared at the twins with more respect for them than he'd ever felt. They were crazy, but man, did they have balls. The twins looked back at him with a huge smile and nodded as if to say *Did that kick ass, or what?*

Yes it did, Bear's smile said.

As Bear, the twins, Annie, and everyone else would look back on this night in the upcoming days, weeks, months, and years, they'd say it was nothing short of a miracle that saved them, but as the woman in the powder blue dress stood and smiled, maybe it was just magic.

CHAPTER ELEVEN

ITHIN THE PAST SEVEN DAYS SINCE HE PLAYED ring-around-the-rosy with his own mortality, Bear hadn't gone back to the pit. It wasn't the trauma of almost losing his life—that still wasn't much of a big deal to him—it was the incident with Cherie. For the past week, he had maybe said three words to her, and they weren't by far the three words that most couples say to each other. He hadn't been back to her place much, either, and was back to sleeping on his bed-roll wherever he felt like sleeping. As it happened, most of those nights were spent on the dock.

Still, even with the dock as his new pad, he would never know about the two bare legs with pants rolled just above the knees that launched another birch bark boat with wild flowers, and a note that read: *I'm Sorry*.

Bret hadn't been seen for some time, either. He'd lost himself in the woods in one of the only places he knew—except for the Boundary Waters—that the hum of traffic could not be heard. It was a quiet that allowed him to do more than just be alone with his thoughts; it drove him to the very core of them, and that was terrifying in and of itself. What he needed to know was whether there was anything left in him worth saving.

Every morning that Martin would come to launch his boat for another day of fishing, he never inquired about Bear's camp at the end of the dock. He figured that Bear deserved an amnesty from the gossip and finger-pointing by people in town who thought they knew what was going on with him and Cherie. Therefore, he continued with his small talk mostly about fishing and the weather. Although their relationship wasn't quite the same as before Elle's death, Martin knew that if he really needed anything more from Bear, he would be able to get it just for the asking, and he was right.

For his part, Bear envied Martin in many ways. Sure, he had a long way to go in dealing with his mother's death, but even so, on the whole he seemed so grounded, so in touch with the natural world around him and his place in it. That was something that Bear was trying desperately to find, but lately, he had found life unappetizing once again. He began to consider his assets in Desire, specifically what he could leave behind if he chose to disappear again. But that was just it: there was nothing to make him stay, but there was also nothing to make him leave. He had come to a stalemate with himself and his life, and this time, those thoughts weren't distorted by the thorny place.

Sitting on the dock, gazing blankly at the tranquil surface of Lake Desire, he held his journal open, but hadn't written a word. He had volumes to write about, but still, taking the pen from his vest and doing it just seemed so insipid somehow.

But there was something else in the inside pocket of his vest that he'd been carrying since it had been given to him, but purposely avoided since. He felt a sort of betrayal, like a spy in his own country, to read her words without her there, without her being the one to give them to him. Right now, though, the need for inspiration overshadowed the need for anything else, and he slowly reached in his vest, and pulled out Elle's journal.

He filed through each page carefully, stopping to read bits and pieces as he went, but nothing in its entirety. She was a better writer than he was, and he was strong enough to respect that, and even admire it.

Her writing, always in cursive, was nothing short of an art form. It was truly elegant, almost calligraphic. Bear's writing looked like chicken scratchings compared to hers, but he could live with that.

As he continued to read the bits and pieces, he became more comfortable, less intrusive. Most of the journal entries talked about the people she knew and cared about, including him. Other entries were drawings of the lake from the island. She even created a poem from her grocery list. It was typical Elle, finding beauty in the everyday things around her.

Unexpectedly, an envelope fell from between the pages, almost as if it willed itself to do so, and landed on his lap. On the front, beautifully lettered, it read ARNOLD. The envelope wasn't sealed, but he wasn't even sure that if it had been, that would have stopped him from opening it and taking out the enclosed letter. Still, he did feel a little guilty and paused to see if anyone was watching before he unfolded the letter, and began to read.

> My dearest Arnold, I have never regretted for a moment forsaking Bret for an eternity in love with you. Even though I did once love him—

This wasn't for his eyes. He stopped reading, gently folded the letter, and placed it back in its envelope, then back into the journal. Perhaps not knowing the contents of that letter would poke and tease him until he finally gave in to his curiosity, but that wouldn't happen that morning.

∽☙∾

THE POUNDING OF CONSTRUCTION, AND THE RESONATING racket of the generator woke Annie from her slumber on the ground in the clearing. She and her king-sized sleeping bag—designed for two but used by three—was soaked with dew. Sitting up, she rubbed her eyes and gazed in amazement at what the twins had already accomplished. They had done the work of twenty men in just a short seven days. They hardly slept, and rarely took time out to even eat. They were completely obsessed with their creation.

In a diamond-shaped platform made from a frame of two-by-fours, Stee was laying the last of the crisscrossed panels of flooring lumber, nailing it to the frame with the nail gun with a loud *thoovd*. On the northwest and northeast sides of the platform, two crisscrossed telephone poles cut to six-feet stumps formed an X along the two sides. Each of the four poles were buried a foot and a half in the ground and anchored with cable. Two thirty-foot telephone poles, anchored two feet in the ground at a perfect fifty-degree angle, formed the upside-down V-shaped legs of the viewing device, which rested each of its poles on the X's.

At the top of the V, twenty-eight feet high, a flat circular piece of wood with an eight-foot diameter held the viewing device. The edging was pounded formed copper to keep the elements from splitting the wood. In the center of the device, seventeen holes were strategically drilled. The bottom of the device was painted black with red lines connecting the holes, which made a rough dot-to-dot outline of two people, hand-in-hand. The top was painted white with various designs, almost hieroglyphical. Painted in an arch on the top of the viewing device was the word CASTOR, and the word POLLUX arched below. The entire structure already had two coats of weather-proofing sealant.

Other telephone poles lay around, not yet put into position. The tops had been cut at a forty-five-degree angle and sanded down to a tabletop finish. They were ready for Annie to paint her designs on them around a group of numbers and letters that the twins wrote down for her on drawing paper and stapled to the top of one of the crossed six-foot poles so she wouldn't lose it.

The instructions read: *RA 7hrs 20min, Dec. 24° 59', Alt. 66° 54', Azmuth 96° 43'.*

They were just a bunch of letters and numbers that were as foreign to her as they would be to anyone else who saw them and did not recognize what they were. But those who would recognize them, would look at the structure, and believe it to have been built by geniuses; they wouldn't be far from right.

The twins used no measuring tools of any kind, and no sky charts, and still their calculations were accurate to within a centimeter. They knew exactly what length to cut things, and at what angle to set the viewing device. They hadn't made a blueprint or a drawing of what the completed project would look like. They worked almost as if something else was creating it through them, as if the structure was willing itself to be made.

Annie crawled out of the sleeping bag, stretched, and slipped on her cut-off overalls over her midriff top. Walking over to her boyfriends, she couldn't help but be amazed at all they'd gotten done since she went to sleep last night.

"Morning, Sleepyhead," Stee said and gave her a kiss.

"Hi," was all she could find to say.

"Pretty amazing, isn't it?" Ven said as he took his turn with a kiss.

"When did you guys do all this?" she asked, trying to avoid any loose nails or other sharp objects as she walked barefoot around the project.

"Last night," Stee said. "We pulled an all-nighter."

"Yeah, I know. I was freezing without you guys," she said wrapping her arms around her, still a little chilled.

Just then, the sheriff's Prowler pulled into the clearing off the back road. They were all thinking the same thought at the same time: If the sheriff was coming down the back road, it was pretty certain that he knew what they had done to finance the project, and the three of them just stood paralyzed, helplessly watching the Prowler pull to a stop just off the side of the back road. They tensed up a little more as the door opened, then breathed a sigh of relief as they saw it was Eddie, not the sheriff, getting out of the truck.

Eddie liked Annie. He never hid that, but also never verbalized it either. All three of them knew it. So did the sheriff, but he didn't care much about that sort of puppy love soap opera crap, just as long as it didn't interfere with Eddie doing his duty. The twins and Annie also knew that Eddie's schoolboy crush could be used to their advantage; he could be controlled. And as he walked up to them, they speculated that the sheriff would never hear of what was going on out here.

"Hey guys," Eddie said, looking directly at Annie.

"Hi. What are you doing out here?" Annie said.

"I was going to ask you the same question," he said, putting on his deputy persona which instantly turned the twins off.

"What does it look like?" Stee said, not trying hard enough to hide his annoyance.

"I don't know. You tell me," Eddie shot back, his eyes now trained on Stee.

"You don't recognize art when you see it?" Ven said with a smirk.

"Doesn't look like any art I've ever seen," Eddie said as he began to walk around and survey their work. "Where did you guys get all this equipment?"

"Catalogs," Annie said immediately. She knew that she had to stop him from probing any further, and she also knew she was the only one who could do it.

She moved seductively close to him. "C'mere a sec," she said with a flirtatious smile, and taking his hand, she led him back to the truck.

The twins watched, actually impressed with their girlfriend. Annie was more than good at using her sexy charm to get men to do what she wanted, and they smiled as they remembered that it worked like a talisman with them. They couldn't hear what she was saying to Eddie, but they could see her hand on his chest and her big, beautiful eyes locking his into her magic. She stood on her tiptoes and gave him a kiss that lingered just soft and long enough to promise that Eddie would now do anything she wanted him to do. Love struck, he clumsily opened the door, and slid into the truck. Annie blew him one more kiss as he drove away, this time down the main dirt road. They never did discover why he came in through the back way, and it really didn't matter now anyway. Perhaps he was just going to take a nap in the one place that he knew the Sheriff wouldn't find him.

Annie walked back up to her boyfriends radiating with pride. "Problem solved," she said with a dagger smile, then walked over and picked up a paintbrush.

👓

Stella had finished *Love, Elusive* days ago, but still carried it with her everywhere she went. It was still speaking to her, still telling her there was hope if she would only lose her apprehension and grab it before it was too late. Mostly, it was still telling her that she needed to find the man who wrote those words that she would have singing in her heart forever.

Sitting at the counter in her empty shop, she took another sip of her still hot cup of coffee that she once again had paid for with change from the bottom of her handbag before picking up the book, and turning to the publisher's page. There, on the bottom, directly underneath the publisher's address, was a phone number that she already knew was there; she had looked at it seven times already. It was a 612 area code. When she first looked, she had expected to see a Los Angeles or New York number, which she would have had to spend months building up the courage to call. But somehow, a Minneapolis publisher wasn't as frightening. They were usually smaller, and better suited to take care of their authors, or at least be open to talking with a fan about them.

She knew she had to call, if nothing more that just to ask, and she knew if she didn't do it now, she might never again get the courage to do it. Still, she just sat there and stared at the phone.

Just pick up the damn phone, Stella. Just do it. It's only a stupid phone call. What are you afraid of?

She grabbed the phone, but then stopped, and tried to get her labored breathing under control. She procrastinated by taking a long sip of her coffee to wet her suddenly parched lips. She couldn't remember a time when she had been this nervous, but she also couldn't remember a time when she displayed this kind of courage. That in and of itself was a triumph. She had picked up the phone. She had taken the first step. Slowly, with her index finger stretched out like a broken branch, she slowly pressed the ten digits of the number, one by daunting one.

The phone rang. Then again . . . and again . . . and again. "Do things to make yourself happy Stella. Stay on the phone," she whispered. The phone rang yet again, and she began to worry as the courage was quickly draining from her. But just as she had removed the phone from her ear, a voice finally answered.

"Lakeland Publishing, how may I direct your call?" an over-sweet but robotic voice inquired.

Stella couldn't get her breathing under control. "Yes, h . . . h . . . hello," she stuttered, but her courage was almost completely drained. Her voice cracked "I, ah . . . I want to . . . um . . ."

She stared into the nothingness of her empty store. Empty. That's how she now saw her life was to be forever. Even the book seemed to throw its hands up in aggravation at believing in such a hopeless prospect.

"Hello?" the pleasant voice on the phone echoed.

"I ah . . ." Stella wasn't fighting her breathing or her pounding heart or her dry, pasty mouth anymore. She was now fighting the urge to simply break down and cry. "I have the wrong number, sorry," she mumbled.

She stared into the nothingness with sad, glossy eyes. Her arm drooped, and she simply opened her hand and let the phone slide from her fingers back onto the receiver. She had found the courage, and then let it slip away. She was disappointed with her-self, and that made her bout of sadness even worse. "Why did you put yourself through that ordeal in the first place? Why did you set yourself up for failure?" she thought to herself. She was who she was and her life was what it was. "Accept it."

Her eyes caught the Post-it Notes on the computer monitor. *Do something fun and unexpected for yourself.* She stared, wondering, "Do these even mean anything anymore?" She looked back at the phone. It sat, waiting, disappointed in her as well.

Her store had never looked so cold, empty, and alone to her as it did at that moment. She couldn't be there anymore today. Business was less than slow, and crawling in bed with the book for the rest of the day until she fell asleep seemed like the only cure to her distress, but even that might not suffice. Still, it was her only alternative, and maybe she'd get lucky and fall asleep early so she wouldn't have to deal with any of this.

Stella picked up the book, dropped it into her shoulder bag, and got out her chair. She looked up to the calendar on the wall, and stared at it while desolation took control of her. She took the black magic marker that hung on a string from the corner of the calendar, and placed an X over today's square marking that yet another day of solitude had bitten the dust.

She looked at tomorrow's square. It had a sticker of a birthday cake with two lit candles stuck to it and the words HAPPY BIRTHDAY written across it. Her wish last year when she blew out the candles on her cake was that that would be the last birthday she would have to spend alone. But she didn't expect it to come true because it was the same wish she made the year before that, and the year before that, and the year before that. Now that she had chickened out on the phone today, she didn't expect that her wish would come true this year as well. She bowed her head for no reason other than she simply didn't want to look at the sticker any longer.

She almost ran out of the store, stopping only long enough to flip the OPEN sign to CLOSED and to lock the door behind her.

☙❧

ARNOLD ONLY CLOSED HIS SHOP EARLY WHEN HE WENT ON his errands in the afternoon, and in the past ten years, there was only one day that he didn't open at all—the day he buried Elle. He found comfort in his work since then, and took pride in how organized and clean his shop was. He sat behind the counter and attached the treble hooks to the thing he was creating with all the colorful feathers. He'd finished it; now he was ready to win the tournament tomorrow. He set the lure on the counter next to the cash register and smiled. "Yeah, that'll win it for Martin for sure," he murmured proudly.

Martin was asleep. He almost always was by this time of the evening. Nine o'clock almost on the dot. Waking up at four every morning does that to a man, especially a fisherman.

Arnold found a special comfort in the solitude of this time of the day. Charlie, who also went to sleep when the sun did, had gone home, so it was just Arnold and the minnows in the shop. In the quiet, he thought more clearly and enjoyed the introspection.

He wiped the counter down with the hand towel with the embroidered bass on it, which was also the same towel he used to wipe the fish slime off his hands on those rare occasions that he did get out for a day of fishing. He took the blue marker that was wedged halfway under the cash register and placed it back on the ledge of Martin's progress board, which read 976. He stared up at it, pleased that in two days, he would very proudly make that phone call to officially report that Martin had broken the record.

Arnold went over to the minnow tanks and placed a clear acrylic cover over each tank to keep the mice that frolicked through the shop every night from falling in and polluting the water. He then went to the peg board lure display and made sure that all the lures were hung where they were supposed to be. Customers were notorious for taking a red and white spoon off the rack, looking at it, trying to imagine the lunker it might bring in, then putting it back on the row of the black and white spoons. It really drove him nuts when people did that, but how could he stop it? Besides, it bought him more time here at the shop; home still felt too lonely without Elle.

But tonight was different. He had something to look forward to tomorrow. The fishing contest would be the first time since Elle's death that he and Martin had gone fishing together, and that was more important to him than the possibility of them winning another trophy. They didn't even need to catch a single fish as far as he was concerned, just as long as they were doing what each of them loved together as father and son.

As he moved to the front door to turn off the lights and call it a night, a dark, ominous figure standing in the doorway surprised him, shocking an onslaught of goose bumps to boil over him. He involuntarily jumped back half a foot as the figure stepped forward into the light.

Bret was filthy, his hair matted and dull. He stood there, looking tired and worn, staring at Arnold with sad, swollen eyes. Arnold looked back at him with a heaping spoonful of sympathy even though his goose bumps didn't fade. It was too obvious that his old friend was in trouble.

What Arnold didn't know was where Bret had been over the last week, and the horrors he'd faced there. He wouldn't have been able to fathom it if he tried; nobody could. Actually, Arnold hadn't realized until just that moment that he hadn't seen Bret since a week ago. Arnold opened the door, and although he never showed it, was instantly repulsed by the stench that only came from sleeping in the decaying earth for a week. That, and the unmistakable reek of a fine Canadian whiskey.

"Bret!" Arnold said with a tone of surprise as he leaned against the open door.

"Can I come in?" His voice trembled, uncertain.

Arnold opened the door wider. "Yes. Of course. C'mon in. I'm just closing up."

Bret stepped cautiously into the shop, then dropped atop the chest freezer next to the door. He sat silently, showing no immediate signs of life.

"Are you okay?" Arnold cautiously asked, genuinely concerned.

Bret swallowed hard. "I don't know what that means anymore."

His stench was overpowering, especially that stale, sweet smell of days-old liquor on his clothes.

"You've been drinking again," Arnold said in a tone more suited for a teenager caught with his dad's beer.

Bret laughed as much as he could. It still wasn't much more than a verbal smile. "Why is it that those with the best intentions in life are always the most cursed?" he asked, staring vacantly ahead.

Arnold could only try to understand what his old friend was going through, but he never came close. All he knew right now were two things: His old friend was in big trouble, and there was no way that this man did anything to Elle's boat.

Suddenly, Bret began to weep in deep, sorrowful, broken sobs. "I loved her Arnold. I really did."

There was only one honest reply Arnold could make. "I know," he said somberly.

Bret's weeping turned into a drunken kind of sarcastic laughter. "Did you know I was going to marry her? Did you know we were going to be happy together?"

"Bret, are we going to do this again?"

"I'm cursed, Arnold. I did an unforgivable thing, and it cursed me for the rest of my Goddamn life. It took Elle away from me. I'm on the cycle again, and I can't do it anymore."

Arnold really wasn't sure what Bret meant. Is he talking about Elle's boat? And if so, maybe he did do something to it. Is Dwayne right? He highly doubted it, but still, it would nag at him. "C'mon. Let me take you home. I'll make us a pot of coffee," Arnold said reaching for his arm to help him up.

Bret laughed again, but this time the laughter rang of irony. "I don't have much of a home left," he said, then looked directly at Arnold, right into his eyes. "I just came here to tell you something I should have told you years ago. I don't blame you for taking her away from me while I was in 'Nam. In fact, I just wanted to thank you for making her happier than I ever could've."

These were not the words of someone who knew he was going to be living for much longer. These were the words of someone trying to reconcile an old debt before it was too late, and Arnold wasn't sure how to handle it. "Bret, you don't have to say that," was all he could think of to say.

"Yes I do," he said instantly, still looking right through Arnold's eyes. "Yes I do."

CHAPTER TWELVE

W HEN BEAR ROLLED OUT OF HIS BEDROLL ON the dock, he noticed a missing note in the symphony of morning. Martin's boat wasn't there clanking against the dock. He had taken it over to the main dock down at the park where the fishing contest was being held.

Martin had spent the better part of the morning preparing it for the contest by making sure the gas can was full, the extra rods and reels were in place, and plenty of jigs and other baits were organized in his tackle box. He spent a good hour sharpening all the hooks with a fingernail file. He also affixed chairs with backrests to the bench seats because he knew his father wouldn't be able to sit on them all day without that support. He made sure there were no frays in the nylon anchor rope, and retied it to the loop in the bow, and to the anchor itself. He didn't know when the next time he and his father would be able to fish together again, and he wanted to make sure that absolutely nothing went wrong.

Bear simply thought that he had missed Martin when he set out to fish, but then remembered that today was the fishing contest, which explained the added number of boats on the lake and the increased traffic noise coming from the direction of town. He could also hear the loud voices of the people who were constructing the stage, and getting the PA system working from the park as they prepared for the hordes of people who had already started to show up, mostly just to hang around and watch the commotion.

This morning's tranquility was spoiled by the added noise, and he simply rolled up his bed, tied it the back of Emily, and rode into town to find a cup of coffee somewhere other than the Sportsman's Café. On the other hand, he couldn't avoid Cherie forever, and maybe it was time to patch things up. But, no, he was still pretty mad at her, and he had a right to be. He questioned whether or not she was still even his, or even if he wanted her to be. One thing he did know was that she would never be the one to say *I'm Sorry*. Even if things weren't his fault, just to keep the peace, he was always the one to say it. But not this time—or ever again. If Cherie had a problem with those words, that was *her* problem. He flat out refused to let it be his anymore.

But, like every morning, someone else wasn't afraid to say that they were sorry, as the two legs waded through the water with pants rolled up above the knees. The birch bark boat was launched filled with wood lilies and astor and the note that still read *I'm Sorry*.

Even as the small vessel carried its builder's remorse across the waters of Lake Desire, other boats were preparing for departure in readiness for the annual competition. At the main dock, the stage was near completion. Large banners announced the contest and the sponsors whose support made it possible. Gander Mountain, being the biggest sponsor of the contest, had the biggest banner.

Between two posts on either side of the stage stretched a banner that read WELCOME TO THE 25th ANNUAL LAKE DESIRE FISHING CONTEST. Strings with multi-colored flags were anchored from it diagonally to the ground. Close by, picnic tables circled the outdoor barbeques, and volleyball nets and food stands were being erected.

Boats of hopeful fisherman began to pull up to the dock, each showing off his boat like a peacock showed its feathers. On the stage, the scales were being tested, and the leader board was power-drilled into place. The PA system was being checked by one of the sound technicians as he pressed his lips to the microphone on the stage, and boomed "Test, one, two. Test," which echoed over the lake followed by an ear splitting screech of feedback.

On Main Street, the town was alive with activity as visitors crowded the shops and the streets. Stella had overslept and opened twenty minutes later than her regular time, but no one seemed to care. Everyone just came back when she had opened, and she couldn't remember a day since last year's contest when she was as busy.

Up the road, the Lunker Lodge opened early, knowing that all day there would be a revolving door of customers wanting sandwiches, snacks, soft drinks, and beer. It was the only day of the year that Barney opened early, and it was well worth it; the fishing contest was an even busier day for him than the deer season opener—a date that by itself kept other bars in northern Minnesota in business.

The Sportsman's Café was full. In fact, there was actually a waiting list for seating; the only other day in the year that happened was Thanksgiving. It was also one of the biggest days for generous tips, and even Cherie, who was in fact was feeling more ornery than ever, donned a rare smiling persona as she ran in endless round-trip circles from the tables to the coffee maker to the cook's window to pick up orders and back to the waiting tables. Jack had brought on another girl, Nancy, who was about Annie's age, to pick up the counter seats, and the other full time waitress, Heidi, had the other half of the tables. Still, they were all running a marathon as Jack rarely waited for a table to even be cleaned before he sat another customer. Like Cherie, they knew that days like this didn't happen often, and as soon as the contest started, it would be all over like a tornado rushing through a trailer court, leaving a swath of devastation and debris in its wake—and them to clean up after it.

Next door, the bait shop was just as busy. Arnold did ten per-
cent of his yearly business on the morning of the contest day
alone. He was out of minnows by 8:00 A.M., even though he
ordered sixty dozen more than his usual thirty dozen a week order
of rainbows, fatheads, suckers, and chubs. The leeches had been
sold out a half hour before that, but he had kept two dozen behind
the counter for him and Martin even though he was pretty sure
Martin wouldn't use them.

In addition to the live bait, the shop had also almost totally
sold out of jig heads, leaders, and line in almost every pound
weight. Most of the rod and reel combos had been sold, too, mostly
to newcomers to the contest who were looking for last minute
insurance in case an unforeseen mishap occurred on the lake.

Charlie was relishing in the attention he was getting as everyone who cared gathered around him listening to his infinite fishing wisdom, unaware that most of his audience listened just for
comic relief. Charlie took this sort of thing very seriously, and he
was truly smug that a few people actually listened intently to what
he had to say. Arnold watched this out of the corner of his eye;
smug as well that anyone who took his advice would not be much
of any competition for Martin and him.

Martin, out of breath from running from his truck that he
had to park on the street down the block, rushed in the front door.

"Martin! Where have you been? We're gonna be late," Arnold
said, putting on his hat with all the colorful dry flies around the rim.

"I was just getting the boat ready. Let's go," he said as he
grabbed his father's tackle box and shoulder cooler.

They hustled to the door, passing a row of jerk baits. "Grab
some of the deep divers," he said. "We may need them if my secret
weapon doesn't work."

Martin grabbed a few of the perch colored muskie jerks as he
balanced his Dad's box on his knee, and threw in the lures haphazardly. "What is it this time?" he said with a spice of sarcasm.

"I'll show you on the lake," Arnold said as they rushed to the
door. He turned to Charlie, who was standing behind the counter

like he owned the place. "Charlie, lock the door behind you when you come down to the lake."

"Right-O," Charlie said with a two-fingered wave as Arnold and Martin ran down to their truck, already late for the start of the contest.

๑๑

A CIRCUS OF FISHERMEN HAD ASSEMBLED BEFORE THE stage. The park was teeming with picnickers, tourists, and people just there to have fun, as they knew that an event like this only came once a year. To most of the town's people, this was better than Christmas. The smell of barbeque sweetened the crisp lake air. The old-timers were involved in separate games of horseshoes, and bocce ball, while next to them a volleyball game was in the middle of play between Paul Bunyan High School, where all the students of Desire attended, and Radisson High School from the town just to the south of Desire.

Eddie was flirting with a group of high school cheerleaders sitting at one of the picnic tables. He propped his foot up on the seat, and leaned on his knee so that the girls could get a good look at his gun.

Arnold and Martin crowded with the other contestants close to the stage. Right on time, the Master of Ceremonies stepped forward and picked up the microphone, causing a burst of feedback after which a consequent hush fell over the crowd.

"How's everybody doing today?" the emcee enthusiastically shouted, earning himself a thundering, cheering applause. "Welcome to the twenty-fifth annual Lake Desire fishing contest!"

As the crowd went up in cheers again, great blue herons and loons looked over from the lake as if checking what the commotion was all about, while the seagulls soared knowing that an inevitable feast of baitfish was forthcoming.

The emcee continued. "We have some changes this year. Arnold Ravenwood has stepped down from judging so we all know it's going to be a fair contest this year!"

Everyone who knew Arnold, and even some of the tourists who didn't, laughed. Arnold shrugged his shoulders and smiled widely as he felt the pats on his back from those around him.

"But seriously, we do have a change in the rules from last year," the emcee continued. "The contest will end promptly at six o'clock this evening. No fish will be accepted after that time. The contest is open to all species of fish, and the prizes are staggered so that everyone walks away a winner. The first prize is five thousand dollars. The twenty-fifth prize is a five hundred dollar shopping spree at any Gander Mountain store, and the fiftieth prize is one thousand dollars in cold hard cash. And for the grand prize, the fishing team that brings in the biggest fish will go home with this grand prize trophy, and a fully decked-out Bass boat donated by Frankie's Marine!"

The emcee held up a huge, three-foot high trophy with gold-plated brass pillars sandwiched between marble slabs, crowned with a brass replica of a bass splashing out of the water. The crowd broke into cheers again, while the contestants each envisioned how that trophy would look on their fireplace mantels.

"Other prizes will be awarded depending on where you place. Before you head out, if you haven't already, check in with Miss Shari Lynn up here to get your official contest hats, and as always our judges' decisions are final, so let's get out there and fish! Good luck everyone!"

The very boisterous crowd followed the contestants to the shore to wave off the boats that within minutes were rushing their favorite spots on the lake, well aware that it might be the favorite of another contestant as well.

But no one knew about Martin's spot. On the map, it only showed up as a little inlet off the main lake that didn't look at all appetizing to anyone intending to bring home any fish, let alone the trophy. But Martin knew from many experiences that just the opposite was true. Knowing, too, that lots of people would be curious as to where they were heading, Martin took his time crossing the lake, pausing a few times as though they'd arrived at their destination, and then quietly moving on a bit further. It wasn't long, though, before getting at their own fishing was more important to the other contestants than wondering where Martin and Arnold were heading, and Martin felt free to glide the boat into the inlet. He killed the motor within casting distance to the shoreline, Arnold threw out the anchor, and that was where they began.

Two hours later, they only had one small two-pound bass between the two of them.

Something was very wrong.

"I don't understand it. This place was hopping with fish yesterday," Martin said with crippling frustration as he cast his spinning jig tipped with a pork frawg into a float of lily pads again.

"Something's gotta be turning them off," Arnold said not with as much frustration as Martin, but more disappointment.

Martin looked up to the sky as he cranked in his line. Conditions were perfect for fishing: mostly overcast without too much hot, bright sun. "I don't know what's wrong. It's the same conditions as yesterday."

"Well, maybe it's time for my secret weapon," Arnold declared as he put down his rod and picked up his tackle box, "You know, son, every family has its traditions. Ours is fishing. It's a good tradition. Separates the men from the boys," he said as he pulled out an old cardboard lure box from the bottom of his tackle box.

Martin, knowing his father all too well, rolled his eyes. "Oh, good God, here we go."

"No, no. Don't judge me yet. I've been working on a prototype of a new lure for the shop. Hey, all the pros have their own line of gear, why can't Arnold Ravenwood?" he smiled as he held up the box.

"Because you don't have your own fishing show and a pile of money from sponsors," Martin said without looking at him.

"I won't need it when the world gets a load of this," Arnold said, holding up a huge lure that looked like it would choke a whale. It resembled a bucktail lure, but more colorful and massive with a crankbait-style head, willow-leaf spinning blades wrapped around a single wire that also held the soft plastic salamander-like body. The tail was an ensemble of red, yellow, orange, and green feathers tied around a number 4/0 treble hook. "Behold! I call it the Muddpuppy!" Arnold announced with a heavy dose of pride as he held it up for his son to marvel at and admire.

Martin couldn't help laughing. It looked like it was the type of lure that attracted the fishermen, not the fish. Arnold was a little deflated, but the test was soon to come, and then his son would finally come to recognize that his old man wasn't as crazy as he thought.

"It looks like a dead chicken," Martin said through his laughter.

"Ha ha. Very funny. Pick up that baitcaster. I would be honored if my son would be the first to field test it on this historic occasion."

Martin still chuckled as he set down his spinning rod, and picked up the baitcaster. He took the lure, held it up, and then looked at his father with a face that asked, *Are you serious?*

"Just humor me and throw it out there a few times," Arnold said, responding to his son's nonverbal sarcasm.

Martin clipped the Muddpuppy to the thirty pound steel leader on the twenty pound test line of the baitcaster. He cast it, and it flew almost to the shore alongside a downed tree.

"There we go. Let's see if she brings home the trophy," Arnold said, genuinely interested in how his experiment was going to work, but hoping even more to impress his fishing genius of a son.

Martin worked the lure like a spinning jig with a slow, steady retrieve. "Well, it certainly feels good. Not a lot of drag. It certainly is flashy," he said as he retrieved it to the boat, then cast it back out to the same spot, and began to work it again along the length of the downed tree. "Not bad," he said, actually a little impressed.

"But I don't think there's a fish in his right mind that would—"

The line went suddenly taut, and Martin leaned back hard into it as he set the hook.

Arnold jumped out of his seat. "Fish?"

Martin waited in his leaned back position for something to happen.

There was nothing.

He whipped the rod back a few times.

Still nothing.

"Naw, snag," he lamented. "It sure feels good to have something on the end of the line after today. Is this the only one you made?"

Arnold drooped in regret—not that the lure might be lost, but that there wasn't a fish on the other end of the line. "Yeah, but it's easy to make more if you lose it," he said trying to reassure both himself and his son.

Martin continued to try to whip it free, but with no luck. "Shit. It's snagged on that tree."

Arnold crunched his face in disappointment, and began to hand crank the anchor up. "The first field test catches a tree. That's gonna sell a million of 'em," he moaned sarcastically, then suddenly stopped.

Something was wrong.

His left arm began to tingle. He grabbed it and gave it a squeeze. His face cramped as a jagged pain erupted in his chest. His face surged red.

Martin looked over at his father, wondering why he stopped cranking the anchor. Alarm instantly overcame him. "Dad? Dad what's wrong?"

Arnold swallowed hard. "Nothing. I'm fine. Just a little light headed. Arm's tingling a little bit. It's been happening lately, but I'm fine. Don't worry."

Although Martin wanted to be relieved, he was still suspicious that his father was just telling him that to calm him down. "You sure?" he cautiously asked.

"Yeah. It comes and goes," he said, actually looking a little better as his face returned to its normal composure. He continued to crank the anchor.

"Why don't I do that, Dad?"

"Martin, honestly, I'm fine. I think I just got up too fast or something. I'm really okay, now."

Martin slowly nodded, then began to whip the rod again. "Maybe I can just rip it out."

Without warning, the drag began to scream.

It wasn't a snag.

It was a fish.

And a *big* fish at that.

The drag didn't stop as more and more line was taken out. "Holy shit! This *is* a fish!" Martin screamed.

Arnold flipped the seaweed mass that had the anchor in it into the boat. "It's a fish!" he screamed, hustling to Martin's side.

"It's a monster! Jesus, she ain't stopping!" Martin screamed. Neither of them had ever seen a fish run like this.

"Work 'im, work 'im! That's my lure!" Arnold sang and threw his arms up in the air.

The drag screamed louder as yard after yard of line was stripped from the reel. Martin never let the pressure off. He knew exactly how to play this beast. He'd been practicing for this moment almost all his life. "I can't move this son-of-a-bitch! It's gotta be a muskie!"

"That's not a muskie. That's a good, Goddamn grandpa muskie! All hail the Muddpuppy!" Arnold shouted with the intent for every other fisherman on the lake to hear.

As the drag continued to scream, Arnold and Martin screamed with it. Then, to both their surprise and elation, the boat began to move. This fish was actually towing the boat, and the father-son team began to laugh with both excitement and a tinge of nervousness.

"This big bastard wants to take us for a ride!" Martin screamed, genuinely surprised.

"Let 'im pull us across the Goddamn lake! We got all day out here! You hear that, fish? We got all damn day!" Arnold laughed like Dr. Frankenstein when the monster first twitched its fingers. It was the purest, most joyous bout of laughter that they had enjoyed in far too long.

୭ଓ

BEAR PULLED EMILY UP IN FRONT OF THE LUNKER LODGE. He had, in fact, chickened out of going to the café, but not because he still wanted to avoid Cherie. He did want to talk to her and iron things out, but not just then. Not after the morning he knew she had to be having. Coffee and a chat with Barney seemed like a much more palatable alternative right now, and he shuffled his tired self into the near-empty bar.

A few of the booths were filled with the seniors of Desire who diligently pulled pull-tabs, waiting for that lucky one that would justify blowing their Social Security checks on their frivolous investment. The mountains of non-winning tabs that piled up on their tables were evidence that it rarely ever came for any of them, but it didn't seem to matter. What good was a grand and a half a month if it just sat on the kitchen table while they spent the day on the porch watching the world go by? Besides, there were just too many damn kids down at the park for the contest festivities for them to entertain the thought of going down there.

Bear bellied up to the bar, dropped himself on the stool, and placed his cold journal on the bar in front of him. Maybe he would write a few words if anything worth writing came to mind, but he doubted it.

Barney, a good-looking guy for almost seventy with a gut held in place by a dirty white apron tied around his waist, lit up when he saw Bear, despite the fact that Bear looked too distressed with his face drooped in his hands.

"Bear. You're up and out early. Beer?"

Bear finished rubbing his eyes. He looked too tired, too spent. "Morning, Barney. No. Coffee, please. Lotsa cream. Lotsa sugar."

"I would have thought if you wanted coffee, you'd go to the café." Barney said as he planted a cup in front of him as well as a handful of creamers and the sugar caddie.

"Cherie and I aren't on speaking terms right now," Bear responded, an edge of lament in his voice.

Barney nodded as he poured the coffee. "You're not going down to the tournament?"

"I might later," he said unenthusiastically as he emptied two creamers and six packets of sugar into his cup, then stirred it to a caramel brown.

Barney poured himself a cup and leaned against the bar. He looked down at Bear's journal. "You wanna share what you're always scribbling in there?"

Bear picked it up, but didn't open it. He didn't want to show Barney that there were more blank pages than not. Good writers don't have empty journals, just the ones who can't find their niche do. "Nothin' huge. Thoughts, ideas, observations, poetry," he said, hoping Barney wouldn't ask him for a reading.

"Poetry? You in love?" Barney asked with a jest.

Bear laughed at that irony.

Barney raised his coffee cup as if to make a toast. "To love. The miracle of civilization—Stendhal."

Bear held for a moment, thinking. He then lifted his mug, and tinked it against Barney's. "Love is only an irresistible desire to be irresistibly desired—Robert Frost," he rejoined with a grin.

Surprised by this, Barney raised his eyebrows as they drank to their toasts. "I am impressed. I never knew you possessed a command for literature."

"Every man has a side he hides, Barney, something that's his alone. A man with no secrets is just a chimpanzee," he philosophized, relishing that truth.

"True enough," Barney said simply, amazed that he had never

seen this side of Bear before. He liked it a lot. There was the flavor of an old friend in the way he conversed. Barney never got to know Bear as much as he would have liked, and therefore, he assumed that Bear was just another rowdy biker that broke his beer mugs and squealed doughnut loops in the parking lot on his bike. But that was evidently just the gang he hung out with. Barney had a hunch that there was another level of depth to Bear, and he was glad to see it finally come out.

Bear took another sip of his coffee, and then picked up his journal again. "You know, I don't think I would have ever written another word if it wasn't for Elle. She always told me something that I'll never forget—'we are all capable of greatness.' That inspired me like nothing I've ever heard before. It motivated me, and got me to start questioning who I thought I was. Emerson once wrote 'make the most of yourself, for that is all there is to you.' I guess I still haven't figured out how to do that."

"It means you have to find out who you are first, and that ain't easy. Because once you find that person you are, you gotta like that person or, better yet, love that person. People are too afraid to dig in themselves because they fear what they might find. That's why the world is full of crazies."

Bear let it all soak in. Talking to Barney was almost like talking to Elle. They shared a parallel outlook on life. But Bear didn't feel much like being philosophical that morning. He did feel the need for a friend, though—a friend like Elle had been. He trusted that Barney wouldn't judge him like it seemed everyone else did. He looked up at him, and quietly let him in on a secret that no one, except Elle, knew about him. "Did you know I was a literature major in college?"

They actually shared a bout of laughter that was unexpected to Bear, but refreshing.

"What was your minor?" Barney asked.

Bear laughed again, but this time only to himself, then took a moment in reflection. "Grand theft," he said, looking up at Barney, waiting to be judged. "Did three years."

But the judgment never came. It wasn't even thought of. "Grand theft? I never knew any of this about you. What did you steal?"

Bear was a little embarrassed to tell him, but the comfort he felt with Barney made it easier to be forthcoming. "Other people's credit cards. I put myself through school with 'em. I got all the way through before I was caught. The Feds actually came to my graduation and hauled me away in my cap and gown."

Still, the judgment never came, but Barney laughed a little at the thought of that. "That must have been a sight."

"Oh, yeah," he took another sip of his coffee. "Earl, he took the easy way out, the expected way out. You know, we have different dads, and his dad's cousin taught him the trade. Me, too, I guess, but Earl's been poking ink ever since he dropped out of high school. I really had no clue what to do when I got out of the joint, and the open road, place to place lifestyle . . ." He paused thinking about the reality of running again. "I guess I've just been there, done that for way too long. I really got tired of running all the time. Then when I was in the joint, coming back here and working in the shop with Earl was all I really thought about. It was home, you know?"

"You wrote a lot in the joint?" Barney inquired.

"Sometimes almost all night long. It kept me alive some days. Hell, some days? It kept me alive every day."

"You ever get anything published?"

"Nothing you would have heard of," he said almost too fast, wanting to avoid the subject.

Barney picked up on this and just nodded. "I thought credit card fraud was only a misdemeanor," he said, freshening up both of their coffees to which Bear added more cream and sugar to his.

"Under five hundred it is. Over twenty grand is five years, three on good behavior."

Barney almost choked. "How the hell did you have access to twenty thousand dollars worth of credit cards?"

Bear smiled. Now it felt like he was bragging, but he didn't dislike it. "I used to date this chick that worked in a flower shop.

When her boss would run the credit card report at the end of the day, she'd press the duplicate button for me."

Barney looked up at Sheriff Walker walking in the door. Bear didn't notice.

"I had an endless supply of them. I was cool about it, though. I took the full rap. They never touched her," he continued.

Dwayne walked up to the bar next to Bear. He leaned on his elbow, which had become sort of his trademarked stance to those who paid attention to that sort of thing.

"Boys. How we doin'?" he said, not really inquiring or caring if he cut into their conversation. He helped himself to a handful of peanuts sitting in a bowl on the bar.

"Not bad," Bear simply said.

"Somethin' for you, Dwayne?" Barney asked.

"Naw, Barney, I'm set. Thanks," he said through a mouth full of what was now peanut butter.

He turned and looked directly at Bear. "I was hopin' you'd be up here 'cause I didn't want to go to Cherie with this," he said as he grabbed another handful.

"What's up?" Bear asked.

He threw the entire handful in his mouth at once. "Have you seen what Annie and the twins are up to?"

Bear shook his head. "Surfing a train somewhere?"

Barney and Dwayne smiled a laugh at this because it wasn't so farfetched to imagine them doing something like that. "No. That'd be easy. Eddie told me it looks like they're building somethin' strange out by the old Springborg farm. Frankly I've been too busy to go check it out myself. You guys have any clue what they're up to?"

"I haven't heard a thing," Bear said, wondering himself what they were up to.

"Me neither. What are they building?" Barney asked.

"Don't know yet," Dwayne said as he shoved another handful in his gaping maw. "But I do know they don't own the land they're building on, and I know that they don't have a building permit, which I really don't give a shit about, but what concerns me is I know they don't have any money to pay for all the equipment they got out there."

Bear instantly looked concerned. If the twins and Annie were doing something wrong, he would be the only person in their world willing to do anything about it to save them. But he didn't have much time to dwell on it, as Charlie burst in the door, completely out of breath. He almost crashed into the bar in the little space there was between the sheriff and Bear.

"Sheriff! I've been looking all over for you. I just came from the tournament, and Marty's fighting something huge. It's gotta be the biggest fish Lake Desire's ever seen! They yelled at me to find you. They're gonna need a bigger boat!"

Dwayne snapped into action mode. "Let's go, we'll get out on my boat!"

They rushed out of the bar, but not before the sheriff turned and grabbed a last handful of peanuts, holding them up to Barney as a gesture of thanks. Barney looked down at the bowl. It was full before Dwayne arrived; now only a few broken hard skins remained. Barney shook his head and mumbled, "He does that every time he comes in here."

◐◑

THE CROWD HAD TURNED INTO A CELEBRATING MOB OF spectators as word spread through town of what was possibly the fishing struggle of the century. Gathered along the lakeshore, the crowd alternated between hushed anticipation and encouraging cheers as they stood intently following Martin's every move. The fish had led the boat into deep water about fifty yards out from the shore, but still close enough for the crowd to cheer every time they heard the drag scream. This would be talked about for years to come; it was history in the making—and the most exciting thing that had happened not only in the past twenty five years of the fishing contest, but quite possibly in the history of the town.

A few industrious people, hearing that a news crew from Duluth was on its way, had created a homemade banner out of a white bed sheet and two broom sticks. They haphazardly painted PLAY HIM MARTIN! in blue paint across it. The cheerleaders that Eddie was flirting with lined the shore with their pompoms, giving Martin a rousing fishing cheer, and six of the football players lined the dock, shirtless, with letters written across their bodies to spell out F-I-G-H-T-! "Fight! Fight! Fight!" they cheered, doing a dance that might turn on an affectionate gorilla. They threw up their arms, and circled them in the air, then all once, did an about-face. Written on their backs was M-A-R-T-I-N. "Martin! Martin! Martin!" they continued to cheer, this time waving their butts back and forth for the benefit of the cheerleaders, then did another about-face, and began again.

A few boats circled the area around Martin and Arnold's boat, some of them videotaping the non-stop action. With all the activity, Arnold wouldn't have been surprised if a news helicopter descended on them. He was getting a little upset that the crowd and commotion were making it difficult for them to work the fish. Some of the spectator's boats were getting a little too close, and several times Arnold had to tell them to back off for fear they could accidentally get tangled in the line.

But somehow, the fish never really left the vicinity of the boat, almost as if it was playing with them. It hadn't shown itself yet, so nobody knew how big that behemoth was, or even what it was for that matter. But Martin knew. Even a big northern pike wouldn't have put up a fight like this. There were only two kinds of fish in this lake that could do what this fish was doing, and that was either a sturgeon or a giant muskie. But sturgeons were bottom feeders, and although it wasn't impossible that one might take a lure like the Muddpuppy, it was highly improbable.

Both Martin and Arnold's hearts were beating like voodoo drums. They had never experienced this level of excitement before, and it was actually becoming euphoric. Half of Martin wanted the fight to be over now so that he could claim his prize, the other half wanted the fight to go on for hours. All he could do was watch the direction the line was going in the water to anticipate the fish's next move. The fish tried to stay one step ahead of Martin. It wasn't so much that the fish knew that it's best move would be to go under the boat—fish don't think that way—but this one apparently did as it charged directly towards the boat.

"Oh shit! He's going under the boat!" Martin cried, reeling in the slack as fast as he could as he leaned back on the rod. The fish charged the boat too fast, and he couldn't get his rod down fast enough to keep the line from rubbing against the rivets on the side of the boat.

"Don't let 'im do it, he'll snap the line!" Arnold shouted, but it wasn't enough. The fish passed right under the boat faster than Martin could reel, and the line went taut against the edge of the boat, singing like a guitar string higher in pitch as more tension was put on it. "Get your rod down! Get your rod down!" Arnold shouted again.

"Dad, I know how to fish!" Martin snapped at him. But Arnold didn't take offense, knowing it was the pressure of the fight that made Martin snap at him.

The sheriff's cruiser burst onto the scene at full power, masterfully maneuvering through the other boats in its way. From the boat's console flashed red orbs of dizzying, spinning light, but Dwayne knew better than to turn on the siren. The crowd cheered as Charlie waved a huge landing net in the air while the cruiser sped past the shoreline.

Arnold looked up to the shore for the first time and dropped his jaw at the mass of people cheering on the shoreline. "Holy shit. Looks like Charlie told the whole world about this. We are gonna win this contest!" he laughed out loud.

Martin looked up and smiled. It wasn't so much the winning of the tournament, or his soon-to-be local hero status that thrilled him. He had a muskie on the line, and that meant that soon, he'd have a Muskie on his wall and finally feel complete as a fisherman.

The sheriff's cruiser pulled up alongside Martin and Arnold's little boat.

"Hey guys, I brought the sheriff!" Charlie exclaimed, stating the obvious as he leaned over and grabbed Arnold and Martin's boat.

"Martin, get on my boat. You can fight 'im easier," Dwayne said as he killed the engine.

Martin grabbed the rod just above the reel so that if the fish made a run, it wouldn't pull the rod out of his hands. He propped his foot on the rim of the cruiser, and effortlessly leaped on board.

"What is it?" Dwayne enthusiastically asked.

"It's gotta be a muskie," Martin replied, trying to shake the circulation back into his hands.

"You haven't seen it yet?" Dwayne asked, astounded.

Martin just shook his head.

Arnold moved to the stern of his boat, unable to resist the opportunity lined up along the shoreline. "Keep fighting him, Son. I'll be right back," he shouted, then cranked the outboard to life, and took off toward the shore where he performed a fly-by past the crowd.

"He's using the Muddpuppy! The Muddpuppy!" he laughed ecstatically. "That's my son out there! That's my son, Martin! Whooo-hoo!" he roared over the cheering crowd.

The news crew from Duluth scrambled to get a feed. They were going live, and the reporter, a young, good-looking woman, was busy getting pampered by her hair and make-up people. "Are we ready to go?" She demanded to her crew.

"Fifteen seconds," the cameraman replied.

The reporter stood in place with one hand around her notebook, the other around her microphone. She smacked her lips and brushed the bangs from her face with the top of her microphone. The crowd of gawkers was already practicing their goofy faces and hand gestures behind her.

Standing next to them, looking out over the lake was the woman in the powder blue dress. She wouldn't have missed this for the world, not only because of the all the action, but because she felt more comfortable in crowds. She blended in and had a smile for everyone. Still, few people acknowledged her presence, and she stood, watching the action on the lake with a certain degree of smugness, as if she knew that it didn't matter if they landed the fish and won the contest or not. It was only the grandeur of a father and son, spending a beautiful and exciting time together that really mattered. Everything else was simply trivial, and if they couldn't understand that, it might have to be taught to them.

"And here we go!" the cameraman said and began the countdown. "In five, four, three—" two and one were signaled with his middle and then index finger pointing her cue.

"Unless they closely follow the annual fishing events of northern Minnesota, most people have probably never heard of Lake Desire. Today, that's almost certainly going to change. Here, at the twenty-fifth annual Lake Desire fishing contest, Martin Ravenwood, and his father, Arnold, are quite literally fighting to make Lake Desire famous as they struggle to land what reportedly might challenge the state record muskie that was caught on Lake Winnibigoshish way back in 1957!"

The camera zoomed past the reporter and out onto the lake. Arnold had tied Martin's boat to the cruiser and had jumped on board. The reporter continued. "Martin has been fighting the fish for almost two hours on a lure called the Muddpuppy that Arnold himself had crafted in his bait shop here in the town of Desire. Martin is not new to setting records, as among others, tomorrow he will tie the Minnesota record for the most number of consecutive days fishing. That record stands at a whopping 978 days. All of this is sure to put the small town of Desire on the map, and we'll stay with the action here at Lake Desire throughout the day. Back to you, Rick and Jane, in the studio."

Martin's hands were beginning to tingle, threatening to go completely numb, and his arms shook every once in a while as the stress of encroaching fatigue began to set in. But he knew he'd never again have the chance to battle a muskie of this size, especially during a fishing contest, so there was no way he was letting it get the better of him. Besides, he knew that if he was getting tired, the fish must be next to exhausted, but it was still fighting the good fight.

Dwayne stood with the net at the ready next to Martin. Arnold and Charlie stood ready for action just behind them. The line gave a little slack, which Martin reeled onto the spool. The fish was making its final moves. "Alright. She's coming up. You ready with that net, Uncle Dwayne?" Martin demanded.

"Right here," Dwayne answered reassuringly, ready to scoop the monster in the boat.

A tingle of adrenaline and actually a little fear rushed through the four men as the fish swam by directly from under the boat out into the lake. It was the first time any of them got a good look at it, and their jaws dropped when they saw it was bigger and more massive than any one of them had assumed. It seemed there was no end to it as it emerged from under the boat. Its dull gray and silvery body moved slowly and methodically, not like a fish that thought it was in trouble.

"Holy shit. Look at the size of that monster!" Charlie said, actually a little afraid.

"That's a sixty incher," Martin said almost without breath.

"Sixty-five. All seventy pounds of her," Dwayne corrected, absolutely amazed.

Martin kept the pressure on the mighty muskie and led her back toward the boat. "I'm gonna bring her around," he said to his uncle. "Get the net over her head, then Dad, you grab her tail."

"She's still too green," Arnold warned.

"It's now or never," Martin demanded.

Martin pulled the rod back again, continuing to work the heavy fish back toward them. Martin let the beauty of his catch seep into him, and reveled in amazement at its massive size as its bright red tail flopped in and out of the water. That was when he noticed something that sent pricklers over his skin. It was only hooked by the tiniest piece of skin; one good shake of her head was all it would take to end the battle. Martin's fatigue wasn't yet getting the better of him, but it was draining fast and, green or not, it was time to try and land his prize before that hook ripped out.

As the behemoth was led closer, Dwayne chucked the net in the water just before it, and to everyone's elation, Martin led the fish directly into it. But true to their concern, it didn't fit. In fact, the fish only fit in to just behind its pectoral fins. Arnold dove for its tail, balancing his gut on the rim of the cruiser.

The crowd on the shore erupted in cheers, while many on the surrounding boats picked up their video cameras and resumed shooting the action. The news crew stood on the edge of the dock, filming as well.

The mighty fish struggled and splashed, drenching everyone but Charlie, who stood back ready for someone to yell an order at him. He still didn't understand how a homemade lure that wasn't even green could catch such a big fish. In fact, he even had trouble fathoming that fish even got that big, let alone that one like this even lived in their lake. But there she was, and as the three of them tried to lift her out of the water, panic engrossed them all as it was instantly apparent that the fish was simply too big to lift, especially without a landing cradle. That and their hands were becoming numb from the cold water and fish slime, making it even more difficult to grab a hold of her. The mighty fish thrashed violently, and in the process was tearing a hole in the nylon mesh of the net.

The muskie shook its way out of Arnold's hands, but he quickly grabbed the tail again. Martin continued to put pressure on it with the rod, wishing he had eight hands as he stood and helplessly watched his father and uncle struggle. The fish had worked most of its head through the gaping hole in the net that grew bigger every time she struggled. Suddenly, in a split second, the hook that had only been held on by a piece of skin ripped out, almost hitting and hooking Dwayne in the face as it snapped loose with sling-shot force. It was the kind of terrifying thing that happened so fast you wished that you could just pause time to fix the problem, but that's not the kind of magic that would happen there today. This was man against beast in its most raw form, and as always, nature would win no matter how many rounds it took.

The fish was free from Martin's capture, but still remained tangled in the net.

There was one chance left to win this fight.

Martin threw down his rod, and took a flying leap at the fish, wrapping his arms around her while Dwayne tried with everything he had to lift up the fish with the net. He knew that the net rim supported only a third of the fish, and if he lifted it any further, the fish would fall out backward into the water. With the fish thrashing so violently, that might happen anyway.

Martin couldn't get a grip on her, but was determined to hang on.

"Damnit! Get 'er up. We're gonna lose her!" he screamed at his father and uncle who gritted their teeth trying to get a grip on it. This wouldn't be such a problem if the net wasn't impairing Martin's access to the gill plates, but there was no way he could slip his fingers under and lift.

And then what he had already known all along sank into him. They weren't going to win this fight. He also knew that the more they struggled with it, the more protective slime they were rubbing off, and if the fish did get away, its chances of survival would be in jeopardy because of it, let alone that a struggle like this would exhaust the fish to the point where it might not easily recover.

With that thought, knowing that his damaged pride was in no way equal to loss of his worthy adversary's life, Martin slowly let go, and stood up. He looked at his father, who looked back at him in surprise.

This wasn't about that fish.

This wasn't even about them winning the contest.

This was about Martin and his father spending a day of fishing together, and with that, further strengthening the bond that could only be held as a family.

This was about healing together.

Martin smiled as he recognized the magic of that day.

"Let her go guys. We won," he said softly, offering that smile to his father.

Arnold smiled back at his son. It was the kind of smile that only a father, overflowing with pride, can give, and he simply let the fish slide from his hands. He put his arm around his son, and then nodded to Dwayne, who, although he didn't fully understand, slid the broken net from around the fish's head, gabbed the tail, and began to revive it as he moved the fish back and forth, rushing water over the gills until she slowly swam to freedom.

From the stage, people, including the emcee gathered around the news crew's video monitor for a better look at the action than they could get from the shore. The woman in the powder blue dress stood behind them watching. A proud smile crept across her face. The emcee looked up out over the lake and smiled. "Now *that* is a fisherman," he said with a heavy dose of respect.

The four men stood there as the boats bobbed in the water, each exhausted, each feeling a sense of melancholy pride that he had never felt before.

"Well, I guess we'll never know if she was the record," Martin said.

Arnold gave him a squeeze. "We don't have to, Son. We don't have to."

Chapter Thirteen

W ITH THE CONTEST ABDUCTING EVERYONE FROM town, and with it being her special day—if she would allow herself to call it that—Stella sat in her lonely, empty store, once again reading through the pages of *Love, Elusive,* and contemplating closing up early again.

The thought of having to spend another birthday alone left her as deflated and lonely as if she was the only person on earth. And her staring down at the phone that looked back at her with a glare of disappointment didn't do anything to help her situation. She still didn't have the courage to pick it up, and it made her scorn herself a little more.

Even the book, the one thing left in her life that made her feel she was worth something, couldn't keep her attention. She read the words without actually absorbing them. She hadn't made up her mind if she would even acknowledge that it was her birthday, let alone even go so far as to celebrate it, or just treat it like it was any other day and go to bed early.

Then, as if something drew her attention to it, she looked

down at the box of Elle's books that Arnold had brought her, and there, on the top of the heap, shining like a biblical beacon, was a book titled *Photography: From Beginners to Pros.*

She looked at it, contemplating her newborn idea. It was a long shot, but it was well worth the try, considering the alternative. She picked up the book and flipped through it with her thumb. A touch of vitality reinvigorated her as she looked up at the birthday cake sticker on her calendar. She hurriedly stuffed the book and *Love, Elusive* into her bag, and almost ran to the door. She flipped the OPEN sign to CLOSED and locked the door behind her as she galloped down the vacant sidewalk.

♋

ERNIE SAT IN HIS DUCT-TAPED RECLINER IN FRONT OF THE television on the folding table in front of him. He was busier this morning than he had been in a long time—since this time last year to be exact, and nobody complained that they had to pump their own gas as Ernie struggled as fast as he could to get to everyone in time. The reward for his hard labors was a thick wad of bills stuffed in his front pocket.

The television was tuned to the news station from Duluth, even though the reception was minimal at best. Ernie wanted to see if there would be any further news on Martin's fish and the contest. But there wasn't. The rest of the news was pretty boring, and was cutting into his *The Twilight Zone* time. He had plans to watch the entire fifth season today after the rush, and so far had only gotten to two episodes, but they were two of his favorites, "Number Twelve Looks Just Like You" and "A Kind of Stopwatch," which was his all-time favorite episode.

He was just about to begin another, this time selecting "In Praise of Pip" when his eye caught Stella walking around the corner toward him. He was a little shocked at first, because Stella, not owning a car, hardly ever came down there. He nervously smiled at her, and combed back his hair with the palm of his hand.

"Good morning, Stella," he said.

She smiled. "It's a little past morning, Ernie."

"I know. Just makin' conversation. Did you see Martin Ravenwood on the TV?"

"No, I didn't. What happened?"

"Looks like he caught a big fish in the tournament."

"Oh," she said, and then paused for an anxious moment before reaching into her bag and pulling out the photography book. "Well, Arnold dropped off a box of Elle's books, and I thought you might like this one, seein' as how you're into photography."

She handed it to him, and he slowly reached for it, almost as if there was something about the book that made him instantly afraid of it.

"A book, huh?" he said as he filed through the pages. "Lotsa pictures, that's good. Well, thank you, Stella, that's real nice of you."

"Yeah. I'm not saying you're not a good photographer or anything. But maybe you can learn something you didn't know before."

Ernie shrugged his shoulders and continued to flip. There was an immediate silence that only Stella took as uncomfortable. She wanted to ask him something, but knew she wouldn't be able to handle it if his answer was negative.

She squeezed the strap of her shoulder bag, unaware that she was twisting it, and then swallowed hard. "Listen, ah, I'm cooking a nice dinner tonight, too much for me alone to eat. Did you wanna come over for dinner tonight? It's my bir—" she stopped, suddenly choosing not to tell him. Sympathy was not what she needed, nor was it what she was after. "Well, I'd just like you to come, if you want. You can read some of the book, and tell me all about it tonight."

Ernie entertained the thought of it. A little dinner company might be nice for a change, and it was a sure bet she'd make something other than an inedible dinner that came from a microwave.

"What time you thinking?"

She shrugged her shoulders. She didn't expect him to agree, and therefore hadn't really thought about a time. "Seven?" she said.

There was something almost undetectable in the way he hesitated with his answer. Something was making Ernie uncomfortable, and she dismissed it as just the general nervousness of being asked on a date—if this could even be classified as a date. "And you want me to read the book before that?" he asked apprehensively.

She laughed a little at the innocence of his question. "Not the whole thing, but it'll give us something to talk about."

"Hey, you know, I don't have a picture of you on my wall of fame," he said, dancing around the subject of dinner and the book. "Can I take your picture for it?"

Stella was suddenly overcome with embarrassment. "Um, okay, sure. Where do you want me to stand?"

He pushed himself out of his chair, walked in front of her, and held his camera up, framing her in the viewfinder. "Right where you are. Smile."

To her surprise, a smile leaked through her perpetual shyness as Ernie snapped the picture. The camera looked like it was sticking its tongue out at her as it delivered the photo. Ernie, without saying a word or even looking at her, took out the photo, and shook it back and forth. Stella waited for him to say something, anything. But he just stood there, staring at her image coming into development as if she had already left.

"Okay, well, I'll see you about seven then?" Stella said, wondering if she was even going to get a response.

Ernie snapped out of his superficial trance. "Okee. That sounds good."

She smiled and began to walk away, then turned as if she felt there really was no closure to their conversation. "Come hungry," she sang.

"I will," he said, smiling at her.

Stella, still smiling as she walked, began wondering what she should make for dinner. She was also thinking about her and Ernie. It really made sense that they would wind up together. Both of them were single, alone, and neither of them had one iota of experience with dating. Maybe something magical would bloom out of this. Maybe she didn't need to call that publisher at all. Maybe she would never have to waste another birthday wish again. What was important over all of that was that she had a date for her birthday, regardless if he didn't even know it was her birthday, and she smiled as that made her as happy as she needed to be. It had been too long a while since she had known hope.

But Ernie, on the other hand, watched her leave with a heavy heart as concern materialized on his face. He looked down at her picture and ran his finger along her pretty, smiling face as it finished coming into full development. Setting the picture on the armrest of his recliner, he picked up the photography book that seemed to weigh as much as a sack of bricks. Slowly, he opened it to the first page, and began to follow the words with his finger.

"C-c-cam-camer-ras h-h-have be-bec-become in-incre-a-s-" The words might have well been written in Arabic.

Ernie's sigh was laced with a heavy dosage of frustration. He looked in the direction that Stella had walked away and felt the darkening approach of overwhelming storm clouds of sadness and aggravation. Worst of all, fueling the storm was embarrassment, and that was just something he would not allow himself to feel. He looked back at the book, and then abruptly pushed it off his lap where it hit the ground. The alarm hose sounded as a car pulled up to the pumps. It was just the diversion from getting in touch with himself that he needed.

⊙⊙

THE TATTOO SHOP WAS DARK, EVEN THOUGH IT WAS STILL open for business. Earl just couldn't take a midday nap with the lights on, though considering how soundly he slept in the dentist chair, anyone could just walk in and help themselves to anything they'd like, and he'd never know the difference. When Cherie walked in, he grumbled and snored, and she rolled her eyes at the pathetic sight.

"Earl," she said loudly, but not loud enough to wake him.

Her patience had worn out as soon as she came in and saw him sleeping, and she wasn't about wake him with any kind of tenderness. She cocked her hand back, and slapped him on his forehead hard enough to echo. "Earl! Wake up!" she screamed.

He jerked himself awake and instantly tried to get his bearings, then cowered back in his seat, startled to see Cherie standing over him, ready to hit him again.

"What?" he said, overly annoyed.

"Where's Bear?" she demanded.

He sat up in the chair. "You woke me up to ask me that?"

"Where is he?" she demanded more fiercely.

"I don't know, it's not my turn to watch 'im." he said through hands busy rubbing his sleep-drained face and the pulsating handprint on his forehead.

Cherie walked around to the counter, looked at his computer, shuffled a stack of papers, and flipped through an address book looking for another girl's phone number, address, anything. There had to be a reason he was avoiding her, and Cherie would never have imagined that the reason would be staring at her in a mirror.

"Has he said anything about me lately?" she coyly asked.

"Like what?" he said, still annoyed.

She shrugged her shoulders. "I don't know. Stuff?"

He shook his head, and snorted at her. "I don't know. You want me to pass him a note in math class and ask 'im what he thinks of you?"

Cherie's shoulders drooped. She really was getting sick of the way he treated her, even though she'd never given him a reason to treat her any better. "Why do you have to be so mean to me all the time?" she asked, almost pouting.

He knew exactly why he was so mean to her. He always had to take second best, or take nothing at all when Bear was around. It was time he found a way out from under that particular shadow, even if he had no clue exactly how to do it. He stared at her for a moment, trying to find some words, any words to keep him from looking like more of an idiot. "I don't know. I'm sorry. I just, ah—when you were young, did boys ever throw rocks at you for no reason?"

Cherie had no clue what he was getting at. "I guess so," she said suspiciously.

"Do you know why?" he said with shy eyes.

"They were just being mean," she said with a shrug of her shoulders.

"No, they weren't," he said softly.

"I wish Bear would throw rocks at me. Then I'd know that he at least he still feels something for me. He doesn't love me anymore, does he?" she said, on the verge of tears, afraid of the anticipated, and known, answer.

Earl was trying to open up to her, but now that she once again brought up Bear, the feeling was lost. "Look, I'm not gonna to get into—"

"He did say something," she sharply interrupted.

Earl stood up and went to the sink not so much to wash the sleep from his face, but rather because he didn't want to face her any longer. "Cherie, look. All I know is he never talks about you when you're not around. You can take that for anything you want."

At that, Cherie began to cry. Earl could hear her whimpering behind him, and slowly, he turned to face her. Her eyes were saturated, and she turned her head to hide it, fearful that he would make fun of her even though his body language communicated something very different. "I would, though. All the time," he said tenderly, yet cautiously.

"Would what?" she snapped, completely missing his invitation to read between the lines.

"Talk about you," he said looking directly into her glowing, tear-soaked brown eyes that had become tiger striped by her running mascara.

They stared into each other, testing the waters of their newfound chemistry. Cherie, caught off guard was instantly hit by the possibility that maybe Prince Charming was not always Prince Obvious.

But Earl?

As she considered this, confusion tempered her burning reaction to simply give in to him. It had been a long time since she had felt wanted, and the feeling was as peculiar as it was intoxicating, even if it was by Earl. But she was still Bear's girl. If she did do this, she would lose him forever, and this was also Earl's concern as well. But love and acceptance from a brother was not the same as the promise of love from a girl that up until now, he could only adore in fantasy. As both continued to stare at each other, both were thinking the same question: *Was Bear's broken heart worth their desire?*

☙❧

BEAR NEVER DID GO DOWN TO THE CONTEST GROUNDS. There was something invasive to him about seeing that many people crowding his solitary place, even if it was around the bend and out of sight of his dock. So he stayed at the Lunker Lodge until just after the news stopped reporting on Martin, by which time he was sufficiently doped up on caffeine and had a chance to brush his teeth and wash his dirty face in the bathroom. Then, knowing that the sheriff was indisposed on the lake, he got on Emily, and headed down the dirt road past his dock that seemed to watch him with a degree of longing, wondering if it did something to repel its best friend.

As he leaned into the sharp curves of the dirt road, his growing curiosity made him drive a little faster and perhaps a little more recklessly. If Annie and the twins were up to something out there, he knew he'd better get to them before the Sheriff did.

When he rolled Emily to a halt into the clearing, his eyes grew wider, and his jaw involuntarily dropped at the sight. It was undeniably beyond anything he envisioned they were doing out there. And it was precisely the reaction that Annie and the twins had desired.

The structure was almost complete, just a few things here and there before they could apply the final sealant coat. Annie wouldn't allow them to call it finished until all of her designs were completed, and she was working diligently to do just that. Stee stood on a scaffold, drilling a hole to screw an eyehole loop into for a cable to thread through that Ven, standing next to him, held waiting.

All at once, they caught the sight of Bear walking toward them sporting his completely captivated face. Annie was truly happy to see him, but the twins became a little nervous, not because they feared he might tell the world their secret, but that he came before the project was complete. They were, after all, relentless perfectionists.

Bear didn't even acknowledge them. He was completely mesmerized by the huge gothic-looking structure.

"Hey, Bear," Annie said with a proud smile, as the twins climbed down from the scaffold and walked cautiously up to him.

Bear slowly turned his attention on them. "What the hell is this thing?" he said, truly shocked.

Annie set down her paintbrush and danced up to him and her boyfriends. "We don't have a name for it yet. Isn't it just the shit?" she said with an exhilarated laugh.

"What's it for?" Bear almost whispered.

The twins looked at each other. If they had to tell anyone about it, they knew that Bear would be the most likely to understand.

"It's pretty complicated actually," Ven said.

"Yeah. I'll bet that," Bear said, still totally awestruck. "What is it?"

Stee looked at his brother, then back at Bear. "When the Mayans set out to build their Pyramids, they used the stars as their compasses."

"They navigated by aligning them and had great ceremonies in worship of them," Ven added.

"So did the Egyptians, and the Greeks created constellations in honor of them."

"Now it's our turn to honor them," Annie said seriously.

"We are twins," Ven said, looking at his brother.

"We are Gemini. We are born from the stars . . ."

"And when we die . . ."

"We return to the stars," Annie added, smiling with pride at her boyfriends.

"This is the pinnacle of our existence," Stee declared.

Bear walked closer to it. Dumbfounded, he gawked up at its thirty feet of height. He walked around to get a side view perspective, and noticed the outlines of two bodies like a police chalk outline painted on the floorboards of the diamond-shaped base. His eyes slanted in confusion of it all. "What exactly does it do?" he inquired.

"We won't know until Steven's birthday," Annie said, which confused the twins as to why she called them both "Steven." But it didn't last very long.

"We were born at 2:22 in the morning on February second," Stee explained.

"And by laying in our outlines and staring up through the viewfinder . . ."

"You'll discover that each star in the constellation Gemini will align perfectly within the holes in the viewing device at exactly 2:22."

"Every February second, from now 'til the end of time," Ven added proudly.

"It is our eternal testament to Elle, and it will prove to the future that we actually did once exist."

"She was the one who perpetuated our love of astronomy," Ven said.

"See? I told you this was the shit!" Annie said with her elated laughter.

Bear stood, speechless for the moment. He walked up to it and placed his hand against it, almost as if he was making sure it was really there. "This is the greatest thing I've ever seen," Bear said with a detectable trace of apprehension in his voice.

Annie and the twins looked at each other. They knew there was something more to Bear's visit as soon as he pulled up.

"But . . ." Annie was brave enough to ask.

"The sheriff was askin' about it. You guys don't own this land. He also asked if I knew where you got the money to pay for all this?"

The twins' hearts sank deeper than Annie's. They knew that they wouldn't be able to keep this place a secret forever, but there was no way they were going to let that keep them from their own greatness. They had never in their lives let the thoughts and hindering ideas of others stop them from doing anything, and this was by far no exception. They also knew exactly who it was that told the Sheriff about this, but didn't even consider feeling any animosity toward Annie. It wasn't her fault Eddie was a first class backstabbing gossipmonger. Not to mention being an all-out asshole.

"The sheriff was asking about this?" Stee asked with a hard swallow.

"How does he know about it?" Annie asked, already knowing the answer, but just wanting to make sure.

"Eddie was out here," he responded, and then turned to face them. "I'm going to ask you guys this once. Did you guys steal the money for all this?"

The way that they all stared at him in silence was his affirmative answer. Bear shook his head, not at the deed, but at the fear of what would happen if they got caught.

"You won't tell anyone, will you?" Annie cautiously asked, using her perfected puppy dog eyes that she knew never worked on Bear anyway, but figured it was worth a try.

Bear just stared at the trio, wanting to say what they wanted him to say, but questioning the wisdom of it. This structure was just way too cool for the law to interfere with, and he knew that it would be its demise if the sheriff ever saw it without them having a legitimate paper trail of expenses to go with it. Even so, the sheriff might just have it destroyed anyway because the fact was, Annie and the twins didn't own this land. But even so, it was worth it for Bear to give it a shot.

Annie and the twins held their breath for his response.

"Guys, I have a little bit of experience in this type of thing, and I do wish somebody was there to take the rap for me," Bear began, then paused to give himself one last out before he said what he wasn't sure he should be saying. But, no. He would not be the one crushing any dreams today, or ever. "If anybody asks, you tell them I gave you the money for it. That's not saying anyone is going to believe that, even if I back it up. I just want to see this thing in action next February," he said with a genuine smile.

Annie and the twins sighed in relief, as smiles widened their lips. Annie screamed laughter and jumped into Bear with a giant hug.

"Thanks, Bear," she whispered in his ear as he wrapped his arms around her.

Annie really was one of the only good things about being Cherie's boyfriend, Bear thought, and maybe it was high time he made amends with her.

CHAPTER FOURTEEN

A S THE EVENING ONCE AGAIN PAINTED THE CIRRUS clouds with its watercolor strokes of purples, oranges, and pinks, Bear was there to witness its grandeur on his dock. The spark to write was still doused with a block of writer's ice bigger than Bear could melt. But that didn't stop him from soaking up the soul-feeding beauty of the sunset, which closed a circus of a day on Lake Desire.

After discovering that the giant muskie was what was causing all of the fish in Martin's secret spot to turn off, they returned, and enjoyed a perfect day on the lake together, bringing in three more contest-worthy bass. At the end of the contest day, Martin and Arnold had placed thirty-seventh and had won two 25th Annual Lake Desire Fishing Contest T-shirts and baseball style hats as their prizes.

But it didn't matter.

They had already won before they even headed out on that water, and even if they didn't land that big muskie and win the tournament, Martin had made the Muddpuppy famous, and Arnold looked forward to selling a million of them, which would also benefit Martin's business as well. But still, as they walked into the bait shop, Arnold detected a bit of gloom in his son.

"Hey, you did good today," Arnold said, putting his arm around his son, giving him a little squeeze.

"So did you," Martin said with a half smile.

"But you're still not happy."

"No. That's not it at all. I was the one that said let her go. But I had her in my hands, Dad—"

"Hey!" Arnold interrupted, "you put up a good fight. You got her to the side of the boat, and you got her in the net. There was no reason for us to take her out of the water and put more stress on her. You've always been an advocate for catch and release, and that's just what you did."

Martin nodded then walked up to his progress board. "Yeah, but thirty-seventh place?" He said with a little laugh at how pathetic it sounded.

"Hey. As far as I'm concerned, we won that tournament before we even entered it because we did it together. Those people out there think you're a hero just for showing them what kind of fish are still in that lake. You've given every fisherman in this county something to dream about."

Martin smiled. He knew what he did today was magical, but still, every wish that comes true still has a little *what if* fairy dust sprinkled on it. He erased the 976, and wrote in 977.

"You caught that fish, and that's the way it's gonna stand in my record book," he pointed to his progress board. "And look at that. Tomorrow morning, you'll tie the record. Morning after that, you'll beat it," he looked at his son with proud eyes and a loving smile. "I'm very proud of you, son. I'm proud that of all the sons in the world, I got you."

Martin walked up to him. "And out of all the dads in the world, I got stuck with you," he teased.

Arnold reached out and grabbed him, mussing up his hair. "Smart ass," he said laughing.

It felt good to laugh, especially together. Laughter between them, they both feared, had died with Elle, and it was refreshing to have it back. Martin looked at Arnold with an expression that could only say *I love you, Dad*, but he never said it aloud.

"I gotta go finish John's head. I told him it would be ready by tomorrow," Martin said softly, then reached and placed his hand on his father's shoulder before walking to the door of his studio.

"You do that, King Muskie. I'll make us some coffee," Arnold said, staring proudly at his son until he disappeared into his studio.

Arnold walked behind the counter, took a filter from the box of coffee filters, and placed it in the coffee maker followed by a heaping scoop of coffee grounds. Sitting next to the coffee maker was a three-quarters full bottle of water, which he looked at, shrugged his shoulders, and poured into the reservoir. It would have taken him an extra step to go to the water pouring from the faucet into the minnow tanks which he usually used to make his coffee, and he smiled to himself with the thought that laziness really did run in the family.

Arnold then opened his tackle box, and grabbed the still-packaged lures they had taken along with them that morning, and he once again twisted his left arm, trying to make the sudden tingling go away. He walked to the shelf and started putting the lures, one by one, back on their designated hooks.

The tingling became irritatingly uncomfortable. As always, he tried to blow it off.

But it wasn't going to go away this time.

All of a sudden, his face surged red as jolts of pain electrified his left arm. His breath had left him, and as he panicked, trying to breathe and knowing exactly what was happening, he stopped and grabbed his wrist. A further explosion of fear erupted over him as he discovered the erratic palpitations. The lures slipped from his hand without him realizing he had dropped them.

"Oh, dear God—Mart—" was all he could whimper before his face cramped from both fear and the excruciating pain of his heart ceasing to function.

Arnold's limp body collapsed into the row of lures as his life drained from him.

After the dislodged lures settled to stillness, a strange, peaceful silence swallowed up the shop, broken only by the coffee maker percolating its last drops into the pot, and then going silent itself.

The silence remained for more than a few peaceful moments, and then was broken by Martin opening the door to his studio, and walking into the shop with a red baseball cap in his hands. It was the first fishing cap that Arnold had given to his son when he was six, and up until that point, it had gone missing.

"Hey Dad, look what I just found," Martin said with a smiling voice.

But the only answer returned was silence.

"Dad?" he said, rightfully suspicious of the silence.

He knew something was wrong. It wasn't anything that he yet had proof of, he just felt it, and therefore walked more slowly than he would have as he looked down the rows of lures.

A crippling moan followed by a burst of horrified tears rushed forth as Martin stood, paralyzed by his father's body lying on the floor with the mess of lures around him. He rushed to his father, and grabbed his still warm, but lifeless arm, knowing that it would be the last time he would feel it.

Martin curled up in a ball beside Arnold, hugging his father's arm, as his tears saturated him blind. As misery completely overwhelmed him, he could hardly breathe as he began to hyperventilate. He wasn't even aware that he was whimpering "Daddy . . ." again and again, as he rocked back and forth, clinging to his father's arm.

And at once, panic chopped its dull, rusty axe into him in a sweeping blow, tearing his being with the sickening realization that it seemed he was now all alone in the world.

CHAPTER FIFTEEN

L ONELINESS, IT SEEMED, WAS PAR THAT NIGHT IN DESIRE. Ernie, dressed in his cleanest shirt to which he had affixed his clip-on bow tie, and un-faded blue jeans that he only wore on special occasions, stood before the Wall of Fame, fixating on one picture—Stella. He ran his finger tenderly along her shy, smiling face, trying without much success to hide his own embarrassment from himself. He really wanted to go to her, if nothing more than to just have a little company for the evening, but something painful stopped him in his tracks.

He looked down at the photography book in his other hand. He filed through it again trying to come up with something to talk to her about by only looking at the pictures. He didn't feel as if he was smart enough to pull it off, and could do without the threat of her knowing his secret, or of anyone knowing about it for that matter. He lost the thought, if only temporarily, when he came across a photo of The Great Wall of China. He was instantly entranced by its majesty and grandeur. He carefully ripped it out of the book and tacked it on the wall over some of the other pictures. A few pages farther into the book revealed a photo of the

Pyramids of Giza. Equally entranced, he ripped that out as well, and tacked it to the wall.

He had never seen pictures of these before, but had heard about them sometime ago in his youth. As he flipped through more pages, a photo of Stonehenge presented itself to him, and as he looked at it, he began to question his response to Bear about how the world came to see him. To his knowledge, nothing in these photos had ever come to him, and he lost himself for the moment, enthralled by what else might lie outside the town limits of Desire. He ripped the photo of Stonehenge out of the book, and slipped that one in the pocket of his special jeans, which reminded him of his impending date.

He looked up at the clock in the shop. It was already 7:45. He had been standing in front of the wall for over an hour, and now he was much too embarrassed to even consider going over to Stella's that tardy. Not only that, but how could he go over there and have her ask about the book, and then have to tell her that he ripped it apart? It was this book that was the problem.

Why did she have to give me a damn book?

He looked back down at it, looking specifically at the words, giving it one last chance to make sense to him.

It was no use.

Overwhelmed with sadness and embarrassment, he walked out of the shop, throwing the book in the garbage can on the way out.

But the book never mattered to Stella. She only gave it to him as a gift to thank him for the favor of saving her from having to spend another birthday alone. She couldn't care less if he set it on fire, or put it under the leg of his kitchen table to keep it from wobbling. She just thought it would be a nice gesture to offer him a simple gift. And how could she have known? Even if she did discover his handicap, she would have taken pride in her offer to teach him, and in no time, his illiteracy would be just another monster of his past. But he would never have the courage to ask her to do such a thing.

So she sat silently in her simple dress with ruffles around the collar and patterned purple flowers, at the head of her table, covered with a pretty off-white eyelet table cloth and set for two, complete with salad plates and wine glasses.

She was afraid to look up at the clock, but did anyway.

7:55.

Ernie wasn't coming, and it took everything she had to fight back the encroaching tears.

The now cold roast beef dinner with little red potatoes, asparagus, and fresh baked bread that she had spent most of the day preparing sat in the kitchen and would never be eaten. Instead, sitting on the plate before her, perfectly centered, was a single chocolate cupcake with vanilla frosting and multicolored sprinkles with an unlit candle sticking out of it.

She stared down at it, then picked up a book of matches sitting next to her plate. She ripped one off and struck it to light, telling herself that she wasn't allowed to cry. She lit her birthday candle, and blew out the match, setting it perfectly on the rim of her plate.

She looked around her house, which was as cold and empty as her shop. She procrastinated, giving Ernie one last chance to show up even though she knew he wasn't going to. With a sorrowful sigh, she blew out the candle.

"Happy Birthday," she whimpered to herself, then at once gave up her struggle to be strong, and she broke down and cried.

The first single tear hit her plate like a thunderclap. It echoed so emotionally loud that it forced her head to fall into her arms on the table, and she cried harder than she could stand.

She never even bothered to make herself the same wish again.

Ernie really hadn't a clue that he had caused so much misery in Stella. He simply didn't have it in him to do something like that on purpose. He sat in his chair in his living room, with an almost untouched microwave dinner before him of which he couldn't get himself to eat more than a few bites. He stared blankly into the glow of the television and clumsily juggled both his guilt and embarrassment. A laugh track erupted from the television, but Ernie had no idea why. He wasn't actually watching it. He was just staring at it to keep himself from dwelling on his own destitution, but even being Ernie, that wasn't an easy thing to do.

He reached into his back pocket of his jeans, and pulled out the photo of Stonehenge. He ran his finger along the standing rocks. *Where in the world was this amazing thing? Texas? I bet everyone but you knows where it is, you damn idiot.*

He sat, actually shocked. He had never called himself that before. But he was mad, and because it was him getting mad at himself, he got damn pissed.

He got up and kicked the power button on the television, turning it off. Then he flipped on the lamp on his way to dig in the closet in the entryway. He knew he'd find what he was looking for in there, because a box on the top shelf contained the only one he had in the house. He stood on his tiptoes and stretched to hook his finger on the rim of the box, which he then pulled and jumped out of the way as the box and its contents crashed to the floor.

The pile of memorabilia from his youth spilled out over his feet. His tattered, stained, and abused teddy bear, his toy battleship, his Mold-A-Rama Alligator that his parents brought him back from a trip without him to the zoo in St. Paul. Board games and assorted toys and other knick-knacks also spilled from the box.

Then, as if the pile was offering it to him, he bent down and picked up the only book he had in the house. It was the one that Elle gave him after one of their talks about their childhood. It was the one about a girl and her lumberjack grandfather. He picked it up and brought it back to his chair.

He strained to read the title.

"Lig-lights in th-the for-rr-est," he stuttered, and then smiled, as he was surprised to feel an unexpected tinge of pride. But still, he had a long way to go before he would feel good about himself after tonight.

He opened the book and began to sound out the first words. It was a frustrating undertaking, but unbeknownst to him, there was a specific sort of magic that came over him that would feed his determination to read that entire book no matter how long it might take him.

It was that specific sort of magic that was beginning to rush over everyone in town, regardless if they recognized it or not, and Bear was by no means left out. But a clouded mind full of insignificant dilemmas led his thoughts elsewhere as he sat on his dock.

He had already realized a Kerouacian lifestyle, which now had all but lost its appeal, even though he held that option just above his thorny place as his "Get out of Jail Free" card. But now, as it had been for sometime, his thoughts lay in Florida where he always knew for some reason that he'd wind up. He had always been enthralled with Hemingway; in fact he saw a tremendous amount of himself in the adventurer's lifestyle. Even his demise in that lonely little cabin in Idaho seemed to recognize itself as Bear's own final solution when the time came.

Everybody needs an out, don't they? Or at least the knowledge of how that out will come to them, which might pacify them into another day of life. But it was way too early to consider those thoughts.

For now, Key West seemed to be an inviting solution to Desire. But what would he do there? Write? He couldn't even get himself to write a word here, and this was his place in the world. And if he did leave again, would the twins and Annie be okay on their own, now that he'd told them he would protect them? Maybe that wasn't the best thing for him to tell them, but what else could he have said? Truth was, there was really nothing else he could have said to them. He would more readily do to himself what Hemmingway did in that cabin in Idaho than be the one to go down in history as the killer of someone else's dreams, especially those of Annie and the twins.

And as he sat there, looking out at the truthful, sympathetic lake, he told himself that he should be writing down all those thoughts he had slam dancing around in his head.

But he didn't write a word.

A block is a block, even if the writer had a subject to write about. And once it has its talons around your neck, there was very little that could be done other than try to put yourself in a separate comfort zone that would turn that block into a Thanksgiving day feast.

But that was the problem.

His comfort was as elusive right then as were the solutions to his problems. And although he didn't really believe it, he worried that he might not ever write another word. One book published was all he was going to get, and what was worse was that he didn't even own a copy of it to give himself a mental boost, although he did know where a copy of it was.

As the ghostly mist rose over the lake, and a lone loon echoed its lonely call, ushering in the morning, it was becoming apparent that his muse was having an affair with someone who simply didn't deserve it. But isn't that always how the story goes?

At least in the thorny place it does.

He reached into his inside vest pocket where Elle's journal always stayed. Perhaps her writings would inspire him the way they used to, and as he once again filed through the pages, reading a bit here and another bit there, the envelope with Arnold's name on it fell into his lap. There was something about it, as if it was calling on him to read it, but that feeling could have only come from his wanting to pry.

He slipped it out of the envelope, and began to read.

My dearest Arnold, I have never regretted for a moment forsaking Bret for an eternity in love with you. Even though I did once love him, I never knew what it meant to be in love with someone until I married you. And it stings to think that I have been dishonest with you.

The sound of hollow, dragging footsteps walking down the dock stopped him from reading any further, and he hurriedly shoved the letter and envelope back into the journal, then turned, expecting to find an energized Martin, ready for the day that tied the record. But what he saw instead was only the crumbling shell of what was once Martin who stood on the dock staring at him through his red swollen eyes.

"Martin. Today's the day, isn't it?" Bear said with an automatic enthusiasm before the evidence sunk in that something was terribly wrong. "Where's your gear?" he asked cautiously.

Martin stared blankly in reply. There was nothing left inside of him. Bear rose to his feet. He'd seen this look in Martin once before, and hoped, that after Elle's funeral, he would never have to see it again.

"Martin? What's wrong?" he said, taking a few steps closer to him, already knowing in the pit of his gut what was, in fact, wrong.

Martin's neck refused to hold his head up any longer, and it involuntarily rolled back, and then bowed as he dropped to his knees. He cried, harder perhaps than he had before, but there were no tears. He had already exhausted them. Bear now knew for sure what exactly was wrong. Martin just didn't react like this to anything else.

Bear was the closest thing Martin ever had to a brother, and like that true brother, he went to the crippled Martin, and wrapped his arms around him. Martin took immediate solace in the comfort.

"How did it happen?" Bear almost whispered.

"I don't know. I just found him on the floor. I think he had a heart attack," he whimpered through his tears.

And then, out of somewhere elusive, an unexpected feeling came over Bear, and he was surprised to find it was anger. It was anger that was aimed directly at himself. He was angry that he had let himself become a practitioner of that trait which he hated most in people, and that was to bathe in pettiness and triviality. He hated this "give me convenience or give me death" culture we live in with its "fuck the environmental consequences, your whites can be their whitest" consumer attitudes, and its cola wars fighting over princess pop stars that break into those intellectually retarded talk shows that perpetuate the damning stereotypes that keep our global family just as dysfunctional as the media needs it to be to enable maximum profitability. And news programs that sensationalize violence to keep the masses in fear so that they become even better consumers of foreign-made merchandise to keep their families safe. It always made him wonder if everyone in the great American super absorbent consumer culture had forgotten what life really was about, or if they even ever knew in the first place.

He hated it all because it was all just a celebration of everything trivial in life. None of it was real, none of it did anything to benefit anyone; it only served to blind us from what was really important. Our culture had become nothing more than a circus of the benign, and what was especially disturbing to him was that there was no incentive in any of it for people to care about each other any more. He never remembered a day in his life that he signed the guest book that welcomed him into that society.

But there he was, holding his broken friend, spending all his time hating everything trivial in life, which in turn made his life just as vapid.

He was angry with himself for worrying about his and Cherie's petty relationship.

He was angry that he spent too much time worrying about a stupid writer's block that was cramping his ability to just sit and absorb and appreciate the natural beauty around him.

He was angry that he couldn't be who he wanted to be in a town that only saw him as someone he was not.

He was angry for not having the guts to ask a certain bookstore owner out for a ride on his bike and maybe a bite to eat. But he took pleasure in that burgeoning anger with himself, because anger had always been his biggest motivator to change. And through this anger, Bear found his strength returning.

That was his epiphany.

From that point on, he wasn't about to waste another minute of his life on triviality. He would never make that mistake again. But now, here was Martin, crying in his arms, and he still was going on about that which only concerned him.

He patted his friend on his back, and looked at him. "Don't worry about a thing. I'll call your uncle."

"No. Don't. I've already taken care of it," Martin said, rubbing his swollen, stinging eyes.

๑๑๛

THAT MORNING, MARTIN'S EYES WEREN'T THE ONLY EYES that were stinging. As the sun had risen a few fingers off the horizon, Bret sat on a park bench at the Little Lumberjack Park on the lakeshore directly across the bay from where the contest was held. He sat on that bench since he left the Bait Shop two nights ago. He hadn't slept—had barely even blinked. He sat through the festivities of the contest, aware that it was happening, but only through a subconscious haze. He sat there, procrastinating from doing what he saw as the only solution to the gridlock his life had long developed into. He sat all night, unaware of what happened to Arnold. At that point, however, it was just a matter of time before he would find out about Arnold by meeting him there. It just didn't seem that there was any magic left in life, but magic never comes to those who sit and wait for it.

Bret's eyes welled up with tears, but only from his unconscious refusal to blink. He was trapped in what vets call "a thousand mile stare." Coming to this place, staring past the children as they played, their exuberant, sincere laughter ringing in the air, was the torture he thought he deserved. He broke his stare only long enough to watch a child run by him from the swings to climb the ladder of the slide, as if that kid would come up to him and simply tell him he was forgiven.

But he didn't need to hear it from those kids.

Sitting on the bench next to him, but keeping her distance, was the woman in the powder blue dress. She loved it here, and came to just sit and watch, and reflect as often as she could. She didn't feel so ignored here. She had a child of her own, but he was all grown up now, and she missed those cheery days when she would bring him here to play. To her it seemed that those times were just a few days ago, and she cringed as she wondered where all the time of her life had slipped away to.

She looked at Bret, knowing that she should say something to him, even though it didn't look like he even knew she was there. But she didn't say a word. She just stared at him with a heavy amount of empathy. She always looked at him that way and felt helpless that she couldn't do anything to directly make all his problems disappear. No one can do that for someone else anyway. They have to find their own way, otherwise the rewards of their accomplishments will not be theirs to celebrate, and there would be no lesson from their failures.

As Bret continued his stare, he didn't notice the man walk up to her and take her hand in his. She smiled up at him. Here, finally, she had found someone who didn't ignore her. The man looked at Bret with the same sort of empathy she did, but there was nothing he could do to directly help Bret, either.

"Well young lady, would you like to accompany me for a pint at the Lodge?" he said with a cordial bow.

The woman laughed, and rose to her feet. "I'd be delighted, if you think we can," she said with a smile.

As they walked away, they gave one last compassionate look at Bret, and for a reason outside his comprehension, he suddenly snapped back with a ravenous appetite for a few shots of a fine Canadian whiskey. Besides, he knew that he needed a little more than that kind of help, but would never impose on his old friend to give it to him. Still, he felt somehow inclined to go down to the Lodge, if nothing else than just to see his old friend one last time. Besides, sitting on the bench, torturing himself into suicide would not be the way he'd ever find that magic, even if he wasn't directly looking for it.

CHAPTER SIXTEEN

I N THE STANDS OF THE PINES THAT BORDERED THE property that Cherie's trailer occupied, two ravens cawed their taunts at each other. They had been playing all morning without anything better to do, beginning their adventures by taking turns sneaking up on a bald eagle and pulling its tail feathers while it tried to dine peacefully on a carp on the lakeshore. With the eagle effectively perturbed, and without either one of them proving their bravery over the other, they had decided on another game to test their audacity—chicken.

With a loud fury of antagonizing caws, they leapt into flight, heading straight for the clouds, high above and directly over Cherie's trailer. When they achieved an altitude of almost two hundred feet, they screamed at each other and folded their wings against their bodies, dive-bombing the trailer at the speed of gravity. The object of the game was to be the last to pull up. If one of them pulled up too soon, he would lose the game. If one of them didn't pull up soon enough, Cherie would have to fix the hole in her roof, that is, after cleaning out a mess of entrails and black feathers.

It was games such as this that ravens loved to play. They were incredibly smart birds, although when games like this were played, that intelligence seemed to be open to question.

Every hunting season, there were stories told in the café of how ravens lead stalking hunters to sleeping game by dive bombing them until the hunters paid attention, then flying in a circle over the hidden game. Ravens had come to learn that a human dressed in blaze orange with a rifle in his hands equaled a feast of a fresh, hot gut pile. They really were quite smart.

But neither of these daredevil birds would be the victor of this particular joust of heroism as the outward explosion of the trailer door bursting open, almost flying off the hinges, scared each of them into pulling up prematurely.

Bear shot out of the open door as if the trailer was on fire. Cherie followed directly after him with her hand clenched around a half empty bottle of rum.

The ravens sat on a pine branch, scolding Bear with spears of anger for interrupting their game. But that was in no way equal to the anger erupting out of Bear. He stormed off in the direction of Emily with his duffle bag full of the clothes that he just had cleaned out of Cherie's closet.

"Bear, Goddamnit, please! Don't quit me!" Cherie whined as she jumped at him and grabbed at his bag in an attempt to stop him.

Bear yanked the bag out of her grasp and kept walking. "Don't make such a big deal outta this. You had to know it was coming."

She leaped onto him and hung onto his back like a sack of meat draped over his shoulder, then slid down his massive shoulders and clung to his arm.

"Cherie, for Christ's sake, show some dignity," he scolded, then shook her off with a snap of his arm, landing her flat in the dirt driveway.

"I don't know how to have any dignity!" she screamed, and then started to weep as she realized just how true that statement was. "You're the bastard that should find some dignity, I gave you everything!" she screamed as her breath whipped up a cloud of dirt that flew up in her face.

Bear turned, and looked down at her. "Like what? Huh? We never had a real relationship. It was symbiotic at best."

"Symbi—? What are you talking about?" she said confused, having never heard that word in her life, and therefore thinking that Bear had just made it up.

"That's just it. When was the last time you and I sat down and had a conversation?"

Cherie struggled to her feet and brushed the clouds of dust from her clothes. "We're not the type of people that sit and talk. When did you turn into the white picket fence type? Jesus Christ, I don't even know who you fuckin' are anymore!"

He looked at her for a brief, solemn moment. "You never have, Cherie," he said with a miserably serious tone, then continued to walk toward Emily.

"What the hell is that supposed to mean?" she said, chasing after him.

He turned, startled to find her so close to him. "Arnold Ravenwood died last night, and it didn't open my eyes enough when Elle died, and you know why? Because I got comfortable. No. I got scared. I'm not going to make that mistake again."

Cherie was taken aback. "Arnold died?" she said softly.

"Yeah. He had a heart attack. He was fifty-eight years old, and just like that, he's gone," he said with a snap of his fingers, then looked directly into her vacant eyes. "I'm not going to waste another minute of my life," he said, taking it as the end, and continued to march toward Emily. But Cherie wasn't going to let him off that easy.

"You mean you're not gonna waste another minute of your life with me," she accused, standing with her arms crossed.

"However you wanna see it," he said without slowing his pace.

Her quiver had run out of emotional arrows except for the one that assumed reverse psychology. "You wanna leave me? Fine. I don't need this anymore, ya know? You sit on that damn dock all night writing who cares what, then you come home to me for an hour before you have to take me to work, and you don't even do that anymore. So you know what? Fine. Go," she condemned, again folding her arms in an arrogant stance, not realizing that the arrow hadn't hit the target. "You're not leaving me. You'll be back here fuckin' the shit out of me in an hour. I'm your drug, Bear, and you know it."

Bear rolled his eyes, but she couldn't see it with his back turned to her.

Seeing that her last barb hadn't worked, Cherie reached back into her quiver and panicked when she found it empty. She had to rely on her wits if she was going to win this, and if that was the case, she had already long lost. "I can do better. I promise. Let's just forget all of this and go back to bed," she pleaded, thinking that it was the best gear to change to.

Bear tried to ignore her. He was almost to his bike and home free, but still, he cringed with frustration and stomped his feet as he walked to let her know that he wasn't stopping.

She stared at him helplessly for a pale moment. When it came right down to it, she really didn't care if Bear stayed or left. She just wanted to save herself from being rejected, and she knew it was a game that Bear would have nothing to do with.

"No!" She screamed running to him, flying onto his back like an attacking cougar. "You're not leaving me!"

"Get off me, Cherie!" he screamed as he spun around, trying to shake her off, but her grip was determined.

"No! Not until you tell me you're not leaving me!" she screamed as she tried to hang on.

Bear scowled. He never expected this kind of pathetic display, but at the same time, he didn't find it surprising. He reached back over his shoulder as if it was his turn to grab an arrow, taking her underneath her arm. With a slight bow of his body and an effortless yank on her arm, he flipped her over his shoulder, and she landed hard on her ass just in front of Emily. Another cloud of dusty earth engulfed her on impact.

He looked down at her. He had never seen her look this pathetic, and a wave of sympathy came over him as he got tangled in her pouty brown eyes as she looked up at him. He had always melted at the sight of those eyes, and he caught himself reconsidering his position and giving it one last shot to make it work. But to his credit, he didn't back down, and he simply stepped over her and got on his bike. She looked up at him, surprised that her eye trick didn't work either. Her face fell as she realized it really was over.

He looked down at her one last time. "Do you know what the word 'emancipation' means?" he asked, already knowing her response.

"No," she said annoyed that he threw another big word at her.

"Look it up," he said through his teeth and kick-started Emily to life.

Completely spent, Cherie rose to her feet. Bear gave her one last look, kicked Emily into gear, and tore off down the driveway. She realized he was never coming back, but that wasn't really the concept that immediately concerned her. She threw her bottle of rum at him, narrowly missing him as it shattered against a tree. "How the hell am I gonna get to work, you asshole?" she screamed.

He smiled as he pulled out onto the street that would lead him to wherever in the world he desired to go, actually a little proud of himself as he wrapped that great feeling of liberation around him like a patriot does with the flag after a victorious battle. But he still had one more harrowing step to go before he could be truly liberated. He headed toward the tattoo shop.

⚬⚬⚬

SOMEONE ELSE ALSO WANTED TO WRAP HERSELF IN THAT flag of victory, especially after last night. Stella never got angry at anything before, not even herself. She just never thought she had it in her, and although she didn't understand his motivations, she wasn't angry with Ernie. She was, for the first time, angry with herself for not being more assertive, for not exposing the strength she knew she had within her, and for compromising everything she wanted in her life. She wasn't even surprised to discover that being angry with herself felt good in a strange sort of way.

It gave her strength.

It gave her courage.

She was determined to find the author who wrote that book that she absolutely had fallen in love with. That would be the self-imposed test of her own strength. When she opened the book to the publisher's page, it was that anger that smothered her apprehension, and she was ravenously feeding on it. Still, some of that apprehension survived, but not enough to stop her from picking up the phone and dialing the number she'd dialed once before.

It rang twice before that sweet, practiced voice answered with "Lakeland Publishing, how may I direct your call?"

"Yes," Stella said with assertive, tight lips. "I wonder if you can help me. I have a copy of *Love, Elusive* and, um, I was wondering if somehow I could contact the author?"

"I can't give out any personal information of our clients," the voice answered, then softening, "but to tell you the truth, I loved that book, too. I actually made my husband read it. I think it saved our marriage. Are you married?"

"No," she said as the cold reality of that question revived her apprehension, but not enough for her to give up.

"Well, it has its ups and downs, but it sure beats being alone. I will tell you this—the author disappeared about five or six years ago; however, I believe his publisher still has contact with him. Hang on, I'll connect you."

"Thanks," she said with the same tingle in the pit of her gut just before you go over the first rise on a rollercoaster.

The connection rang once and then was picked up with a deep, groggy voice that said "Tom Ringling."

Stella paused, then willed herself to continue. "Hi. My name is

Stella Holmstead. I have a copy of *Love, Elusive,* and I wanted to try to contact the author," she said, nervously fidgeting with everything around her.

"Ah, yeah. Rob Harper. There's a name I haven't heard in a while. Good book, wasn't it?"

"Yes. I own a book store, and I've never read anything like it."

"Well, he retired to a small town up north, but I still e-mail him every once in a while. I'm trying to get him to write another book for us. Would you like me to forward a letter to him?"

She smiled with all the zest of her success. "Yes, I'd like that."

"Just e-mail me at Tom at Lakewood dot com. Real easy."

"I'll do that. Thank you," she said, writing down his address.

"My pleasure. I'll forward your letter as soon as I get it. I'm sure he'd like to know he still has fans out there."

She could hardly talk through her smile. "Well I'm one of them. Thank you for doing this," she said both to him and herself.

"Of course," he said.

"Bye," she said not really wanting to hang up. She wanted to ask him everything about this Rob Harper guy, but he had already hung up, and besides, she didn't want to press her luck.

She set down the phone, exhilarated with her first genuine smile in what seemed forever. Even if this Rob Harper were sixty years old and married with children and nothing that she had fantasized about, this would come true, it didn't matter. She had made the first step to curing her inability to enjoy life, and that was what was important. Who knew, maybe she would simply have a life-long pen pal if nothing else. Maybe she would just have a new friend, and maybe, just maybe, it might be something more.

She looked at all the Post-it Note affirmations on her computer monitor. There was one in particular that she wrote to herself while she was bathing in her thorny place. She ripped it off and read it one last time. *If love is blind, how will it ever find me?* She took great pleasure in ripping it up into as many pieces as she could.

ᗡᗡ

THAT NOTE COULD'VE BEEN STAMPED AND ADDRESSED TO Earl, who, as he finished up with Lorin's back for the day, couldn't get a particular waitress out of his mind and wondered if he deserved anything that might come from it.

Lorin winced as he slid his T-shirt over his bandaged back, as the grumble of Bear's bike pulled to a halt in front of the shop.

"Stay off your back for a few days," Earl directed, standing over the sink, washing off that powdery substance that coated his hands from the inside of the latex gloves. Lorin detected something somewhat preoccupied about him this session, but didn't inquire about it—he simply didn't care.

"That's easy," Lorin said, stretching into his shirt. "I'm never the one on my back," he laughed like a weasel.

Bear walked in, but not like he owned the place. He waited like a client for Lorin to finish and leave.

"S'up Bear? Back for more porno?" Lorin said with his weasely laugh as he walked out the door.

Earl looked up at him from the sink. "Where you been all day?" he asked in a pseudo-nagging tone.

"I want you to buy me out," Bear said matter-of-factly.

Earl grabbed a towel and began to rub his hands. "Of what?" he asked, already knowing the answer, but not wanting to acknowledge it.

"Whadda ya think? The shop. I'm gonna be leaving."

Earl laughed at him. He knew that his brother was a runner and therefore had been expecting that this day would come. Even so, he didn't at first recognize that this was what in fact was happening. "Why're you talkin' crazy? Did Cherie hit you upside your head with something again?"

"Cherie's no longer in the picture." Bear said in that same emotionless monotone.

"Where the hell did this come from all of a sudden?" he said, surprised, but internally happy to hear that news.

"It's not all of a sudden. I just don't belong here anymore."

As much as it would be to his benefit to have his brother out of the picture as far as he and Cherie were concerned, he also knew that when it came right down to it, brothers come first, women come second. "Yes, you do. That sign says Earl and Bear—"

"It's not Bear anymore," he interrupted. "It's Rob. Look, I don't expect you to get it. Just—"

"What's there to get? I knew that you'd do this some day. You're not that hard to figure out, Professor," Earl said.

At that point, Bear detected something different in his brother. It was a vivacity that had never revealed itself before, a confidence that made Bear uneasy only because he could no longer appraise his brother's mentality. It was also a strength that immediately demanded compliance even if, at first, Bear didn't give into it.

"Look, it's not like you're going to lose the business. You were doing fine before I got here," Bear argued.

"This has nothing to do with that. Bear, you always run from everything. When are you gonna say enough? Huh?" Earl said, once again demanding compliance.

"This is my choice—"

"I hate to burst your bubble, Bro, but we're not the kind of people that get choices. You got nothin' else but this. And that's the way it is for both of us."

"Earl, all I'm asking you to do is buy me out. I'm leaving either way," he said, reaching for the easy out after realizing that this was not going to be as cut and dried as he had thought.

"Look, if you wanna leave, there's nothing I can do to stop you. But when are you gonna take a stand?" Earl challenged, expecting a rebuttal that never came. "You just can't keep running from everything, man."

Bear just stared at his brother, surprised at Earl's insight. Still, he'd made up his mind. Key West was calling, and so were all points in between. Besides, this role reversal with his brother was just a little too much for him to take right then, and all he wanted was an out. "You don't need to understand, Earl," he said decisively.

"Then get me to understand!" Earl stabbed. "Why are you leaving, huh? Just answer me that."

But Bear couldn't answer it, not in any way that Earl would understand. Even so, Bear repeated Earl's question in his mind just to see if his answer did, in fact, make sense.

"Just answer me that," Earl repeated more calmly, taking Bear's hesitation as a sign that he really didn't know why.

"Because this isn't who I am. This has never been who I am," Bear answered, straining to make it sound like his resolve was stronger than it was.

"Oh bullshit! And so what? You think anybody out there really knows who the hell they are?" Earl asked, again expecting an answer that never came. "You wanna know who you are? I'll tell you who you are—you're my brother. We're blood, and blood doesn't do this kind of shit to each other."

Bear stared at him. He didn't come here for a lecture, nor did he need one, even if Earl was making more sense than he ever had before. Still, he had to ask himself if he deserved this interrogation, and he found that his patience was wearing thin, even with himself.

"You gonna buy me out or what?" Bear demanded.

"No," Earl simply responded. "I don't have that kind of money, and you know it."

"Fine," he said, and then walked toward the door. "Keep the shop. I don't need your money anyway."

"Hey!" Earl yelled at him.

Bear stopped and slowly turned to face him.

"I don't want you to leave, man." He pleaded only because he truly meant it. "Please? You gotta find a reason to stay."

CHAPTER SEVENTEEN

C HERIE WAS ON HER OWN AGAIN. IT WAS A SITUATION that she despised only because she knew herself well enough to know that she simply couldn't rely upon herself for anything. There always had to be someone there to do things for her, and most of the time, there always had been. But now, she had to try and find strength within herself to figure things out, and as she ran across the parking lot of the café, late for work once again, responsibility had to be first on the agenda.

Her shoe flipped off as she ran, and momentum carried her a few steps beyond it before she could stop. Everyone in the café was watching her through the picture windows, even Jack. Some of them smirked and a few even laughed as they watched her run back for her shoe, noticing that the back of her work dress was unzipped revealing the black lace of her bra. There was no one left at home to zip it for her, and it left her dress hanging loosely from her shoulders. She'd figured that she would just ask Jack to zip it up for her and maybe even get his jollies off in the process, but Jack wasn't anywhere near jolly as he stood by the register watching her run in the door cradling her shoe and balled-up apron.

"In my office. Now," he seethed.

Jack led her in, and marched behind his desk. He threw himself into his chair. Cherie took a few steps more inside the cold, bland office. Her heart instantly began to palpitate.

Please don't fire me. Please don't fire me.

She was about to sit in the chair opposite him in front of the desk, but Jack abruptly stopped her. "Don't bother. You won't be staying long."

"Look, I know I've been late lately, but I'm aware of it and—"

"This has nothing to do with you being late, however it does make this easier. First of all, you are fired," he said, aroused by his own power.

"What?" Cherie said almost involuntarily, as if it jumped out of her mouth.

"Don't look so surprised, Cherie. I can put up with a lot, but I can't and won't put up with thieves."

Cherie was taken completely aback. "What are you talking about?" she said softly, full of both suspicion and concern.

"Every night, I ask you to run a credit report for me, right?"

"Yeah, and I do."

"But that's not all you do, is it?" he said as he flipped a printout with a list of credit card numbers typed in black, with a chuck of numbers in the middle of the list typed in red. Cherie picked it up. She had no clue what she was looking at other than that it was a black and red list of credit card numbers. "I got that printout from our credit company showing a history of our credit reports. A few weeks ago, somebody pressed the duplicate button, and apparently stole a copy of the day's credit card numbers," he looked at her for a reaction that he didn't get. "Do you want to explain why you did that?"

Cherie began to tremble. She'd been blamed for a lot of things in her life, and most of them she was actually responsible for. This, however, was an accusation of a jailable offense that she did not commit, and she had no one to turn to for help.

"Mr. Hanson, I swear I have no idea what you're talking about," her voice trembled as fear produced the tears that welled in her eyes.

"I thought you'd say that," he said, shaking his head. "At least have the dignity to admit you did it."

Look at me. Why does everyone think I should have any dignity?

A few tears trailed down her face, making Jack roll his eyes, thinking it to be a too pathetic display. "Why do you think it was even me?" she whimpered.

"Because you were the only one working that night. And frankly, Cherie, you're the only one here I don't trust."

She couldn't look him in the face any longer, so her eyes dropped to her feet as her head drooped. "I've worked here for eight and a half years, and never once have I stole so much as a coffee cup from you," she whimpered, wiping at a tear even as another fell directly in its place.

"Look, it's really simple. This credit card thing isn't my problem, it's their problem, so I don't give a crap what they do about it, but I can't have people working for me that I can't trust. And that's the bottom line," Jack stated flatly.

Cherie raised her head and looked back at Jack with condemning eyes. "So that's it, just like that. You're not even going to listen to—"

"You've already been replaced, Cherie," he interrupted with a stab of cruelty. "I don't think we have anything more to discuss," he finished, taking inward pleasure that he had at last made her pay for that night when everyone had so much fun laughing at him.

Cherie just stood there wondering why she didn't just walk out right now. But the pile of bills that she had stacked up on her kitchen table with PAST DUE stamped red on the envelopes, her empty refrigerator, and the cost of fixing her waterlogged truck all reminded her how much she needed this job. Still, she couldn't think of any magic words to make Jack change his mind. The reality was that there weren't any words that she could have said to him, not even from on her knees before him.

Jack got up and walked to her. "C'mon, I'll walk you to the door," he said, reaching for her arm. Cherie ripped it away from him as if he had dog shit on his hands.

"Don't touch me! I know where the Goddamn door is!" she snapped and ran out of his office.

Cherie looked directly at the floor as she ran through the café, sure that all the staring eyes were quietly judging her. Everyone knew what just happened, but no one really knew why. They'd have to wait until Jack came out of his office, ready to tell anyone who asked. But first, he had to solve an impending dilemma: Where the hell was he going to find a replacement for Cherie?

೧೯

CHERIE WALKED NUMBLY DOWN MAIN STREET ONLY A ghost of herself still cradling her one shoe and balled-up apron, giving her a bag lady limp as she walked up on her shoe, and then down on her loose sock. She felt the eyes of people on the street boring into her, but she never consciously acknowledged them. She was trapped in her thorny place, held tight by the sharp vines of self-demolition that strangled themselves around her heart, squeezing, cutting into the flesh of her being.

Her thorny place was worse than just about anyone else's. Bear wouldn't even be so gallantly brave as to play in there. It was a perfect mutilating garden of self-devastation. Her thorns had razor-sharp edges and venomous spider fangs that constantly injected the poisons of doubt and sorrow into her, and what was worse, she believed everything that the fangs injected, especially then. Those thorny vines were nourished by her submission to them. They fed upon her guilt and her indignity, and therefore got stronger as she got weaker. But she wasn't completely lost. Not yet, anyway. There was still meaning to her life, and twenty years earlier, she named that meaning "Annie." And at the moment, that particular sack of mental herbicide was completely unaware of the place she held in her mother's life. She was absorbed elsewhere, clueless that while her actions might not backfire on herself and the twins, they came close to destroying her mother.

Absorbed as she was, Annie didn't know that she was being watched as she got up from the embrace of the twins and went to the cooler to grab another beer, only to find it empty. The structure was complete. The scaffold had been taken down and discarded, and most of the equipment had been ditched in the woods. The twins sat on the ground resting their backs against the Gemini Observation Device, passing the last bottle of beer back and forth over the place between them that Annie had vacated. There was a pride about them that few people ever got to enjoy in their lives. They looked truly content, savoring a richness of life they couldn't know was so rare they might never know it again. With a heavy dose of bliss, they took a deep inhale of the sweet, damp forest air, and settled into the self-satisfying perma-smiles of a job well done.

"Hey, we're out of brew! Let's go into town. Cherie'll probably buy us breakfast," Annie yelled to them.

The twins eagerly nodded in agreement. What better way to enjoy this accomplishment than with a free feast? Full of joy and laughter, the three raced each other to their snowmobile. They sped off down the damp dirt road, and just as they were out of sight, the sheriff's Prowler pulled into the clearing.

This time, however, it wasn't Eddie.

Sheriff Walker stepped out of his truck, staring wide-eyed at the structure. He had been watching the three of them for the past hour, and was truly amazed by what he saw. Even so, his jaw involuntarily dropped. He walked up to the gothic-looking structure, looking up at it until his neck couldn't tilt back any farther. He had never seen anything like this before. He couldn't help but to break out in a dumbfounded smile.

But still, he was the sheriff, and he had a job to do. As he walked up to it and touched his hand to it, he knew that, magnificent as it was, this was just too big to sweep under the carpet. He began to hate his position for having to do what he saw needed to be done.

⊙⊙

CHERIE CONTINUED TO HOBBLE DOWN THE SIDEWALK, oblivious to the magic at work that would finally show her what was really important in life. That's the thing about those thorny places—they go for our eyes first, blinding us from finding the power to dull those razor sharp thorns.

Cherie walked past Stella's bookstore without even realizing that she did. She wasn't even cognizant of where she was going.

Stella, on the other hand, was consumed with where she was going. It burned crystal bright in her mind while she sat behind her computer, completing her e-mail with hopes of love in her heart. She read it again for the third time and sighed to herself as she moved the cursor to SEND. She paused, entertaining the thought of reading it again just one last time, but she knew that it was only a procrastination method. With a deep breath, she clicked the button on her mouse and sent the letter into the void of cyberspace. She watched the monitor until the notice popped up that told her that her mail had been sent, then leaned back in her chair.

"You're a stupid girl, Stella. You're a stupid, stupid girl," she sighed, testing to see how sharp her thorns still were.

CHAPTER EIGHTEEN

T HE LUNKER LODGE WAS ALMOST AS EMPTY AS IT was every day around this time. Barney took this time to catch up on the dish washing and tune in to either the History Channel or the Discovery Channel, which were the only reasons why he bought that damn satellite dish in the first place. Every time he paid that bill, he laughed to himself that he was paying all that money for two hundred channels, and he only ever watched two of them. Sometimes he did tune in to the news, just to thank his stars that he had the smarts to live in Desire. He did have to admit that sometimes he had a chuckle when he caught *The Simpsons*. But at that moment, he was deeply enthralled by *Walking with Prehistoric Beasts* on the Discovery Channel.

His attention was distracted by the front door opening wide, but no one coming in. He walked down the length of the bar to get a closer look and saw Bret standing in the doorway, pausing before he walked in, and then came over and sat on a stool at the bar.

Barney was surprised to see him. The last Bret had told him he was back on the wagon, "sobered" by Elle's accident. But nothing could be further from the truth. Bret just didn't care anymore what Barney, or anyone else in town, thought of him.

"Bret?" Barney said as he approached the tattered, worn-out crust of his friend.

"A beer. As a chaser from the double whiskey yer gonna pour me," Bret said looking up at him with lifeless, bloodshot eyes.

"You sure?" Barney asked both suspiciously and concerned.

"You ask all your customers if they're sure they want a drink?" Bret retorted sarcastically in the way that only old friends can get away with.

"Nope. Just the one's that've been scared sober."

"I'm not sober anymore," Bret said, bowing his head. To him it sounded like *I'm not alive anymore.*

Barney walked over to the shelf and pulled from it two low-ball glasses. "What was it this time?" he asked.

"A doll. Out in the woods," he answered rapidly, not wanting to relive, or even rethink, the incident. "Barney, if you're really my friend, just pour me the drink, leave the bottle, and leave me alone to finally finish the job that was started thirty years ago."

Barney set one of the glasses in front of him. "That's Earl talkin' shit."

"It's the only thing he's ever said that's right," he said solemnly.

Barney crunched his face at that comment. He certainly didn't believe it, but he was concerned that Bret did. He grabbed a bottle of Canadian whiskey from the shelf. The good stuff. Buddies don't serve that well crap to each other. Especially buddies that were vets. He free poured into Bret's glass.

"I hate doin' this Bret. But I ain't your paw," he said as he then poured himself a shot, and then lifted his glass to make a toast.

"Here's to fightin' the war within ourselves," Barney offered.

Bret slammed his shot then motioned for another, which Barney poured, followed by another one for himself. He knew exactly why Bret was there. Bret had been in this position too many times before, but Barney still took it seriously as every time it happened, it got a little worse, and he never knew when it was going to be the last time he'd have a chance to talk his friend out of doing something stupid. Therefore, he maintained a calm confidence about himself, knowing that people in need of help don't take it from someone who doesn't appear more stable than they are.

"You know, you and I are a rare breed. We're the warriors who are left to wallow in the misery of survival," Barney said as he took a sip.

"I'm not worthy of surviving," Bret muttered, then slammed his drink.

"That's what I used to think. When I got back from Korea—years after I got back—I thought of suicide every day. I lost my wife over it and a lot of other things I'll never get back. But one thing always stopped me from doing it."

"What was that?" he said, fully expecting a lecture that he knew he needed.

"I simply wanted to see how the story ends," Barney said with another sip. "I knew there was peace out there, and you're sittin' in the closest I ever came to it," he said, and then leaned on the bar, looking directly into Bret. "There is peace out there for you, Bret. But you're not going to find it here."

"Barney, there are some people in the world whose life was just an accident because they have caused more pain and suffering than they're worth," Bret said helplessly. He paused, trying to swallow, but was only able to smack his lips. He trembled, trying to keep himself from breaking down. "It's that orphanage I thought was a VC hideout that I open fired on," he paused and tried in vain to swallow again, then looked directly at Barney as the tears made themselves present. "I killed a bunch of innocent children, Barney. And that one little girl—she was all bloody, dying in my arms—I can't get her face out of my head. That's why the doll set me off again," he choked as his voice cracked. "All it would have taken was a second. Just one Goddamn second to look inside, and those children would still . . ." He paused again, fighting the urge to scream. "Just one second cursed me for the rest of my life, and I just can't drink them out of my mind like I used to be able to."

"Bret, you've been battling that for thirty years. When are you gonna finally forgive yourself for that?"

"How can I? It's cost me everything—my job, my friends," he paused for a stale moment. "And it cost me Elle," he said under a veil of torment.

Barney sighed in empathy. "Bret, regret is something that has killed more men than all the bullets of any war. We can do a lot of things, but the one thing we can't do is go back into the past and change things we wish we never did. That's what forgiveness is for."

Bret looked directly into Barney. "You think Dwayne's ever gonna forgive me? Huh? How 'bout those kids? How about Elle?" He looked even deeper into him. "Do you think God is ever gonna forgive me for all that?"

"I don't know the answer to that," Barney said lamentfully.

Bret grabbed the bottle, and poured himself another drink. "Well, we're about to find out," he said, and then slammed his drink so fast that half of it spilled down his chin.

"I do know that you can't expect anyone to forgive you until you forgive yourself," Barney quietly said as Bret poured himself another.

"You've been a good friend to me, Barney," he said, downing the drink. "I'm gonna miss you."

"You don't want to see how the story ends?"

"This *is* how the story ends," Bret insisted.

Barney fought to retain his cool on the outside, but inside he was panicking that he was losing Bret. He always thought that suicide was the coward's way out, and by no means an honorable ending for any soldier, especially those who already had survived in battle. But he knew other people, particularly those in agony, didn't see it that way. He certainly hadn't see it that way when he had gone through what Bret was going through now. But Bret had an advantage: he had the help and advice of a friend, something that Barney never had when he went through it.

During that dark time in his life, Barney never found religion as so many others had because he found it to be trading one prison for another. But what he did find was his own spirituality to help him down that road, aided by the wisdom that accompanied it.

Now as Barney stared at his broken friend, he knew that he had one more shot to try and save him. If he couldn't get that one thought that saved him across to Bret, his friend would, in fact, be lost.

He leaned closer to his friend. "Let me ask you a question, Bret. Do you believe in heaven?"

Bret had never considered it and was a bit surprised by the question. "I certainly hope so," he said with a sigh.

"Then you have to ask yourself why you're giving up on this life, but yet you wish for another that'll last forever."

To Barney's relief, Bret slowly set down his drink, unwilling to take even one more sip. That statement hit him more profoundly than anything that anyone had ever said to him. He had never considered asking himself that question, therefore, he hadn't an answer to it.

There was no answer.

Bret stared at Barney, those words echoing in his head. He didn't notice the woman in the powder blue dress or her new friend sitting just behind them, staring at them, still waiting for their pints. But as they watched him, Bret began to understand why he felt compelled to come here, and that was the magic that would continue to perpetuate his life.

CHAPTER NINETEEN

E RNIE SAT ON THE FRONT STEP OF THE SHOP IN HIS duct-taped recliner just the same as he had done everyday, but that morning, something from his everyday routine was missing. He never bothered to set up his TV on the folding table. Instead, he sat with *Lights in the Forest* on his lap, trying to get through the fifth page.

He looked up every so often, concerned that Stella would come to ask him where he was the night before. If she did, he was prepared to tell her his secret, no matter what she might think of him. But she never came, and he simply stuck his nose back in the book and continued his reading.

Off in the distance, getting closer, was the unmistakable rumble of the twin's snowmobile. As Ernie saw it come around the bend and pull up to the pump, he coyly slipped the book into the magazine pocket on the side of his chair before walking up to them.

"'Morning, boys, Annie."

"It's a little past morning, Ernie," Annie laughed gently, already knowing Ernie's reply.

"I know. Just making conversation. Fill up?"

"Yeah. Thanks," Stee said, unscrewing the gas cap.

Annie danced herself off the snowmobile. "I gotta pee," she said and waltzed to the ladies room, which was also the men's room.

Ernie took the hose out of its holster and plugged it into the gas tank. "The sheriff was out here looking for you guys earlier this morning. He was askin' 'bout that thing you're building out in the forest," he said as he leaned against the pump, relishing in that beloved *ka-ching* sound, and then the bass line to "Money."

The twins looked at each other with instant concern. "How long ago was he here?" Ven anxiously asked.

"Few hours ago. Said he was on his way out to see you out there. He asked if I saw Martin, but I told him no. Did you run into him?"

They simultaneously shook their heads. "No, we haven't seen him," Stee said uneasily.

To the twins immediate distress, the sheriff's Prowler pulled into the station as if from out of nowhere.

"Shit," the twins whispered to each other as Sheriff Walker rolled to a halt directly in front of the snowmobile.

Dwayne stepped out of his truck with his girth poised out before him. He grabbed dual handfuls of his belt and yanked his pants into comfort as he walked up to them. Ernie could feel that there was tension in the air, and even though their tank was full, he simply reached up and turned off the pump so he had an excuse to stay and watch.

"Ernie. Martin been around since I last was here?"

"Nope, still haven't seen him."

He looked at the twins. "Have you guys seen Martin around?"

"No. Why?" Stee asked.

"You guys haven't heard about Arnold?"

The twins shook their heads in confusion.

"If you see him, let him know I'm looking for him." Dwayne said, not wanting to offer any more information until he knew what was going on with Martin. Desire was a small town. News of what happened would spread fast anyway.

"We've been out in the woods and haven't heard about really anything that's going on around here," Stee said, hoping that Dwayne was only here to inquire about Martin's whereabouts. But they weren't going to get that lucky this time.

"Yeah, I was just out there. That's quite a structure you got out there," he said, genuinely impressed, but also knowing that it would be taken as sarcasm. "What's it for?"

The twins knew it would not be so easy to talk their way out of this. "You wouldn't understand the mystery," Ven said half-heartedly, already knowing what the sheriff had come to do.

"Try me," he said and propped his foot on the ski of the snow-mobile as a gesture to show that he had all the time in the world for their explanation.

"On the surface, it's a device for viewing the constellation Gemini," Stee said, annoyed to be put on the spot.

"But underneath that it's the pinnacle of our existence," Ven added.

The sheriff was actually intrigued. "How so?" he asked, and leaned on his knee in another gesture to show that he wasn't going anywhere.

"It's our mark on the world."

"To prove we actually did exist once."

Their effort to appeal to his sympathy didn't seem to be working as well as they hoped. "It's how we were gonna live forever," Stee said with a dash of quiet sorrow.

"And it's a monument to Elle," Ven added with the same dash.

"C'mon, guys. How is that a monument to Elle?" the sheriff asked suspiciously, not buying into their pity party.

"She was the one who taught us who we are." Stee said, knowing that the sheriff simply would not understand.

Annie danced out of the bathroom and abruptly stopped dead in her tracks at the sight of the sheriff interrogating her boyfriends. She cautiously walked a few steps closer, trying to keep her distance so that she could hear them without their knowing she was there.

Sheriff Walker sighed, knowing that he was about to drop the bomb. "Guys, I got a job to do here," he said as he took his foot of the snowmobile. "Now, it's a great idea what you guys are doing. It really is, and I'm really impressed," he paused, giving the twins a second of hope that died with the sheriff's next statement. "And that's why it kills me to tell you that you have to take it down."

Annie jumped forward. "What? Why?"

"Because, Annie, you guys never checked into who owned that land you're building on. It's owned by the state, and you can't go and build a permanent structure on state land no matter how great the project is."

The twins didn't show any reaction to this news. They just stared blankly into nothingness. The sheriff picked up on this, and frowned to himself. He truly hated having to do this. He went over scenario after scenario of how he could let them do this, but he also knew that Annie and the twins did not fund this out of their own pockets, and his ass would be on the line if he let them keep it up.

"I'm sorry. I wish it were different. You also have a lot of power equipment out there. Do I dare ask where you got the money for all that?"

"Bear gave us the money for it," Annie said confidently.

"I don't recall him saying anything about it," Dwayne said, taking it as a lie.

"We asked him to keep it a secret," Annie said.

"When do we have to take it down?" Stee asked.

"Right now. Guys, I hate being the bad guy all the time, but this is bigger than you guys skinny dippin' or train surfing or dangling off suspension bridges. I like you guys. I really do. You keep me young," he briefly smiled at that, then continued. "So if you agree to take it down, I won't proceed with any investigation. That's the only thing I can do for you guys. I'm sorry."

"What investigation?" Ven demanded.

"I'm going to have to investigate how three kids that have never filed a W-2 form could afford to build a structure like that. My gut says my findings would not come out in your favor."

The twins broke their stare to look at Annie. They knew that the sheriff would do what he said he would do, and if they did nothing, he would find out that Annie had stolen those numbers for them. They didn't care so much about what might happen to them, but they did care about Annie.

It came down to a decision of them having to either destroy their dream or jeopardize their—and Annie's—freedom, and they weren't about to have that happen. They looked back at the sheriff, recognizing that he gave them an option instead of arresting them on sight for suspicion of one thing or another, and actually felt few hard feelings toward him.

"It's not even finished. We'll never know if it actually would have worked," Annie said sorrowfully.

"It would have," Stee said, knowing that it would never be proven.

"I'm sorry, guys," Dwayne said and began to head back to his Prowler. He turned to face them, sympathizing with the deflation in their eyes. "If you see Martin, let him know I'm looking for him."

BUT MARTIN, WHO WALKED AIMLESSLY ALONG THE DIRT road that wrapped itself along the far shore of the lake, didn't want to be found. He wasn't even very cognizant of putting one foot in front of the other as he ambled along in search of nothing. He was alone in the world, and right then, the world seemed so much bigger now that it was empty.

Martin had jumped head first into his thorny place, and for now, he had barricaded the exit. He blamed himself for everything, especially Elle, and it wasn't the type of regret that you tell yourself you really don't believe, that you're just being too hard on yourself.

He believed it.

He believed everything he thought about it.

If he hadn't always disappeared into his studio all the time, he would have been there to try to save his father. He knew CPR. He could have done something, anything. But the truth was that three separate clogged arteries strangled Arnold's heart, and nothing could have saved him once his heart suffocated, but Martin didn't know that. All he knew was that he should have been there. He should have spent just a few more moments with him every day just to talk about anything at all. He should have just once told him that he loved him. But he hadn't done that since he was seven years old.

He continued to shuffle one foot in front of the other, oblivion guiding his steps.

And what was death anyway? What's the big Goddamn mystery for? What's the big deal if we know what happens to us after we're gone? Would we not live our lives to the fullest anymore? Hell, who does that now?

He didn't. And that thought hollowed him out a little more.

Martin looked down at his hand. Grasped loosely within it was the Muddpuppy, the only part of his father that he had left, and if his trek took him to the other side of the world, that would be the only thing he would want to have with him.

A distant thunder and the rising brown dust clouds from the road over the horizon seized Martin's attention. From over the rise, a hoard of bikers approached him. He didn't acknowledge their arrival, even though the rumble was becoming deafening. He just slowly moved to the side of the road to let them pass, and hoped that that was what they would do. But the gang, led by Earl, encircled him as they approached him. Martin didn't even so much as look up at them until he heard his name.

"Martin," Earl said with a tone of empathy.

Martin slowly looked up at him, but didn't say a word.

"I ran into your uncle this morning," Earl told him. "He said if I saw you to let you know he was lookin' for you." He paused, and cleared his throat. "He, ah, told me about your old man."

Martin just stared at him.

"He was a good man, a fair man. That can't be said about a lot of people," Earl continued and offered a small smile to him, but Martin couldn't return it.

Not knowing what else to do, Earl offered his hand to Martin, who looked down at it and slowly took it in his.

One by one, the bikers extended their hands to Martin, grasps accompanied by a pat on the back or a touch of his shoulder that said louder than any words that his world wasn't as vacant as he thought. Martin even cracked a little smile as that realization flooded into him.

"You'll let us know when the funeral is?" Earl asked.

Martin paused. "There isn't going to be one," he stated flatly.

CHAPTER TWENTY

AVING COMPLETELY LOST THEIR APPETITES, THE
twins dropped Annie off at the café on their way back
out to the clearing to decide what to do and how to do
it. They hadn't spoken a word about it since leaving
Ernie's, except that Annie should go on a reconnais-
sance mission at the café to see what the situation was there. When
Annie walked in, she was surprised to see Jack with an ever-present coffee pot in his hand and a server's apron around his waist.

"Hey, Mr. Hanson, where's Cherie?" she suspiciously asked.

"She's not going to be working here anymore, Annie," he said
almost regretfully as he was learning quickly the hell her job really was.

"What for?"

"I'll just let her explain that to you," he replied, not wanting to
get into a conversation about it with her.

"Well, do you know where she is?" Annie asked, and then was
interrupted by a voice in the background.

"Jack, could we get some more coffee over here?"

Jack cringed in the same way that Cherie used to when that
phrase would reverberate through the dining room.

"Try looking under a bottle at the Lunker Lodge," he said sarcastically and then hustled to the table to refresh the ungrateful customer's coffee.

Annie paused. She wasn't surprised that Cherie was fired, but she was a little afraid of the reason why. If she knew her mother—which she did more than Cherie realized—she knew exactly where she had gone, and it wasn't the Lunker Lodge. She sighed at the thought of having to find her, but it was also something that she felt she needed to do, even though she assumed that Bear was handling the situation and therefore she didn't have to take part in it. But to her credit, she ran out the door, heading for the spot where she knew she would find her mother.

Bear, however, was about to be faced with handling a completely different situation as he pulled up in front of the shop with Emily weighed down with his duffle bag and bedroll, ready for another outing on the open road south.

He walked into the dark, empty shop, and went directly behind the counter and plopped himself down in his chair. He flipped on the computer, and as it warmed to life, he looked around the shop at the equipment and bottles of ink on the shelf, and the tattoo designs on the walls in which he and Earl took so much pride, and his calendar with the picture of his old bike and the two naked women, which he decided to leave behind for his brother. Everything was so familiar to him, and because of that, it was comfortable. But getting comfortable is what started his problems in the first place, or so he tried making himself believe. Still, he was surprised to find he just might miss his old shop, but not enough to make him change his mind.

The computer beeped that it was ready, and he logged onto his e-mail account. He had to send out an e-mail to all his buddies in the joint that his e-mail address was going to change, and he'd let them know what his new one was when he got to wherever destiny would land him.

While his e-mail began to download, he watched Nicasa as she patrolled back and forth along the glass. He gently tapped the glass, following her darting nose.

"How you doin', Nicasa? I'm gonna miss you little girl, you know that?" he said with a melancholy smile. He thought briefly about taking her with him, but that wouldn't be practical or fair to her to have to live in a pillowcase all the way across the country.

His e-mail prompt beeped. He kicked his chair back to the computer, and frowned a bit seeing that he had only one e-mail from an old friend of his who still sent him letters every once in awhile, always wanting the same thing out of him. But it was addressed FW: FAN MAIL, so he decided not to simply delete it as he had intended.

He clicked on it and began to read, and with every word and with every sentence, his eyes grew wider in amazement until he laughed out loud. At first he thought it was a joke, but as he read it again, he realized that it was anything but, and he began to question every plan he had made for the rest of his life.

He looked out the window at Emily. Everything he owned was packed and waiting for him to leave, even though he never promised her that he would. He sighed as the thought invaded his mind once again that maybe leaving was just a placebo for his problems.

He looked at Nicasa again, and then around the shop, and laughed to himself at the irony of his little brother's voice echoing in his head *You can't keep running from everything, man—You gotta find a reason to stay.*

That e-mail was more than inviting him to stay.

But still he sat, and hesitated.

CHAPTER TWENTY-ONE

S HERIFF WALKER STOOD AT THE SHORE OF LAKE
Desire looking over to the rocks that ended his sister's life.
Bear's dock sat unoccupied just up the shore. He thought
about going back to the twins and letting them know they
could keep the structure, but if he did, would they ever take
anything he said seriously again? Would his ass really be on the
line if he just looked the other way? Probably. His was an elected
position that he'd held for almost thirty years. He just couldn't
jeopardize it on this, no matter how bad he felt about it. Besides,
he knew that they acquired the capital to build that thing through
some illegal source, and that's what would come back to bite him
on the ass. He was already compromising his integrity as a law
officer by not investigating that aspect. Nobody would want to see
him arrest Annie and the twins anyway. It was a good PR move on
his part to do what he did, and he left it at that.

Dwayne also thought about Martin. That was really why he
was there. If Martin was to turn up anywhere, he knew that eventually it would be on the lake. But so far, there was no sign of him,
and with every passing hour, he became more concerned.

He also thought about Bret.

He found a small part of himself that questioned if he was right about his hunch, but as he looked out to those rocks, his anger blinded him again. He knew that if Bret knew he was the key suspect, he would probably leave town, and therefore Dwayne had avoided him altogether while he tried to build up a case around him. But Bret was a soldier, and Dwayne thought that someday, the guilt would consume him, and he would do the honorable thing and confess. But waiting for that confession became harder and harder as the days passed, and Dwayne began to entertain the idea of simply arresting him for questioning. If he did, though, word of that would spread around the town in less than an hour, and Dwayne didn't know if he would have popular opinion on his side for doing such a thing, especially if his hunch turned out to be wrong, and that might hurt him when election time rolled around again. In any case, his patience was at an end.

Interrupting his thoughts and the tranquil sounds of the lapping water, he heard footsteps crunching on the gravel shore behind him. Expecting to find Martin, he turned, and then frowned, as it was instantly apparent that Bret was not interested in avoiding him.

"Dwayne?" Bret said trying to keep his strength.

Dwayne looked back over the lake, directly at those rocks. He stayed silent, as Bret again questioned his own wisdom for going there. But Bret had something to say, and if he was going to survive to live, not just merely exist, he had to make his peace, and he wasn't leaving until it was done, or at least until he was satisfied that he had tried.

"Dwayne, I wanna tell you I'm sorry," he choked.

Dwayne said nothing at first. He just looked out at those rocks. "You could have saved her, Bret."

Bret took a brave step forward, but was still apprehensive to stand side-by-side with him. "Look, if I could go back and change what happened, I would. But I can't go back and change the things I regret, and that's what forgiveness is for, right?"

Dwayne paused. He didn't want to waste time with apologies. He wanted his confession, and he set his hand slowly on his handcuff holster in preparation for it. "That's all you got to say?" he asked, leading him to his admission.

Bret knew he was going to be slapped in the face a few times before—if—he got through to him, but he didn't understand what Dwayne meant by that question. "What else do you want?"

"You have nothing to say about the night before it happened?" Dwayne said, looking at him from the corner of his eye.

"What about it?" he said, truly confused.

Dwayne turned to face him. His patience had expired. "Don't play games with me, Bret. I know what you did."

"Of course you know. You fired me for it. Don't you think that eats me alive every day?"

"That's not what I'm talking about, and you know it," Dwayne challenged, beginning to think that Bret was just playing with him. This was a small town full of gossips, how could he not know what he was getting at? "Have you been living under a rock for the past coupla weeks?"

"No." Bret said, truly in the dark. "I've been living under a rock for the past thirty years. And I can tell you things are gonna be different now."

Dwayne had heard those words from Bret too many times before. "No they're not," he said, then turned back to the lake for no reason other than he just didn't want to look at Bret any longer.

"Look, I know I've made mistakes—"

"What you did was not a mistake," Dwayne snapped.

Bret's shoulders drooped along with his head. He could think of nothing more to say to get through to him, and his distress emanated in a long sigh. "Is it going to be this way forever, Dwayne?" He asked unconditionally.

Dwayne did not respond. He didn't have an answer to that question, but as far as he was concerned, the answer would be the one that Bret expected. But still, Bret wasn't leaving until he heard it, or until he heard anything from him that would give them both a little peace. The more that Dwayne held his silence, though, the angrier Bret became.

"Goddamnit, Dwayne, talk to me!" he yelled.

Dwayne just stood there, holding on to every ounce of self-control.

He killed your sister. Take him down now. You're not going to get another chance.

If Bret wasn't going to confess to that, Dwayne had nothing more to say to him.

Bret was getting nowhere with him, as he should have known might happen. He turned to leave, then hesitated and asked the one question behind why he'd wanted to find Dwayne in the first place.

"How long are you gonna hold this over my head?" Bret asked directly.

Dwayne did have an answer to that, and he turned to him to make sure it became lodged like a bullet in his head. "As long as she's still dead," he said through clenched teeth, then turned his back to him thinking that that ought to do it.

And it did.

Bret stood motionless for a brief second, trying to find something more to say. Anything more to say. But he could think of nothing worthwhile that wouldn't result in them strangling each other. But at least he tried, and as he walked away empty, he would have to make his own peace with that.

༄

BUT FOR CHERIE, FINDING PEACE WITHIN HERSELF WAS AS elusive as that magic wand that was only available to those who believed in them.

She didn't believe in anything anymore.

As evening began to threaten the day with its darkness, she sat on the curb under the dull, urine yellow glow of the streetlight by the old abandoned sawmill, wallowing in her own desolation. She hated crying, but was getting used to it, and that in and of itself made her cry a little harder. She had exhausted her struggle to escape her thorny place and had let those razor sharp vines squeeze the life out of any hope of serenity she had left in her. She sat with her head on her propped-up knees, rocking back and forth, mournful about everything trivial. She was yet to understand that only one thing really mattered in her life. It was the one true thing that she had neglected time after time.

It was her magic wand that she had possessed all along.

"Cherie?" Annie said as she walked around the corner of the mill.

Cherie looked up at her daughter walking toward her, and turned her head to wipe her tears, too embarrassed to let her daughter see her cry.

"It wouldn't hurt to call me 'Mom' once in a while, would it?" she said sniffling while Annie sat down on the curb next to her. "I guess Elle's the only one that earned that title from you, huh?" Annie shrugged her shoulders at that, and Cherie didn't want to press it. "Where's Steven? I thought you guys were inseparable," she said with as much of a smile as she could muster.

"They went back to the clearing," Annie said, now wondering why she didn't go with them.

They sat in silence for a moment. They didn't know how to talk to each other on this level, but both of them knew that it might be the last chance they had to figure it out.

"I know you got fired," Annie began cautiously, a little afraid that she'd hit a nerve that would set her mother off. But Cherie just sat there and let another tear roll down her face.

"And Bear left me," she whimpered.

"When did this happen?" Annie asked, surprised that she hadn't heard about it yet.

"Today, this morning."

"What a bomb," Annie said with more compassion for Bear than for the woman sitting beside her. She had seen her mother go through this one too many times, and had become insensitive to it. As for Bear, she loved him as the only father figure she ever knew, and became a little frightened that he might not be around anymore. She even entertained the thought of getting up right at that moment to go find him, but something forced her to hesitate.

Cherie laughed a little through her tears. "He didn't even give me a ride to work, so I was late again. But I guess that doesn't matter now, does it?"

"Is that why Jackass fired you?" Annie said, a little afraid of the lean times ahead. But she still had some credit card numbers left undesignated, and she smirked at the thought that they'd be okay for a while if it came down to that.

"No. I don't understand it. He said that I pressed the duplicate button and stole a list of credit card numbers."

The smirk dissolved off Annie face like it was melted off with acid. She paled, her eyes involuntarily growing wide.

"He wouldn't even let me tell him I didn't do anything," she said, flying off into another crying fit.

Annie couldn't say a word. It surprised her, but her first thoughts were not about going to warn the twins that Jack had found out about the list. Nor did she think about packing a bag and seeing if she could go with Bear, and if not, leave with the twins somewhere until things cooled down. Her only thought was the crippling notion that she had caused this turmoil in her mother. And with that realization, a tear fell down Annie's face as well.

Cherie looked out into the dark void beyond the light. "It just seems like everything in my life, everything that I've ever tried to do, I've always screwed it up somehow. I'm such a Goddamn failure, and I don't even know why."

Annie wiped her tears. She could say nothing, and felt more helpless than she could stand.

"You know, I wanted Elle to die. I did. Because I knew she was more of a mother to you than I'd ever be. And I hated her for that. Now I feel even worse for ever thinking that," Cherie confessed.

Through her tears, she looked into her daughter's eyes for the first time in too long. "And when I think about my life, and the disaster I've made of it, I know that the best thing that I ever did in my whole life, the one thing that I ever did that was right . . . is you."

Annie completely broke down in tears. She had wanted to hear her mother say something like that to her for too damn long. She needed to hear it. And as she bowed her head, still looking up at her mother, Cherie reached out to brush back the drooping hair out of Annie's face with her fingers, but hesitated. She didn't know her daughter well enough to touch her.

Annie sensed this, and slowly leaned her head forward, and Cherie slowly reached over and touched her daughter for the first time since she was eight. She forgot how beautiful her daughter had become, and it made her smile.

It was miraculous, as at that moment, with that single, simple touch, Cherie had grown the muscles to rip herself out of those wicked razor-sharp thorns, and thus obtained the strength to hold onto that magic wand forever.

Annie leaned over and held her mother who lovingly wrapped her arms around her.

"I love you, Annie. I really do."

Through trembling lips, Annie choked "I love you, too . . . Mom."

After a few moments, Cherie leaned away from her, and looked at her again. "I am going to get through this life. You wanna come with?"

All Annie could respond with was a half smile and a reassuring nod. Even though her eyes were saturated, they were wide open in the distress of the choice she had to make. She could either have a fleeting life with the twins—a life that had the prospect of going nowhere, especially now with the possibility of jail hanging over them, or she could have something that she'd only ever wanted, something that she'd never had before—a mother. Her choice was bittersweet, as she knew that their new-found relationship would forever falter without repair if she ever told her mother the truth of what she had done. Still, as she comforted herself in her mother's embrace, at that moment, she felt that she had chosen wisely.

Chapter Twenty-Two

A FEW DAYS LATER, AS EVENING ONCE AGAIN threatened the light of day, Bret loaded the last box into the back of van, hearing Barney's words in his head again and again.

There is peace out there for you, Bret, but you're not going to find it here.

Talking with Dwayne had just proven that.

He stared at the shack he had called home for too long. There wouldn't be any point in trying to sell it. No one would want to buy this place anyway, and it would just take more time than he wanted to commit to it. He thought about just burning the place down, but in the back of his mind, he knew if he left it standing, he would always have a place to come home to. But when morning broke, he wanted to be as far away from here as he could. He wanted to get as far away as possible from everything he had and everything he had become. Then, he looked at all the boxes holding everything in the world he owned, and questioned why, if he was leaving to get away from all of this, was he taking it all with him?

❦

BEAR RODE EMILY DOWN THE ROAD WITH THE FIRST GENUINE smile he had produced in a long time. His vitality seemed to once again be restored in him, and just maybe, Florida might have to wait.

Clenched between his hand and the handlebar, he held a bouquet of wild roses that he picked along the lakeshore, but he wasn't ready to give them up just yet. He was on his way out to his dock to bid the evening tranquility a welcoming salutation. Coming up on the café and bait shop, he noticed Charlie standing despondently alone in front of the dark shop. Bear turned his bike around and rolled into the parking lot, stopping just in front of him. He got off his bike, and walked up to him, not surprised to find tears filling Charlie's eyes.

"Hi, Charlie."

Charlie slowly turned to him, but said nothing.

Bear looked into the dark shop. His eyes scanned across Martin's progress board, which was stopped at 977 days. The record, 978 days, was frozen, unachieved. Bear sighed with a great deal of condolence, saddened at the many losses this place had known. His eyes continued moving through the shop and stopped at the minnow tanks. The aerators had been shut off, and the thin white bellies of all the minnows floated lifelessly on the surface. The pile of lures that had fallen on Arnold still lay scattered on the floor. All Bear could do was shake his head helplessly.

"Where am I going to go now, Bear?" Charlie asked with quivering lips, pointing with the bunch of ox-eye daisies he held in his hand to the sign on the door that read FOR SALE BY OWNER. Bear didn't know that Martin had planned to do that, but if the situation were his, he would probably do the same thing.

Bear motioned to the sign. "Why don't you stay right here, Charlie."

Charlie had already thought about that prospect, but somehow having someone else suggesting it to him made him consider it as a real possibility. But still, he said nothing, and simply bent down to add his flowers to the group that had already accumulated in front of the door along with a few candles, and mysteriously, a birch bark boat, full of wild flowers with a note that simply read, *I'm Sorry*. Bear took instant notice of the boat. He had seen one just like it on the shore behind his dock about a month ago.

"Who put the boat there?" Bear asked.

"I don't know. It was already there when I got here this morning," Charlie responded.

Bear looked at the group of wild roses he had clutched in his hand. With a half smile to Charlie, he bent down, and set them against a camouflaged helmet that in black magic marker read DESIRE across it.

ঙ৩

JUST BEFORE THE SUN BEGAN TO DISSOLVE INTO THE landscape, Bear had managed to make it out to the dock to witness it. He felt like writing again, and it filled him with an eagerness that was like helium. Positioning himself against the dock pole, he inhaled the sweet, effervescent lake air, and scanned the tranquil, satin water. He noticed that Martin had parked his boat at the dock down the shore. Was Martin trying to avoid him? Bear didn't think too much about it. Perhaps Martin, knowing Bear was living on the dock, didn't want to disturb him.

Bear reached into his inside vest pocket, and pulled out what he thought was his journal, and it wasn't until he opened it that he saw it was Elle's. Her crumpled letter to Arnold immediately caught his attention, and he slowly pulled it from the pages of the journal. He stared at it, then up to the lake. His curiosity once again overshadowed his discretion, and he began to read.

> My dearest Arnold, I have never regretted for a moment forsaking Bret for an eternity in love with you. Even though I did once

love him, I never knew what it meant to be in love with someone until I married you, and it stings to think that I have been dishonest with you.

There is no easy, poetic way to tell you what I should have told you years ago, and I write you this letter out of my own shame for not finding the strength within myself to overcome my fear of letting you know the truth.

They say the secret of a secret is to know when and how to tell it. I have never known either, so I will just say what I have to say.

I discovered that I was pregnant just before I married you, and I've known since then that Bret is Martin's father.

Bear's eyes ripped open in shock. Even though Elle always shared her secrets with him, this one she would not want anyone to know, obviously not even Arnold. He instantly recognized that he was holding a letter that was not intended for anyone's eyes but hers, but still, he couldn't get himself to stop reading.

I have been troubled by the intense fear of letting you and Martin know the truth. Perhaps things are better left unsaid anyway, because in the end, don't we all invent our own truth?

I can't imagine the pain and confusion that you and Martin will feel because of this. That is why I may never show you this letter. Maybe I wrote it more for me than you anyway.

Just know that I will love you forever, Elle.

Bear set the letter on his lap and looked out over the pink water. He couldn't bring himself to believe it, and he questioned if it was really a confession letter that she had written or maybe something else? He reread the line again about Bret and Martin, and he could imagine her trembling hand as she sat out on Arrowhead Island writing that letter to Arnold. Knowing Elle, she was probably wearing her powder blue dress. She always wore that dress. She used to say it made her feel magical.

She came to be known, in some circles, as simply *the woman in the powder blue dress*. She was a very magical person. Everyone who had ever talked to her had to admit that.

As Bear looked down again at the letter, he wondered what he would now do with it, or more importantly, what would Elle want him to do with it? Could he tell Martin about this after what he was now going through already? Would it hurt him more to know the truth? And what about Bret? Should he know? Perhaps there really were some things that are better left unsaid.

He sighed, and looked up over the lake. The movement of Martin untying his boat on the far dock grabbed his attention. He sat up and watched. He knew Dwayne was looking for him, but he shied from letting Martin know he was there, especially after what he just read.

Then, at that moment, he saw the sheriff walk up behind Martin.

"Martin?" Dwayne called as he walked toward him, noticing the wooden urn on the dock at Martin's feet.

Martin, startled, turned to him. "Uncle Dwayne," he said softly, a little distressed that he was there.

"What are you doing?" Dwayne asked, looking down at the urn.

Martin didn't answer. He had something gruesome on his mind, and he just couldn't live with it anymore. "Uncle Dwayne, I gotta ask you something. Do you still think it was Bret that did something to Mom's boat?"

"I'm pretty sure of it," Dwayne said with a stiff lip.

Martin caught himself from breaking into tears. "It wasn't him," he looked up at his uncle. "I was the one who took her boat out that night," he whimpered as tears began to form. "It was day 865. I hadn't yet taken my boat out of storage. It was dark and I hit a log. I didn't get a chance to tell anyone about it. Then I got the news the next morning, and I was afraid to tell anyone about it."

Dwayne's eyes grew wide, then sloped in anger. Not at the confession, not even that it was Martin that did it, but that he was so blind and so quick to crucify his old friend. His head bowed, too heavy to hold against the shame that weighed it down.

"I killed her, Uncle Dwayne. And now I wasn't even there to save my father," Martin wept.

Dwayne looked at him, searching for something to say, but found nothing. He reached out and wrapped his arms around his nephew. "It's okay Martin," he said in the most calming voice he could muster.

He held him, and looked over the lake, trying to control the creeping disgrace that was boring itself into him. He then sighed, deep and long. "We'll call it an accident. And that's just the way it's gonna stand," he said, not sure if he was reassuring Martin or himself. "You didn't kill her, Martin."

Martin pushed himself out of his uncle's support. He looked directly into his eyes. "Yes, I did," he stated bitterly. "I never even stopped fishing. I even went on the day of her funeral."

"Do you think she would have wanted it any other way?" he said, knowing for a fact that she wouldn't have.

Martin dried his face with the back of his hand. "I'll never be able to forgive myself for this."

An answer to that came immediately to Dwayne's mind, and he choked a bit, trying to swallow. "Someone just told me that we can't go back and change the things we regret. That's what forgiveness is for. Pretty strong advice," he said with another hard sigh, teased by the grievance that he had ignored it when it was pleaded to him.

"Who said that?" Martin asked, touched by the assertion.

His uncle didn't want to remind himself who said it, let alone tell Martin. All he could to do was reflect on its meaning, and that was what Martin was already doing.

Dwayne began to untie the boat. "C'mon. It'll be dark soon."

Martin picked up his father's urn, and then looked at his uncle. "Uncle Dwayne," he said quietly. "I think this is something I need to do on my own."

Dwayne hesitated, staring into his nephew's swollen eyes. Then he nodded, trying not to let his own remorse overwhelm him.

Martin stepped into the boat and lovingly set the urn on the floor just in front of his seat. He yanked the pull cord, and the out-board revved to life. Martin gave a brave, but melancholy smile to his distraught uncle who tried to offer one in return. Martin turned the throttle, and headed out onto the polished orange and pink stained lake.

Bear respectfully rose to his feet as he watched Martin glide over the lake. He looked down at Elle's letter in his hand, and it became instantly clear what he should do with it.

He slowly reached in his outside vest pocket and pulled from it his Zippo and snapped it to flame. After a moment of hesitation, he introduced the letter to the flame and smiled as he set it adrift in the sweet lake air as it burned into ashes.

Meanwhile, in the clearing, another test was being challenged as the twins stood before the Gemini Observation Device, which was dripping with fresh gasoline. Empty gas cans were thrown all about except for the one in Stee's hand that he used to saturate the torches that they had made from lumber scraps and their ripped T-shirts.

The twins each took a step forward, then paused as they made very sure that this was in fact their final option. They had little choice, and as they prepared themselves, Ven took his Zippo from his back pocket, and with a heavy dose of anguish, flicked it to light.

Stee shared his brother's despondency and touched his torch to the flame setting it alight. Ven hesitated, but his brother nodded at him, and he reluctantly took his time in lighting his own torch.

They walked to the structure together and reverently touched the flaming torches to it. They were instantly blinded by a tower of luminescent flame that rose ten feet over the thirty-foot structure. As the heat grew more and more intense, the twins moved farther and farther away, walking backward but never taking their eyes off of it. Neither of them had much of any thought in their heads. They simply stood and watched their dream burn, unaware that the glow from the fire could be seen for miles all directions.

Especially from the lake.

Martin didn't notice it right away. His head was bowed, looking deep into the purple water, his hands clenched tightly around the urn. Through a stream of tears, he slowly opened the box and held it above his head.

A tender breeze stroked his face, telling him it was time, and he screamed through his clenched teeth as he let his father go.

Arnold's ashes flew from the box like a swarm of sparrows, and covered the golden lake. The lake welcomed him, and seemed to look back at Martin as if to tell him not to worry, that it would keep his father safe.

Trembling, Martin set down the urn and then picked up two birch bark boats, each filled with wild flowers that he had picked earlier in the day. Wood lilies and asters, purple lupine and white trillium, among others. But only the flowers. This time, there wasn't a note.

He leaned down over the side of the boat, and as he had done every morning since the accident, he set them afloat as the tender breeze sailed them off into the tranquility.

As he watched them sail to the horizon, the mysterious glow from the burning Gemini Observation Device over the ridge in the woods finally caught his eye, and he stared at it in absolute wonder like it was divinity itself incarnate. His face lit up with renewed vigor, and he smiled a bit through his tears at the brilliance of that vision.

"Lights in the forest," he whispered, lost in sheer amazement.

As he actually began to laugh a little, a blooming relief flew into him like a thousand fluttering butterflies.

And it told him that things were going to be all right now.

CHAPTER TWENTY-THREE

BEAR HAD STAYED ON THE DOCK ALL NIGHT WITHOUT doing much more than dozing off from time to time. So, when the symphony of morning began to tune its instruments, Bear was up and waiting for it. In his thoughts were the events that had happened since Elle's death, and the only word that he could describe it all with was magic—there was a magic in it all, a real magic. And that magic told him that Elle was still somehow watching out for everyone she loved, and everyone that loved her, and that offered him a great comfort.

And as the morning mist began to rise off the lake like a sacred spirit, and the sky was just beginning to lighten, Bear reached in his vest pocket and pulled out his journal and pen. He opened it to where he left off and began to write.

> It's strange how we fight harder for our desires than we do for our quest for truth. But we will find that when our desires are dissolved like sugar in vinegar, it creates a rise to a new, unexpected beauty that demands us to reinvent what it means to exist. Such is the beauty in the experiment called humanity. But

every experiment has it flaws. Ours are that we fight every negative episode in our lives with such fierce determination that we forget to listen to its offerings, especially when we find that negativity within ourselves. We miss the good that might be part of the bad, and we may never discover all that is strengthened by the choice to overcome. But when we do arise from that malignant disability, we will find that that unexpected beauty will propel us toward an understanding of our own enlightenment.

Bear stopped writing and thought about Bret and Sheriff Walker at the same moment that the sheriff rolled his Prowler to a stop in front of Bret's shack.

Dwayne wasn't in the mood for humble pie for breakfast, but he was more than prepared to dig in. He was about to make the biggest apology of his life, and that was something in which he had very little practice.

He stepped out of his truck and walked around the back of Bret's van. The back doors were wide open, and the boxes Bret had put there were stacked up to the roof. It looked like he caught Bret just in time.

"Bret," he called out, but there was no answer.

He walked in the house, and called again. Still no answer. He began to go room to room, halfway expecting him to be passed out in one of them. But after finding the place to be vacant, he walked back outside.

"Bret!" he called louder, but still there was no answer.

Dwayne had missed Bret by only an hour. Walking down the dirt road that wrapped around the far side of the lake, with an old, tattered backpack draped over one shoulder, Bret felt free for the first time in a very long time—thirty years to be exact. As he lifted the sagging backpack back onto his shoulder, he smiled with the thought that he had answered his question of why was he taking it all with him. It was the most liberating feeling he'd ever experienced to just abandon everything and leave it all behind. It didn't mean anything to him anymore, anyway.

An old pickup truck pulled up alongside him, and he instantly recognized it as Arnold's.

Martin leaned over and rolled down the passenger-side window. "You need a lift?" Martin asked.

Bret smiled at him. "Yeah. I could use a lift," he said as he opened the door and climbed in.

"Where you headed?" Martin asked as Bret got himself situated.

"I haven't decided yet," Bret said with a euphoric feeling of freedom.

"Neither have I," Martin said with a genuine smile.

Martin put the truck in gear and accelerated down the road.

Standing behind them, watching them drive away, was Elle, radiant in her powder blue dress. And standing next to her, was the one man that she had found who never ignored her. Arnold put his arm around her as they smiled with pride as they watched Martin and Bret disappear around the bend into the forest to a destination unknown, together.

Bear turned his mind again to his writing and continued.

And that enlightenment also comes from recognizing and demolishing the roadblocks that generate the vacancy in our own happiness. And once we accomplish this, we will find that through our own self-contained divinity, our desires can be achieved, and we will come to accept that everything happens because it is supposed to happen, and not necessarily because we want it to. And in time, we will find a living power that blooms from the forgiveness that offers us the power to make peace within ourselves and will lead us to the discovery of new desires that have yet to be conceived.

Bear thought about the twins, and how their dreams had been incinerated the previous night. He would later learn of how they sat utterly despondent at the bar at the Lunker Lodge with two cups of coffee before them that they hadn't yet touched. They sat in silence, struggling to come to terms with the loss of their dream. They didn't hear the door open behind them, much less notice who had come through it.

"I've, ah, been looking for you guys," Ernie said, walking up to them with a smile.

"What for?" Stee said emotionlessly.

"I have something for you. I know that whatever it was you were building out there meant a lot to you, and I'm into photography, do you know why?"

The twins shook their heads, wondering what he was getting at and frankly not caring.

"There's this one *The Twilight Zone* episode, it's called 'A Kind of Stopwatch' and there's this guy that gets a watch that can stop time. I so wish that I could do that. So, I guess that's why I like photography, because the camera captures a piece of time happening, so it does kinda stop time, ya know?"

The twins looked at each other wondering what any of this had to do with anything.

"I knew that you guys wanted to live forever through that thing out there, so I snuck out there, and took a bunch of pictures of you guys building it, and there's also ones of you burnin' it," he said as he handed them a stack of Polaroids.

The twins took the photos and began to file through them. With each picture, a small tinge of happiness was restored inside them.

"So now you guys can live forever. These pictures prove that you really did exist," Ernie said with absolute conviction.

The twins looked up at him full of astonishment, their eyes overflowing with gratitude.

"Ernie, you are the most brilliant person I've ever met in my life," Stee said in almost a whisper.

"Thank you for this," Ven added.

Ernie's lip began to quiver as a tingle of emotion ran through him. He looked as if he was about to cry.

"Did . . . did you just call me brilliant?" he stammered.

"Yes, I did," Stee said, wondering why Ernie was responding like he was.

"Nobody in my whole life has ever called me brilliant before," he said as a tear took a trip down his cheek.

Ernie smiled through his tears and simply turned and walked to the door with those words invigorating his being.

"I'm brilliant," he said again as his smile enlarged.

Ernie danced down the street, and for the first time ever, he was high on his own greatness.

Bear resumed writing.

> It is also the same with recognizing what is meaningless, and what is significant, and which one of these our desires serve. Only the significant leads to the truth, and once we realize this, we will discover a magic that offers us the answers to the complications of our existence. And what we will find from this is that those desires may be answered from the most simple, and unexpected of places.

Bear looked up to see a pair of loons call out, wishing the lake its good morning with their chick riding lazily on her mother's back. It made Bear think about Cherie and Annie, and how pleased he really was that his brother had taken his place in that scenario.

In their trailer, Annie sat at the kitchen table sipping a cup of coffee while Cherie was busy flipping pancakes on the stove. It was the first breakfast they had shared together that didn't come from a microwave or from the café.

They laughed like they had never laughed with each other before. They were getting to know each other again, and they were happier than they had ever been. But Annie now would have to live with a ghost that would continue to haunt her with the question she might one day have to answer: *Can a lie really be easier to live with than the truth?*

A brief knock on the door was followed by Earl peeking his head in before he stepped inside. Cherie's face began to glow as he produced a flower arrangement for her from behind his back.

She took them and wrapped her arms around him in an enthu-
siastic hug—a hug he immediately returned. As she watched,
Annie didn't even roll her eyes as they kissed.

As Earl helped himself to a cup of coffee, Bear continued.

And when we begin to celebrate our existence instead of holding it in contempt, we will only then discover that magic that
offers us a fresh baked epiphany that propels us towards an
understanding and appreciation of our own being. With that,
will also come the realization that there are so few things in life
that are truly important, and so many things that are irrelevant,
and once we appreciate this, we'll discover the revelation that
life does not have to be as complicated as we make it out to be.

The sun was painting its arrival above the tranquil, lapping
waters of the lake in masterful strokes of oranges, reds, and purples meshing into the cirrus clouds. The arrogant sky admired
itself in the mirror of the lake, approving of the artistry that fed its
vanity.

The symphony of morning was well into its program as the
white-throated sparrows sang accompanied by the oboe of the
loons, and the clarinet of the red-winged blackbirds harmonized
with the plucking cello strings of the green frogs, and the trum-
pets of the Canadian geese heralded the day as they flew overhead
in a V formation.

Bear really did love it here. This was his spot in the world, and
he wasn't going anywhere. Hearing the hollow footsteps on the
dock behind him, he turned and with an immaculate smile, was
reminded why.

Wearing her ankle length dress with the pretty purple patterned flowers and Bear's oversized motorcycle jacket, Stella
walked up to him sharing in his smile.

She cuddled up next to him, and Bear wrapped his arm
around her, then put his journal on her lap, and continued to
write. As he did, she read along.

Eventually, the truth will be revealed that our lives, with our virtues and our failures, our courage and our fears, and with our severe loathing for our own insignificance, we will find that, in the end, our desires consists in ultimately accepting the changes that make us who we are. And that acceptance becomes the recognition that we are all capable of greatness.

She looked up at him and smiled, and Bear leaned down and kissed his new muse tenderly on her forehead. They sat and enjoyed the tranquility of the morning symphony together both knowing that from that beautiful moment onward, everything was possible.